For Hilda, my nana, who loved animals,
people and life.

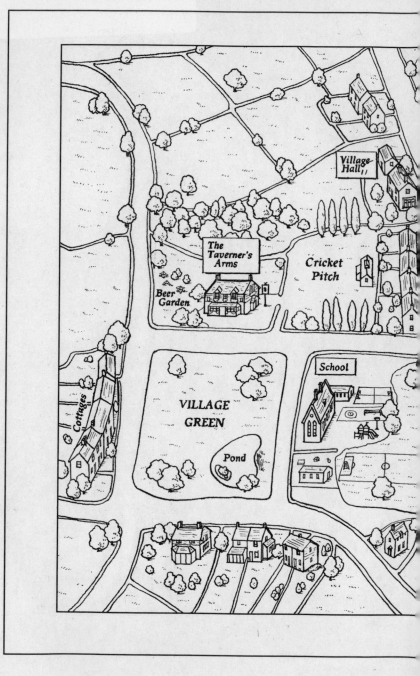

# Blackberry Picking at Jasmine Cottage

## Zara Stoneley

A division of HarperCollins*Publishers*
www.harpercollins.co.uk

Harper*Impulse* an imprint of
HarperCollins*Publishers*
The News Building
1 London Bridge Street
London SE1 9GF

www.harpercollins.co.uk

This paperback edition 2017

First published in Great Britain in ebook format
by HarperCollins*Publishers* 2017

Copyright © Zara Stoneley 2017

Zara Stoneley asserts the moral right to
be identified as the author of this work

A catalogue record for this book
is available from the British Library

ISBN: 9780008241087

This novel is entirely a work of fiction.
The names, characters and incidents portrayed in it are
the work of the author's imagination. Any resemblance to
actual persons, living or dead, events or localities is
entirely coincidental.

Typeset in Birka by Palimpsest Book Production Ltd,
Falkirk, Stirlingshire

Printed and bound in Great Britain

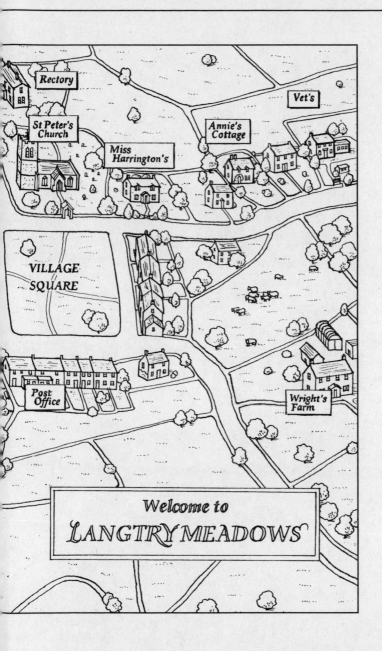

Rectory

Vet's

St Peter's
Church

Annie's
Cottage

Miss
Harrington's

VILLAGE
SQUARE

Post
Office

Wright's
Farm

Welcome to
LANGTRY MEADOWS

# Chapter 1

Lucy Jacobs stared out of the window, and tried to ignore the little shiver of excitement that had sent a rash of goosebumps down her arms.

Could she do this? Was she brave enough to cut the last tie, change her life for ever?

The words danced about in her head in much the same way as the chickens in the garden were doing.

Yesterday they'd flounced in indignantly when the first spots of rain had fallen. They hated the damp, and had spent most of the day sulking and shivering, but this morning after poking their sharp little beaks out, and craning their necks, they'd discovered sunshine. She'd had to laugh as they'd jostled their way out, like a group of pointy-elbowed bargain hunters in the January sales.

Today the good weather had put a skip in their step – they were scratching around in the soil, with an occasional dash across the garden if they suspected one of their group had found something worth fighting over. And the news had brought a secret smile to her lips, she couldn't help it. This could be the start of a massive adventure.

'Are you still there? Miss Jacobs?'

She was still here. And she knew it was time to stop behaving like a hen and to make a decision. If she did this she was shutting a door for good. Moving on. Which was exciting. But scary.

'Miss Jacobs?' The tetchy tones scratched their way over the airwaves.

'Yes, sorry.' She tried to concentrate on what the estate agent was saying, and block out all the conflicting thoughts that were bouncing around in her head.

She much preferred talking to the young, jolly Simon Proofit who made everything sound like a good idea, than to Mr Bannister who had never told her his first name, and insisted on calling her Miss Jacobs and making her sound like some old spinster.

It was strange really, Mr Bannister had lived in the village of Langtry Meadows all his life, but his whole manner suggested a brusque, efficient city type. Whereas Simon, who had over an hour's commute from a suburb of the closest city, always made it seem like working in this tiny village was the best thing that had ever happened to him.

'I suppose you need time to think about it?' The

sharp words were followed by a resigned sigh that rolled towards her in large waves of disappointment. Mr Bannister really wasn't the man you wanted to start your weekend with. He was enough to rain on anybody's parade, as her gran would have said.

The hen that she'd not-so-originally nicknamed Squeak darted forward and tried to wrestle a long worm from Bubble's beak. They looked like lovers sharing a strand of spaghetti. Bubble flapped with indignation, and Squeak, well squeaked before bustling off in a huff to scratch under the apple tree. She kept cocking her head to one side though, keeping a beady eye on the other hen. Just in case.

Lucy smiled to herself. Who'd have thought she, Lucy Jacobs, would become an expert on poultry? Well maybe not an expert, but her life had changed beyond recognition in the last twelve months. She'd swapped the hustle and bustle of a city centre school, nestled next to the M6 motorway, for a tiny primary school overlooking a village green, and somehow found time to look after a pig, goose, chickens, cat and a fat, naughty pony.

Taking on a teaching position in the village of Langtry Meadows had, it was fair to say, changed her life. Renting Annie's cute home, with its overflowing cottage garden and menagerie of animals had, at first, seemed a step too far from her clean and tidy semi-detached house

– the only reminder of her old life she'd hung on to.

She'd rented her home out, fully intending to go back there one day – after her cover position at Langtry Meadows Primary School came to an end. But she'd accepted a permanent position now, and whilst the rent was handy she was beginning to wonder if she'd ever go back there.

And one day, in the not too distant future, Annie would return from her travels, which could leave her in a bit of a mess if she wasn't careful. She really did need a plan.

The city would seem so large, impersonal now. Although she knew that was partly what had originally drawn her there. But living in Langtry Meadows had changed her, she'd realised that this close community of caring people was what she wanted in her life. Not anonymity. And she also wanted a rather gorgeous vet called Charlie sharing her breakfast table, which was part of the problem...

She hoped her sigh hadn't travelled down the phone, and decided she better say something just in case he had heard, and thought she wasn't interested.

'Well, no. I mean yes, I ...' If she did this, if she bought the house that Mr Bannister had told her had just come up for sale in the village, and she sold her house, she was saying goodbye to her old life. She didn't need to keep a foot in the past, just in case things didn't work out, did she?

No, no, she really didn't. After a fabulous summer of getting to know Charlie Davenport, the village vet, she had to admit, she had dreamed up this strange fantasy that when, if, she settled permanently then it would be in a cottage made for two. Not one.

But his life was far too complicated for that at the moment. He had a child to consider. *They* had a child to consider. Adorable little Maisie had to be their main priority.

Lucy knew what it was like growing up with only one parent, thinking that she wasn't good enough, thinking she wasn't loved, wasn't wanted – and she was determined that Maisie would never feel that way. The little girl would know that Charlie, her father, loved her with all his heart. That Lucy wasn't going to steal him away.

When Josie, Charlie's ex, returned from her six month contract abroad, then it would be the right time for her and Charlie to spend more time together, be more involved, maybe, just maybe, settle down in that dream cottage together. But for now, making sure Maisie felt secure, was happy, was what really mattered.

She felt the small smile creep over her face as she thought about Charlie. They'd agreed at the start of the summer that they'd take things slowly, see how it went and it had gone – she knew her smile had grown – wonderfully.

But they didn't know when Josie would be back, didn't know what would happen when she returned – whether she'd settle locally with Maisie or not. And until they did, it was hard to see what the future held. What if Josie moved away? What if the only way Charlie could see his daughter was to move as well? What if she couldn't find a new job close to where they went? What if, what if, there were just so many 'ifs', which Lucy wasn't keen on at all. For a girl who liked to have a plan, be organised, the uncertainty was difficult. But she was learning, getting better at taking each day as it came.

So really, if she was going to be sensible about this, she had to decide what *she* really wanted. Now. And worry about the future later – after all if she bought a cottage now, she could always sell it.

She really had never thought the whole question of buying a house would raise its head for months though, years!

The estate agent's crisp tone cut into her thoughts. 'It would be in your interests to move quickly. It does, as I have mentioned, require a fair amount of modernisation, but opportunities like this don't come up very often. A cottage for sale in Langtry Meadows is a rare occurrence, and I'd have normally already contacted interested parties, but Miss Harrington persuaded me to give you first option. I'd advise you not to dally about too long.'

Ah. So that explained the unexpected phone call from Bannister & Poole's Estate Agency. She'd made an offhand comment to the elderly Elsie Harrington about needing to look for a permanent home, and as if by magic a solution had appeared.

'I won't, dally that is. I'd love to look round.' It really was an opportunity she couldn't pass on, she had to at least look. And 'modernisation' might mean that it had an outside toilet and a well – which would put it way beyond her humble budget.

'I'll email the details through, although they are currently just draft ones, they haven't been approved.' She could hear him shuffling papers in the background. 'I can meet you there at 11 a.m. if that suits?'

'Well, I.' She would really have liked to share the news with Charlie first, see what he thought, but he'd be busy seeing clients. And she *did* want to stay in Langtry Meadows, whatever the future held for her and the man she'd fallen head over heels for. 'Today? This morning?'

'We do close at midday, it is Saturday you know.'

Which meant Charlie couldn't go with her, but she could check it out first. It could be totally unsuitable anyway. 'That suits perfectly, and er, thank you, Mr Ba—' He cut her off mid-sentence, and Lucy slowly took the phone away from her ear and stared back out at the garden, knowing she had a stupid grin on her face.

Lucy glanced down at her pyjama bottoms, then up at the kitchen clock. This was not how she'd expected her last weekend of freedom to start. The new school term started on Wednesday, and they had an inset day on Tuesday, and she was officially the teacher of Classes 1 and 2. The last few days of the holiday were supposed to be about relaxing, chilling, preparing herself for the chaotic weeks ahead. She hadn't factored in being woken up by a phone call from a bossy estate agent, and the kind of stomach churning, exciting news that had left her feeling all butterfly stomach-ey and jittery.

Her brain wasn't exactly functioning either, which was how she always felt before the first strong coffee of the day. Lucy was not a morning person, she wasn't really a night owl either. She was guaranteed to be the one that had to be in bed by midnight or she risked falling asleep on the shoulder of the nearest person and no doubt snoring and drooling in a very unattractive way. She was the one the rest of the students had drawn a moustache on when she was at college, as she slept through oblivious.

Her mobile gave a cheery bleep announcing an incoming message. Coffee. She needed coffee and a chance to wake up properly, then she'd shower and dress, and then she'd read the email that the efficient and officious Mr Bannister had already pinged off from his clean and tidy office, determined to disrupt the peace of her sleepy cottage in Langtry Meadows.

She'd only got as far as the bottom of the stairs, when a loud honk stopped her in her tracks. A warning honk, not the kind of gentle 'go away' noise that Gertie the goose often directed at unwelcome visitors. This had more urgency. And volume.

Rushing to the front door, Lucy threw it open, expecting some kind of carnage.

Gertie was having a fit. The type she normally reserved for straying men – as in they'd strayed on to her property and nothing to do with their morals. Well, to be more precise the goose was flapping her big white wings like some avenging angel and dipping her head backwards and forwards towards a mysterious object just inside the garden gate. Gertie didn't like mysterious objects. She didn't like most things, to be honest. And Lucy didn't know if that was a 'goose' thing, or just a Gertie thing.

Lucy folded her arms, relieved that it was nothing more serious. 'What have you got?'

Gertie glared back accusingly.

Lucy was used to parcels being left just inside the gate. Her regular postman knew all about how to deal with Gertie, but most strangers took one look at the bird as she hurtled round the corner of the cottage in response to the click of the gate catch, and scarpered. She couldn't blame them.

'Okay, I'm coming.' She slipped her feet into the pink wellingtons that were in the porch. The wellies were her secret defence – with them on Gertie was putty (well not exactly putty, but no longer quite as lethal) in her hands. Gertie loved the boots; they were, as Annie had told her, the first thing she had seen and she thought they were her mother. She would happily follow them anywhere.

The parcel moved. Rocked. Gertie gave it a prod. It made a strange, wheezy noise and the goose drew herself up to her full height, gave a loud honk, then turned on her heel and marched off in search of something more interesting.

Frowning, Lucy lifted a corner flap cautiously. It sounded like there was something alive in there, and for all she knew it could be a box of snakes. Or worse. Rats.

Two eyes stared up at her out of the dark shadows of the box. One chocolate brown, the other the clearest blue she'd ever seen, spring water in a crystal clear stream.

Quiet trusting eyes.

She stooped down and opened the flaps of the box wider. It was a puppy, the blinking of its eyes the only movement as it gazed up at her. Over one eye was a patch of black, but most of its coat was the softest grey, splashed with black as though a careless artist had tired of finishing the painting, its paws and chest a damp, stained white with a smudge of tea-stains.

The puppy shivered and its chin sank down onto its paws as though it was exhausted.

'Hang on.' It didn't respond. Not even the slightest wag of its fluffy tail, which sent a shiver of alarm through Lucy. Her instinctive response would have been to reach in and cuddle the poor animal, but something told her not to. It was poorly, very poorly.

She reluctantly closed the flaps of the box back down as gently as she could and ran back inside, grabbing her mobile phone as she dashed up the narrow stairs. She couldn't ring Charlie to discuss something like a house for sale, but this was altogether different. 'Charlie?'

'Morning, gorgeous, you're up early for a non-school day!'

'I know you're not open yet, but ...'

'Are you okay?' His voice lost some of its cheery tone as he picked up the worry that tinged her words.

'Somebody's dumped a puppy in the garden. It's in a box, but it looks really sick, it's just lying there and shivering, and it's ...'

'How sick?' The cheeky edge had gone altogether now, replaced with professional concern in an instant, and she could imagine his frown, the narrowing of his eyes as he ran his fingers through his hair.

'It looks like it's been sick in the box, all its chest is damp and stained,' she put the phone on speakerphone and dropped it on the bed, rifling through the drawer for clean underwear, 'and it looks so thin and pathetic. I know I'm no expert, but it hardly even moved when I opened the box up, puppies just aren't supposed to behave like that, are they?'

'Bring it straight down, Luce.'

'I'm just getting clothes on,' she was breathless as she yanked her jeans up, fumbling with the zip with one hand, 'I'll be there in five minutes.'

Vet Charlie Davenport headed out of the surgery as soon as he spotted Lucy. He got the same familiar rush of pleasure he always did when he saw her. Along with the desire to take her in his arms and kiss her. Which would be very unprofessional.

He'd not expected to see her until the evening. It was the last weekend of the school summer holidays, and he knew that Lucy, organised as she was, would be busy with spreadsheets and lesson plans, getting ready for the new term of fresh-faced children, excited after a summer of freedom.

He felt the muscles in his shoulders tighten. This term that included his daughter Maisie, and he was dreading it.

He'd been over the moon when his ex, Josie, had finally let him see Maisie again. The daughter she'd told him might not be his, the daughter she'd refused to let him see for months.

When she'd asked him to look after Maisie while she worked abroad for a few months his whole world had seemed brighter and he'd been naively expecting it to be just like it had when they'd been a family.

Maisie had moved in with him at the start of the summer holidays, and it had been a big adventure. Now, with the new term approaching the reality had started to sink in. She was starting a new school, she wasn't going back home to the friends she loved. She had a new uniform to pick up on Monday, and a bright new book bag that she didn't like at all. It was the wrong colour. It had the wrong badge on it. Mummy hadn't picked it.

They were both struggling, him with how to deal with the unexpected tantrums, and her with adjusting to a different life.

He sighed. After Maisie had begged, then told him it wasn't fair, then stared at him with her big brown eyes brim-full with tears, and her lower lip trembling, he'd relented and allowed her to spend Friday night with a friend from her old school. He still wasn't sure he'd done the right thing. He'd cocked up; he should have spent all summer ensuring she made friends with the children in Langtry Meadows. But it had seemed wrong to expect her to take the move in one massive step.

He was already proving pants at this single parenting lark. He was heading for disaster.

When Lucy had suggested they spend Saturday evening together, then take a picnic out on Sunday afternoon, fly the kite he'd bought, have some fun, he'd jumped at the suggestion as quickly as his daughter had. Maisie loved Lucy; he wasn't convinced she held him in quite as high esteem.

'It's been sick again just in the time it's taken me to walk down here.' Lucy ran through the open doorway, out of breath, going straight through to the consulting room, where she put the box down and slowly undid the top. As though worried about what she'd find.

Charlie glanced in and frowned. This was worse than he'd expected. He reached for some gloves, then carefully lifted the tiny scrap out of the box. A gangly, skinny bundle of dirty fur that seemed to weigh nothing in his hands.

It shivered violently, the shakes travelling down its whole body. 'Has,' he paused, glancing up at Lucy who was pale, biting her lip, 'she been in contact with any of your other animals?'

'No, I'd only just found her when I rang, well Gertie found her. But she didn't touch her, the box was still done up. I left her by the gate while I rang, she just looked so poorly ...'

He nodded, relieved. 'Good. You didn't clean her up, then ...' He had to be sure.

'No. Should I have done? I just panicked and ...' She stared at the gloves.

'No, no. You did exactly the right thing, didn't she little one?' Charlie stroked one finger gently over the tiny puppy's head, but it barely reacted.

'What's wrong with her, Charlie? Why are you wearing ...?'

'I'm sorry Lucy, the gloves are a precaution.' He softened his tone. He didn't want to upset her, but he had to be honest. 'I can't be sure, but there's a chance this little mite has got parvo.' He wanted to hug her. But he couldn't.

'Parvo?'

'Parvovirus. It's pretty lethal when it comes to young animals like this, and from a quick look at her she's not very old at all. No idea where she came from?'

'None.' She shook her head, and her blonde ponytail swung from side to side. 'The box was just dumped by the gate.'

'Well she can't be local, nobody here would do that. They must have driven in from outside the village.' He frowned, angry at the callousness of some people. 'How much effort would it have taken to have the animal treated, to have taken it into a local surgery?' He knew the rough edge was back in his voice, but he couldn't help it. 'Instead of abandoning it to its fate. If you hadn't been at home, it could have been dead within twenty-four hours.'

'It's that serious?' Lucy leaned forward to look at the pup, her voice soft, and he knew she was finding it hard not to reach out, touch it, reassure the tiny scrap.

He nodded, tried to be brisk, business like. 'It's good that you got here quickly before morning surgery started.' Charlie quite liked Saturday morning surgery, usually it ran at a nice steady pace. People bringing cats and dogs in for vaccinations, and consultations about neutering or teeth cleaning. At this time of year though there were often young animals and the last thing he wanted was the risk of a parvo outbreak in the village. 'Look I need to get her on a drip.'

There was the tring of the bell as somebody opened the surgery door.

'Sally?'

Sally, the practice receptionist and animal nurse appeared at the consulting room door, her normal ready smile spreading across her face as she saw Lucy.

'We need to get this little one isolated.'

The smile faded. 'Parvo?' As she spoke she dropped

her bag on the chair and reached over to grab a pair of gloves. Carefully she took the unprotesting puppy into her arms, and headed out of the consulting room into the back.

'I'll call you later, Lucy.' She was still worrying at her lip, her eyes glistening, and he really did want to hug her. Instead he peeled off his gloves and then put his hands on her arms. 'If you've handled her make sure you wash your hands properly won't you?' She nodded. 'This virus is highly contagious and we really don't want it to be passed on to any of Annie's animals.' He dropped a kiss on the tip of her nose, and wished more than anything he could stop, reassure her, but he knew he had to do his job. Save the puppy.

'Will she make it?' The words were soft, and he wouldn't have heard them if his forehead hadn't been resting against hers.

'I honestly don't know if it's parvo. Let's hope it isn't.' He brushed his thumb over her cheek, then pulled back reluctantly. 'God, what a horrible start to the day for you. Look, I'm sorry, I'm really going to have to go.'

'I know.' Lucy was staring after him, as he elbowed the door through to the back of the surgery open.

'I'll call you in a bit, okay?' He shot an apologetic glance over his shoulder as he headed through.

She nodded.

'Still on for tonight?'

'Sure. Is Maisie any better?'

'Fine, well she's had a sleepover at a friend's and I've got to go and pick her up after lunch. She's getting a bit uptight about the new term, she wants to go back to her old school.' He grimaced. There'd been tears at bedtime more than once, and he didn't know if he'd done the right thing agreeing for her to go and visit a friend from her old school. 'It's just been like a holiday, having those couple of weeks at Langtry Meadows Primary at the end of last term, then the summer break. She wants to go back to her old life now, and I don't know what to say.' It bothered him. 'Am I doing the right thing, Lucy? Have I got this wrong?'

'You're doing the only thing you can, Charlie.' Her voice was soft, it was her turn to reassure him now, but he could see a trace of worry in her blue eyes. 'She's bound to miss her mum, and her old home, it will take time. It's a big change for a little girl.'

'I better ...'

'You had, go on, go! We'll talk later, and we'll make sure she has a great time tomorrow. I'll make cakes!'

He opened his mouth in horror. 'Oh no, not Lucy cakes.'

'Sod off, I have mastered fairy cakes now,' she paused melodramatically, 'I have watched a whole series of *Great British Bake Off* back to back I'll have you know.'

'You'll be in the WI next!' He winked, thankful to

her for lightening the atmosphere, even though he was more worried than he'd let on. Then turned back to the matter in hand. A very poorly puppy.

# Chapter 2

Jasmine Cottage lived up to its name. The sweet-scented white flowers spread a delicate flush of colour over the old red brick as the plant snaked its way round the old window frames, over the ramshackle porch and up towards the roof. In amongst the feathery leaves of the summer jasmine were thicker, woody stems that Lucy was pretty confident were winter jasmine. Six months ago she wouldn't have had a clue, but after spending all her spare time trying to tame Annie's garden she discovered she'd taken in more details from the gardening books she'd found in the tiny bookcase under the stairs than she'd have thought possible.

If she remembered correctly, winter jasmine had yellow flowers, which meant that once Christmas was over she could look forward to a flush of cheery bright colour.

Since she'd spoken to Mr Bannister on the phone, she'd been completely distracted by the puppy and hadn't been able to give the cottage (or him) another thought. In fact, she'd not even remembered to mention it to Charlie. But now she was here every doubt about whether this was the right thing to do fled her mind.

Which could be bad news, given the state of the overgrown garden, and peeling porch and window frames.

It might be a good job she enjoyed a challenge she thought wryly, as she pushed the small gate, and it rocked alarmingly on its one hinge and squeaked in protest.

'Morning, Lucy.'

Jumping at the cheery greeting, she spun round to see the tall, lanky figure of Simon Proofit.

'Simon, am I glad to see *you*!' Which could be taken as rude. 'Not that, well, I was expecting Mr Bannister.'

Simon grinned as though her reaction wasn't totally unexpected. 'Alf couldn't make it.'

'Alf,' Lucy felt the smile twitch at the corners of her mouth, 'that's his name?' That made him seem much more human.

'It is, he inherited more than just the business from his grandad. What do you think?' Simon gestured at the cottage. 'It's the type of property we say,' he put on his 'estate-agent' voice, 'has got oodles of charm and character.'

Lucy laughed, the last trace of the jitters disappearing

from her stomach at his disarming smile. 'I bet you do. Along with dry rot and rising damp?'

He chuckled. 'The plumbing has character as well. Want a look?' He strode past her, and was opening the front door before Lucy had a chance to answer.

Lucy stepped from the stone flags to the warmth of the old oak floorboards and fell head-over-heels in love with Jasmine Cottage.

'It's beautiful.' The words came out on a sigh.

'It is.' Simon's tone had softened, lost its normal slightly bombastic strength, and he walked over and settled into one of the armchairs by the fireplace, sending up a plume of dust that danced in the sunlight. 'It's been empty since May had to go into the nursing home, and her family haven't wanted to part with it. I think they've hung on because giving up on the place would be accepting she'll never come back.'

'How sad. I don't think I know her, she must have left before I came to the village.' Lucy wandered over to the window; she had the perfect view of the green, of the bench where she and Charlie had sat so many times. For a second something caught in her throat, a sadness she didn't want to acknowledge. Charlie had to go where his daughter led. If Josie took Maisie away, then he'd be leaving the village too. She was sure he felt the same way about her, as she did about him. That he'd want her to go with him. But it wouldn't be easy.

They both had busy lives. And leaving this lovely place would be hard.

For the first time in her life she felt like she belonged somewhere. That Langtry Meadows was her home.

'Oh, May's been gone a couple of years now.' Lucy turned her attention back to the estate agent, and he waved in the direction of the fireplace. 'You could put a nice wood burning stove in there.'

She gazed round the room. 'It would be so easy to make it cosy.' She could reach the beamed ceiling if she stretched up, but the place felt safe, and comforting, even in its present neglected state. 'I could soon clean up the floorboards.'

A few bright rugs scattered around, a bookcase in the corner, some new curtains would transform the place. She could even squeeze her desk into the alcove.

'Want to see more?' Sensing a sale, Simon jumped to his feet, and waved her on enthusiastically.

The kitchen was bigger than she'd expected, and brighter, with a lovely large window which she was instantly drawn to and found herself looking out over the small cottage garden. Next to the house was a York paved patio, with a small, round wrought iron table and chairs and a mass of colourful pots all different shapes and sizes that she could imagine overflowing with summer bedding plants.

Lucy turned back to study the room. There was a

mix of old fashioned cupboards, and under her feet the red quarry tiles seemed to glow, leading her gaze straight to the cream Aga.

'Wow, is that a proper Aga?'

Simon grinned. 'It is, May's daughter told us it's been looked after, but it runs on coal so you might want a more modern version.'

'Oh I love it, just as it is, it must be so cosy in the winter in here.' She could sit, on a chair by the Aga, reading a book or doing her marking, and gaze out at the cute back garden. Charlie and Maisie would adore the place, though she really, really mustn't think that way, their future could be far away. But the pup would love it here, it would be heaven for a dog.

Oh God, she mustn't think about that, the poor thing was really ill, and she still didn't know quite how poorly it was. The way it had looked at her, so trusting, lifting its head even though it was so weak. She blinked. She mustn't think about it, she'd had her heart broken once before as a child, when she'd lost her dog, her best friend. Her and her mother had moved, and not been able to take Sandy with them, and now she really didn't know if she was ready to risk the heartache again. Even thinking about the poor little scrap, the thought of it dying...

She gulped away the feelings and stroked a hand along the old stone sink.

She'd love it here. She just knew she would. And buying it was something she'd be doing for herself.

'I've got to warn you that the bathroom isn't up to much.' Simon was heading up the small staircase as he spoke, ducking to avoid the beam. 'It was originally outside the back door of course, which is now a brilliant storage shed, I'll show you in a minute, but they squeezed one in up here about forty years ago.' He turned to wink at her. 'Modern development.'

The small bathroom was far from modern, but she could imagine how it would look if she got a claw foot bath near the window, if she stripped out the thin green carpet, the olive-coloured tiles, and the avocado suite that might well be as old as the bathroom itself.

'You'd need a survey of course, but the place is basically sound as far as we can tell. The family did look after it for May, it just needs a bit of updating and a few throws and cushions and stuff, not that I'm into interior decorating, but my mum is a whizz with a bit of soft furnishing. Only started to appreciate it when I started going into other people's houses and realising how much difference a few bits and bobs could make.'

Lucy couldn't help but smile at his enthusiasm, and he blushed, ushering her into the next room.

'Master bedroom, nice view over the green and pond, you can peer round the net curtains and keep up with business better than Elsie Harrington can. Must drive her mad being hidden away by the church.'

'She does get to see what goes on in the square.'

'True. What do you think then?'

'Honestly?'

'Honestly.' He sat down next to her on the little window seat.

'It's amazing, Simon. I could see myself living here. But ...'

'But?' His shoulder nudged against hers, as though chivvying her on, willing her to say yes.

'Well Mr Bannister, Alf, said it would sell quickly and I'm sure he's right, and I'd need to sell my own house first.'

'Don't worry about that. If you really want it, get yours on the market and we'll sit on this for a few days.'

'But you can't ...' She frowned. 'It's business, you ...'

'It's much better for the village if the people who live here own the houses. Especially these ones. We can't hold on to it for ever, but if you're serious ...'

'Yes.' She looked around, and nodded. 'I'm serious.' There was a little flutter of anticipation deep down in her stomach. This could be her home. Her real home. Not some characterless block of bricks that was little more to her than a symbol of her achievements. 'I am.' She could hear the conviction ring out in her own voice. 'I'll ring the agent who's letting mine out as soon as I get home, I'm sure he can give me an idea of how long it would take to sell, and confirm a price.' Although she had a fair idea of how much the house would be worth. Hopefully she'd be able to keep the same level of mortgage and she'd have a little bit of equity to spend on the work the cottage needed.

'Great, Alf will be pleased.'

She raised an eyebrow, and Simon laughed.

'He's okay, just a bit of a grumpy git on the outside, but his heart's in the right place. He'd far rather somebody we know buy it, and so would May's family.'

Lucy felt a little glow spread up through her body. Somebody we know. She hadn't been in the village that long, less than a year, but she *did* feel she belonged, she did feel she knew people – which was something she'd never expected at all.

'Feel free to come and collect the key if you need another look.'

'I will, thanks Simon. I'll let you know this afternoon what the agent says, although you're closed aren't you?'

'Officially, according to Alf. Here,' he held out a card, 'take this, it's got my mobile number on it.'

The banging on the door was followed by the sound of it creaking open, and a cheery 'hello.' Lucy gave up on staring at the email from the estate agents, not that she'd been concentrating on it that hard – with the poorly pup on her mind – and closed the lid of her laptop with a sigh, just as Maisie flung the kitchen door open and dashed in, a small brown dog at her heels.

'I've been to see my friend, have you got any cakes? Daddy says you've got cakes.'

Lucy grinned. 'They're for the picnic tomorrow.'

'Hi!' Charlie, looking much more relaxed than he had earlier at the surgery, ruffled his daughter's hair. 'You've had enough cake, and what happened to "Hello Lucy, how are you?"'

'I don't need to say that, she's got a happy face so I already know.' Maisie rooted through the wicker basket of toys near the back door. 'Daddy says your puppy's a poo.' She giggled. 'Poo and Roo go together. Come on Roo.' Picking out a tug toy she waved it at the dog, before making a dash for the back garden.

'My puppy's a poo?' Lucy raised an eyebrow. Not sure about the poo, or the fact Maisie had called it *her* puppy.

Charlie shook his head, trying not to smile. 'It is indeed, well that's my best guess, I think it's a cockerpoo, a cocker spaniel poodle cross, and I have good news.'

'About the puppy? She's going to be okay?'

'Yep. I thought I'd deliver the news in person, along with this.' He held up a bottle of wine, then after a quick glance out of the window he leaned in and planted the softest of kisses on her lips. It was a gentle caress, the slightest brush of his dry lips against hers, but it found its way all the way down to her toes.

'Oh.' Lucy's stomach gave a little flip, and the single syllable quivered. They'd said they wouldn't get too involved over the summer, for Maisie's sake. But they'd failed miserably. Not that the little girl had been affected. Charlie's parents had been overjoyed that Josie was away. She'd always limited the time they could spend with their only granddaughter, and as soon as they'd known the coast was clear they'd been on the phone to Charlie – begging him to let them spend as much time as they could with Maisie over the summer. So Maisie had spent several weeks with her nana and grandad, and Lucy had spent rather a lot of time with Charlie.

Now, after two weeks of him spending as much time as he could with Maisie, and her spending rather more time than she wanted to with her spreadsheets preparing for the new school year, she had a very unladylike urge to jump on him.

He winked, as though he'd read her mind. 'I really need to get my hands on you, think you'll be able to cope with my animal urges once Maisie's fast asleep tonight?' The rough edge to his voice brought a rush of goosebumps to her arms.

'I'll do my best.' She grinned as the heady atmosphere of anticipation lifted a bit. 'Think you'll be able to cope with all my demands?'

'Oh, I'll certainly do my best.'

They grinned at each other. Then he remembered

the wine. 'Open it now, finish it later?'

She smiled back at the question in his voice. She'd fallen in love, and she felt happier than she could ever remember being. But she also knew they had to keep this as low key as they could for Maisie's sake, now she was back.

Lucy knew only too well how it felt to be abandoned by somebody you loved, what the upheaval from your family home could do to you. At least Maisie's dad loved her, both her parents loved her, and her move to Langtry Meadows was to a lovely welcoming place. Nothing like the nightmare Lucy had experienced.

When she was not much older than Maisie, she'd been sure that nobody loved her. She'd thought her dad had abandoned her, and that her friends hated her. She'd lost her dog, her home, and her mother was working every hour she could to scrape a living. Lucy's whole world had crumbled. Which was why, when she'd graduated, she'd buried herself in the anonymity of a city.

But she'd learned recently that the truth was far more complicated. Wasn't it always? That her mum had feared for their lives, and fled her domineering and brutal husband. That starting a brand new life, severing all their ties had been what had saved them. Even though for years it hadn't seemed like that.

Maisie's situation was quite different. But Lucy knew that the little girl needed as much of her father's attention as work allowed. For now, she had to be there for support, a helping hand, not her father's lover. Which would be confusing, more than confusing as she was also going to be Maisie's teacher.

Tonight though was special. They'd agreed that they needed to distract Maisie from the fast approaching start of term. Charlie and his daughter would stay with Lucy in the cottage, then in the morning they'd make a picnic together, before heading off on an adventure.

'Sounds nice.' She grabbed a corkscrew. 'Is she okay?' Lucy kept her voice low, even though Roo was barking and Maisie was squealing excitedly.

Charlie shrugged. 'She's been a bit subdued.' The smile dropped from his face, the fan of laughter lines she loved so much faded away. 'It's my fault, she's probably spent far too much time with Mum and Dad this summer and in between I've let her see too much of her old friends, and not got her to mix with the kids here.'

'It's not your fault.' She chided him gently, wishing she could take the worry away from his eyes. 'Everybody is away over the summer anyway, and she needs to know her old friends are still there for her, young kids need to feel secure, it helps them cope with change.' She glanced down. 'I lost all my friends when I moved.' It had been horrible, she'd come to terms with it, discovered why it had been that way. But she could still remember how it felt. The hurt. The feeling of being cast aside – and even the logic of knowing it wasn't actually like that couldn't rewrite the memories. Which was why she had to resist the temptations of the gorgeous Charlie Davenport, and make sure they did this right.

'I know.' He put a warm hand over hers, squeezed, and brought a lump to her throat.

'We can chat later, when she's in bed? Come up with a plan.'

He laughed then, a warm, deep laugh and looked straight into her eyes. More tempting than a box of her favourite hard caramel chocolates. 'You and your plans, you haven't got a colour coded spreadsheet in mind, have you?'

'Of course.' She took his lead, moved on from the difficult topic that she was sure occupied most of his waking hours. 'So, how's the puppy?'

'She's not got parvo.' His words were muffled, as his head was in the cupboard. 'We'll have to keep her in a few days, but then she's all yours. So, what are you going to call her?' He reappeared, holding two wine glasses.

'All mine?' She frowned.

'You are keeping her, aren't you?' He raised an eyebrow. 'Well, if you can't I suppose I can get Sally to ring the dogs' home, but they won't be keen with all the care she'll need, she's really poorly. Needs some TLC and building up.'

'Stop.' Lucy held up a hand. Okay, she had been thinking about keeping the pup, after all hadn't it been one of her thoughts as she'd stood in Jasmine Cottage? But it had just been a passing thought. 'Just stop, I know exactly what you're playing at. I'll look after her for now, okay? Then we'll find another home. And you can stop smirking.'

He grinned, and poured the wine. 'You were really upset when Elsie Harrington told you that somebody else wanted that podgy retriever pup of hers.' His tone was a gentle tease.

'No I wasn't!' The last of Elsie's litter of puppies had been adorable, and for the first time in years she'd actually started to wonder if a dog in her life might not be a bad thing.

'You were. You got your sulky face on.'

'I don't have a sulky face.'

'You did that *I can cope, leave me alone*, thing.'

'Charlie!'

His grin broadened until the dimples appeared at the side of his mouth. 'It's okay,' he leant forward, his broad, suntanned forearms resting on the table, 'I know you're a soft touch under that strict school teacher exterior.'

'You'll be getting detention if you don't behave.'

'Oh, yes please, now you're talking.' He chuckled, and the shiver of goosebumps shot down her arms again.

'Stop being naughty!'

'I can't help it when you're around.' His gaze grabbed hers, held her, for a moment serious, and she couldn't miss the meaning.

'You're bad.'

'You make me that way.' The husky tone made her wriggle in her seat. 'You're in so much trouble later.'

'Promises, promises.'

'You betcha.' He touched the tip of her nose with one warm finger, shook his head then pulled away reluctantly and turned his attention back to the wine. 'I know you didn't want to give Elsie her puppy back, even though you wouldn't admit it.'

Lucy tried to scowl, but he was right. He knew her too well. She'd grown quite attached in the few days that she'd looked after Elsie's dog Molly, and her puppy. She was fairly sure that Elsie had been plotting to persuade her to home the dog, but when a neighbour was devastated by the loss of her own Labrador, Elsie had felt she had no choice but to offer her Podge, as Lucy had named him. But she'd decided it was for the best.

A tiny, malnourished runt of a puppy with mismatched eyes and an aptitude for projectile vomiting wasn't for the best. Even if she couldn't stop thinking about the animal.

'She's stopped being sick now.' Charlie grinned, as

though he'd read her mind.

She sighed. 'I haven't really got time though have I? Being sensible. Term starts in a few days, and there's bound to be tons of work to do, and parents evenings and ...' and possibly a new home to renovate.

'She'll be good company for you.' His voice was soft, but it hung between them. The unspoken agreement, she'd be company for her because he couldn't be right now, he had Maisie. 'Sometimes it's better not being too sensible.'

'I have got all the other animals.'

'The other animals aren't yours, they're Annie's. And anyway, a dog is different.' He was right. A dog was different. The sound of Maisie and Roo filtered through from the garden. She'd played with her own dog Sandy when she was that age, and she'd been heartbroken to leave him behind when they'd moved. She'd sworn she'd never get attached to an animal in that way again. But maybe now was the right time.

Things had changed since she'd moved to Langtry Meadows. She'd changed.

'So?'

She shook her head at him, but couldn't help the smile that came to her lips. It *was* the right time. 'Piper. I'm going to call her Piper.'

'Let's drink to Piper then.' He raised his glass, his eyes seeming to assess her, and it was there, that moment when she knew that whatever happened, she'd always love him. She gave herself a mental shake. 'You look like you need a drink, are you okay?'

'Well actually,' this was a brilliant time to concentrate on the other big issue, and distract herself, and her urges. 'I've had a bit of a strange day.' She sighed.

He was studying her, looking serious. 'What? Has something else happened?' His voice was soft, concerned.

'My house, the one in Birmingham?'

'Oh no, it's not been trashed or anything?' He put his drink down, laid a warm hand over Lucy's.

'No, no, it's not that.' She hadn't been able to believe the response when she'd rung the agent who was letting her house out, within the space of an hour she'd had a return call, and an email confirmation in her inbox. 'The people who are renting it from me might want to buy.'

It was all so much to take in. In the space of one short day she'd found an idyllic home, and it looked like it was hers for the taking.

When she'd taken a temporary job at the school in Langtry Meadows, Lucy had had no intention of hanging around. She liked working in Birmingham, and as soon as the opportunity arose she'd be back there like a flash. Which was why she'd let her home out. But the village had got under her skin, and she'd soon found herself accepting the permanent position that

Timothy Parry, the headmaster had offered. Now it was hard to imagine living anywhere else.

'That's fantastic!' Charlie paused, his eyes searching her face. 'Isn't it?'

'Well yes ...'

'But?' He frowned. 'You've take a permanent job on here, and you can't live in this place for ever, can you? I mean, what happens when Annie comes back? Selling yours means you can afford to look for a place, doesn't it?'

Which was true, Annie had planned to be away for at least a year, but beyond that who knew? That had been fine when she'd only planned on staying a term, but it was a rather different situation now. She'd already been in Langtry Meadows for six months, what if Annie and her husband were back next spring? 'Well yes, I mean I have got a job. But the school's still got an uncertain future, even knowing it's not on the list they're considering closing this year.' And it was the final step. Letting go of the security blanket that had cloaked her insecurities of the past.

'That could be the same anywhere.' His voice was gentle, with a question at the end of it. 'What's the real problem, don't you want it to work out?' The way he said it, the way he was looking at her with that slightly unsure edge to his voice, said it all.

He knew, they both knew, that the problem wasn't

just about letting go of the dreams she'd put in place to protect herself – the big school, challenging kids, promotion prospects. It was him. Charlie Davenport, and his daughter Maisie. Them.

Or more specifically, it was Josie. What would happen when Maisie's mum came back?

It would break her heart if Charlie moved on, and she couldn't follow. And it would be beyond awful if Josie moved back to the area, and made things difficult for them.

'Of course.' She squeezed his hand. 'I do want it to work out.' Those gorgeous brown eyes of his were studying her intently. He cared, she knew he cared, but that didn't alter anything. 'But it is complicated, isn't it?'

He nodded. 'It might be.' She knew he'd understand, know she wasn't just talking about houses, jobs. 'But nothing we can't handle.'

Lucy hoped so. 'Well,' she paused, 'the other bit of my strange day,' how much drama could a girl cram into one short day? 'One of the little cottages opposite the green has just come up for sale. I could buy it.'

'Wow,' Charlie sat back, and ran his fingers through his hair, 'you have had a busy day! But that's perfect timing, isn't it?'

She nodded slowly. 'It's gorgeous too, but, well, should I wait until ...' It was a massive step. She should do it, just for her. But he was part of her life.

He put his glass down, and gave her a funny lopsided grin which she didn't quite understand. 'Wait? Why? So you don't want to commit to life here? I thought ...'

'You thought?'

'Well, me and you, I thought you'd be around to help me with Maisie, and for, well, us.'

She felt like he was squeezing her heart. 'I do want to be here for us.' She wrapped her arms round him. Rested her forehead against his. 'I do.' But what if the immediate future didn't have a Charlie and Lucy shaped gap? Loving Charlie was one thing, but coming between him and Maisie was something she'd never want to do. 'But should I wait until Josie comes back, until we know ...'

Charlie shook his head, his forehead brushing against hers, his dark gaze hitting her head on. 'Josie's dictated to me for long enough. You know Maisie means the world to me, I'll never give her up, but you mean the world to me too, whatever we need to do to make this work we will. Yes? Do it, if it's what you want to do?'

She nodded, looking at him through the tears she hadn't realised had sprung into her eyes. 'It is.'

'Good.' Then not even glancing up to check whether Maisie was nearby, he kissed her.

# Chapter 3

'I wondered where you were!' Jill smiled at Maisie, who was kneeling down in the playground, clutching Roo to her chest. The tears that had been building in her big brown eyes spilled over, as she sensed the inevitable. Her grip tightened on the little dog. 'I need your help, Maisie.'

Lucy stood back. Yesterday morning, the little girl had been more than a little reluctant to leave her dad and dog, and she was sure there had been a muttered 'you're not my mummy', so today she had decided to use different tactics.

'Our guinea pig isn't at all well, and I'm sure somebody told me you were the best person to help. But, if they're wrong I can always ask one of the other children.' Maisie's grip loosened on the dog, and she stood up, taking the hand that Jill was holding out.

Lucy could practically see the whoosh of tension leave Charlie's body as his daughter disappeared into the school building.

'Morning.' Lucy smiled at Charlie. 'You'll go bald if you're not careful.'

He gave a wry smile, but stopped running his fingers through his hair.

The first few days of the new school year had been chaotic and Lucy had been glad the term had started on a Wednesday and they hadn't had a full week to cope with. The children, and staff, had been exhausted by the end of Friday. And now they were already into the second week, and were starting to settle into a routine. Apart from Maisie.

'She seemed fine last week, but this week ...' He shrugged, looking at a loss.

'I know. She was very quiet over the weekend though. She's bright Charlie, she was mulling it over.'

'I thought bringing Roo with us might help, but if anything it's made her worse.' The little terrier looked up at the sound of his name, and Lucy patted his head.

'She'd be hanging on to you if Roo wasn't here. She'll be okay, honest. She just needs time, and Jill will keep a close eye on her.'

'I hope so.'

The school bell rang, and the last of the children started to make their way towards the entrance door. 'Shoo, go, and make sure you bring Roo with you when you pick her up!'

'I wanted to bring Roo in to school.' Maisie was looking down at the desk, and Lucy knew it was to hide the shine of tears. 'Roo will be sad.'

'I'm sure he will.' Lucy squatted down. 'Daddy will look after him though, and he'll be very happy to see you this afternoon, won't he?'

'Daddy's busy.' She gave a large theatrical sigh, but Lucy was glad to see that the threat of tears seemed to have abated. 'He's always busy. Why can't dogs come to school?'

She was just trying to formulate the best answer to that, when Rosie chipped in. 'They can.' She was doodling away industriously at what looked like a picture of a sheep, or it could have been a legless dog, or even a very hairy guinea pig, and didn't even look up. 'Our other teacher let us have a pet day. We always have one. I brought my rat in. Do you like my picture, Miss?'

Lucy stared, and wondered if looking at it from a different angle would help. 'Very good, I thought we were all drawing our favourite animals?'

'He is.' She scribbled harder until the point of her pencil snapped off. 'He's the furry caterpillar I found on the fence on holiday, he was enormous.' She picked up a brown crayon. 'We stayed in a big caravan. But Mummy wouldn't let me bring him home. That's why,' she glanced up at Lucy, 'I'll have to bring our rat to pet day. It's pet day tomorrow, isn't it Miss?' She nodded at Maisie knowledgeably. 'You can bring Roo, as long as he's not going to try and eat my rat.'

Lucy looked up at Jill, who shrugged apologetically, then pointed to the large calendar.

How on earth had she forgotten that tomorrow was pet day?

'My mam says caterpillars are a bleeding nuisance.'

'Sophie, we don't say that, do we?'

'A bleeding' she paused, and frowned, 'pest. They eat our lettuces.'

'I wish my mummy was here.'

Lucy put an arm round Maisie, swallowing down the lump in her throat. She remembered wishing her dad had been there when she wasn't that much older than Maisie. The little girl was only six, what kind of mother just upped and left her child for six months? Josie had to have a good reason, she had to. 'Draw her a lovely picture of Roo, and you can show her on skype can't you? I'm sure she's missing you and Roo.'

'Lunch time meeting.' Liz Potts stuck her head round the door, then was off before either Lucy or Jill had time to question her.

'What's that about then?' Jill raised an eyebrow.

'Your guess is as good as mine.' But even as she said the words, Lucy felt a twinge of anticipation. It was Tuesday, the children had been back at school five days now, and five days into the new school year had an ominous ring to it. It was the earliest date that the Ofsted inspectors could come calling.

Lucy sank down with a sigh onto one of the comfortable staffroom chairs. Would anybody notice if she put her feet up on the table?

The first week of the new school year was always a killer. After a long summer of late nights, lie-ins, walks and general lazing about it was nice in a way to get back into a normal work routine. At her previous school, the first few days were always hard work, particularly when you had a new class, over thirty new names to learn, personalities and capabilities to assess. Behaviour to manage. Here though, even after only a few short months of working at the school, she at least knew most of the children by name – and she was carrying on teaching the class she'd had last year. It was a small school, and several of the classes had been merged, which meant she had Class 1 and Class 2. But there were a few newcomers, a few changes, and the children always seemed to grow over the summer and learn new tricks. Even the sweetest of children liked to test the boundaries, in fact the butter-wouldn't-melt ones were often the ones who pushed hardest. And then there was Maisie. Sweet little Maisie who had giggled her way infectiously through the summer, but now wasn't quite sure why she was still here in a strange place, without her mummy.

Lucy tried to force the frown away and relax, and found herself yawning.

'Keeping you up?' Jill, her classroom assistant, laughed. 'Budge up. Any idea why Timothy has assembled the troops?'

'Nope. I was hoping you'd be able to tell me.'

Jill shook her head, then nodded towards Liz Potts, the school secretary who had just bustled in with an armful of papers. 'Looks like Liz knows.'

'Thank you for getting here promptly everybody.' Timothy Parry, head of Langtry Meadows Primary School coughed, straightened his bowtie and tugged at the cuffs of his shirt which were peeping out of the sleeves of his tweed jacket. 'I won't keep you long, I do appreciate how much, er, fun, the first couple of weeks back are. Now,' he motioned to Liz, who handed over the papers. 'I have a copy here of our SEF, which Lucy very efficiently updated at the end of last term.'

Lucy grimaced as her stomach hollowed in anticipation. With the small village school still at risk of closure they'd all thrown themselves into making sure they were fully prepared to hit the ground running before they'd closed for the summer break. The school's self-evaluation form had been updated, a new improvement plan put together, and every file in Mrs Potts's system gone through to ensure they were ready for anything. Anything, it seemed, involved an early Ofsted inspection.

A small smile twitched at the corner of Timothy's mouth. 'As I think Miss Jacobs has already guessed,' they all turned to look at her, 'we have been informed that the Ofsted inspectors will be calling rather earlier than anticipated. We appear to be in demand, top of the list.'

A ripple of a groan spread round the staffroom, peaking when it reached their youngest member of staff, who clamped her hand over her mouth as she realised she'd gasped rather louder than she'd meant to. Liz patted her arm comfortingly.

'Don't worry dear, it's not all bad, they're not the ogres they used to be.'

'Says who?' Jill whispered rather too loudly in Lucy's ear.

'Ahem.' Timothy coughed to restore order. 'After the huge success of our summer picnic I pretty much think we're on track to safeguard the future of our school, but a good report would be the icing on the cake. Which reminds me, the Right Honourable George enjoyed his visit so much that he sent us a rather delightful letter. Liz has very kindly framed it and put it on the wall so that we may remind ourselves how wonderful we are,' he paused, 'if the need arises.' He glanced around the room, his face serious, but something Lucy was sure was mischief danced in his eyes. 'George always did like to make himself heard, which I think Lucy has done a splendid job of utilising.'

Lucy blushed and studied her hands. It had really been Elsie Harrington and Jim Stafford who had been responsible for the reintroduction of the Summer Picnic – without their help the idea would never have occurred to her. She would never have known that so many past attendees of the school, like George, now had rather prominent and influential positions on the numerous councils that had the power to control the future of the school. But Elsie, a colourful, elderly villager who seemed to know everybody's business, and school governor (and councillor) Jim who had a finger in every pie, had soon pointed her in the right direction. She still wasn't quite sure if she'd been manipulated, or made the decisions, but it didn't matter.

How could George recommend Langtry Meadows Primary School to be the next closure, after the nostalgic reminder of his childhood? As guest of honour George had excelled himself, his speech had been longer than a presidential inauguration, and had definitely made prolific use of the word 'great'.

'I rather thought we should invite him back to the school nativity, and ask him to switch on the lights if nobody has an objection? Keep him in the loop, as it were.'

'Nativity?' Lucy hissed to Jill who had a broad smile on her face.

'Oh you're going to love Christmas. But don't worry about donkeys and the rest of the mayhem yet, we've got this half term and Ofsted to get through first.'

Which sounded ominous. 'Donkeys?'

'And cows.'

'Right ho.' Timothy clapped his hands together. 'Let's smash it.'

'Smash it?' Lucy raised an eyebrow at Jill as they made their way to the door.

Jill grinned. 'He's been spending too much time with his nephews over the summer. He'll be high fiving us next and telling us how many Pokémon he's caught. Don't worry he'll be back to normal within a couple of weeks.'

Lucy rather hoped he'd be back to normal by tomorrow, before the Ofsted team arrived.

Five minutes after they'd got to the classroom, the first of the children started to run in – hot and excited from running about in the sun, and within a further two minutes the head scratching began.

'Looks like we've got little visitors.' Lucy pulled a face at Jill. 'Not only have we got bring-your-pet-in day tomorrow, we've also got head-lice now. Just what every Ofsted inspector likes to see.' She automatically reached a hand up to scratch her own head. They definitely weren't a welcome addition to her classroom.

Jill laughed. 'I thought I saw one or two of them scratching earlier, but didn't like to say. I think we've got more livestock in Langtry Meadows Primary School than there is in Charlie D's waiting room.'

Lucy shook her head. 'I'll ask Liz to write a letter to the parents.'

'Talking of Charlie,' Jill watched as Maisie was escorted to her seat by Rosie, who seemed to have taken her under her wing, 'is that man really going to let Josie waltz straight back in and take his daughter away from him again?'

Lucy frowned. Hoping the villagers wouldn't speculate about the return of Charlie's daughter had been a bit unrealistic. The daughter he'd kept a secret. The daughter his ex had said wasn't his. She didn't know how far *that* last nugget of information had spread, but she really hoped that it wasn't a topic of conversation in the village shop.

She shook her head. 'I hope not, I don't think he's going to give up without a fight, but who knows what will happen when she comes back from her travels. If she's not his daughter though, will he have much say in the matter?'

'He doesn't know yet? He hasn't had a DNA test?'

'Nope, he says she's his, whatever.' It worried her, and

she knew that it worried Charlie. He'd always been wary of Josie and her intentions, and they hung over them, a threatening black cloud.

'Miss, Miss, I've just found a nit on Rosie's head.'

'And what are you doing messing with Rosie's hair, Ted?' Jill made her way over to the children and Lucy clapped her hands to get their attention.

'Right, who is bringing in a pet tomorrow? Hands up!'

# Chapter 4

'Guess what?' Sally beamed, and actually did a happy dance on the doorstep when Lucy opened the cottage door. Sally, Charlie's receptionist and right hand woman, was like that. She was unfailingly friendly and breezy in the vets (but always professional), and fun outside of it.

She'd also been the first person that Lucy had properly talked to when she'd moved to Langtry Meadows the previous spring, the person that had dragged her out of her new home and into the community. *That* made it sound like she was part of a rehabilitation programme, which in a way was true. A few months in Langtry Meadows had given her a new lease of life.

Sally didn't wait for a response. She grabbed Lucy in a hug. 'Piper is ready to come home!'

'No!' Lucy shrieked, peering round Sally to see if the puppy was actually with her, then pulled herself together. 'Sorry, sorry, come in.'

'Don't worry, I've not got her with me, the weekend seemed a better idea. Look, I know you've only just gone back to work, Loo, but that's a bit of an extreme reaction!' Sally grinned and gave her friend another hug. 'Bad start to the school year?'

'No, well yes. We've got nits.'

Sally giggled. 'At least it isn't fleas.'

'And it's bring-a-pet-to-school day tomorrow.' Lucy put her hands on her head, feeling like her brain was about to boil over.

'Piece of cake when you're used to herding Annie's lot. What are you worrying about girl? I think a glass of wine is in order.' She started to steer Lucy towards the kitchen.

'I can't drink!'

That got Sally's attention. 'You're pregnant!'

'No I'm not bloody pregnant.' Lucy couldn't help it, she laughed, then shook her head. 'Nutter. It's worse. We've got Ofsted tomorrow.'

'Ofsted and bring-a-pet-to-school? You definitely need a drink. Chill, you've got this, you spent half the summer break preparing for all eventualities. I've seen the colour coded spreadsheets.'

'There isn't any kind of colour coding to cope with Ofsted and animals at the same time.' She frowned and peered at Sally as the comment sank in. 'I'm not that anal am I?'

'You are, but we all love you for it.' Sally put an arm round her shoulders and handed her a far too big glass of wine.

If she drank all that she'd be as entertaining tomorrow as one of the worms that little Ted liked to keep in his trouser pockets.

'I promised to take a pet in as well.' Lucy sank down on one of the kitchen chairs. 'Though heaven knows what. Gertie will chase any inspectors off the premises, no way can I take a fat pony, so Mischief is ruled out. The chickens are total hooligans, and Tigger the cat will have a field day if any of the kids take in fish, mice or hamsters.' Which was what she hoped most of them would take in, anything bigger could be calamitous.

'How about Pork-chop? He's got a harness, and he's cute.'

The pig was quite cute, she had to admit it, and he spent a lot of time just grunting and sitting down, which was a definite bonus.

'Hell, I'm being pathetic.' She looked up. 'It just feels like there's still so much at stake, we need an outstanding from Ofsted, and then we'll be completely in the clear.'

Sally shook her head. 'Totally pathetic.'

'Sally!'

She fought a losing battle to keep a straight face. 'It's okay, you're allowed to have moments of weakness. It makes you more human.'

'What do you mean, more human?'

Sally flung her arms round her in reply, and squeezed. 'Less perfect.'

'I'm not per—'

'We all like to see other people lose it a bit now and again, you know weep, explode, scream.' Sally shrugged. 'You keep it in most of the time.' She tutted. 'Not fair.'

'You're mad.' Which made two of them. She had all this to cope with, and she'd agreed to have a dog?

'At least Piper's stopped being sick now. We can keep her until Friday for you, she's no bother.' Sally grinned, as though she'd read her mind. 'Anyhow, I hear you should be celebrating. Charlie says you've sold your house and found a new one.'

'I've got an offer, I've not said …'

'You don't look very happy about it.'

'I'm in shock, that's all.' She tried a smile, and knew from Sally's rolled eyes that it wasn't convincing. 'Well you know how I like to plan.'

More rolled eyes. 'Don't I just! Sorry,' she laughed, 'carry on, go on, tell me.'

'Well making my own mind up that I want to do something is different to suddenly having it dropped in your lap, and somebody else almost making the decision isn't it?'

'It's bossy teacher syndrome isn't it? You like being in total control, don't you Lucy Jacobs, and this is freaking you out. God knows how poor Charlie copes with you in bed.'

'Sally!' Lucy tried to glare. 'But you've got a point about being a bit freaked out. I feel like I've been backed into a corner and my hand's being forced. Though I'm sure you'll be delighted about that, me showing my human side.' She had actually been pondering over the summer about the possibility of selling the house, but she hadn't quite got to the point of knowing it was what she wanted to do. Now this had happened. Which was fantastic. But scary.

Sally sat down at the kitchen table and studied her, looking serious. 'You know I was only joking.' Her voice was soft, concerned.

'Yeah, I know, well I know there's an element of truth in there too.'

'So, what's the problem? I know, you don't want to become a country bumpkin like me.'

'It's not that.'

'I mean, you *live* here now, don't you? And it's not often a nice place comes up for sale in the village. Gawd I'd kill for a chance like that.'

Sally's words had a wistful edge, and Lucy instantly felt herself colour up with guilt.

'Could you and Jamie get a place together?' Lucy knew that Sally and Jamie's relationship had positively exploded, and left the whole village agog. Not that they weren't all pleased, and very relieved that the couple had finally started to date – after all *everybody* knew they were *perfect* for each other.

Sally and Jamie had known each other since they were children, but both had been worried about admitting that they wanted to be more than just good friends. Until Sally had finally taken the drunken plunge and admitted how she felt. After that they seemed to have been intent on making up for lost time. Lucy had never known two people so obviously madly in love with each other.

Sally shook her head. 'Rentals hardly ever come up and the amount I get paid it's hopeless. Jamie's trying to save so that we can put a deposit down, but farming isn't exactly the best job to be in right now.' She sighed. 'At this rate it'll take bloody years, and lovely as they are I am getting a bit sick of living with Mum and Dad. Have you any idea what it's like being asked what time you'll be home when you're my age?' She rolled her eyes and Lucy laughed. 'And don't start me on the comments my dad makes about my clothes, you'd think I was twelve years old still. He actually asked if I was wearing a skirt or a belt the other day, how old is that line? And it was nearly down to my knees!' She shook her head in disbelief, then gave Lucy her direct not-to-be-messed with receptionist look. 'You'd be mad to pass on it.'

'I know. But what if the school closes?'

'That could happen anywhere. What if the world ends tomorrow? You get run over by a tractor? You get nits?' Sally's voice was gentle. 'What's the real issue here, Lucy? It's not just about the house is it? Is this about Charlie?'

'Charlie, what's it got to do with ...' She stopped herself short. It had everything to do with Charlie, well maybe not everything, but quite a lot. 'Charlie needs space for him and Maisie, a village is a small place.' Lucy grimaced. If she was honest, she needed to know she had a bolthole, options, if it all went wrong. If she wasn't wanted. Again.

In the last few months she'd finally managed to get rid of a lot of her insecurities, but there was still that lingering doubt. She'd spent a good chunk of her childhood feeling dispensable, as an adult knowing she had some security had always been important, *the* most important thing.

'You don't need to tell me that.' Sally rolled her eyes dramatically.

'What about when Josie comes back, what if it seems a better idea to move?'

'Then move. But you don't have to go back to your old place in Birmingham, do you? You don't have to hang on to the past and look backwards, Lucy. The world's your oyster.'

'It's just a bit of security, having that house.'

'So keep it. Carry on renting it out.'

Which was what her head kept saying, but some part of her heart was telling her to let go. To be really brave, braver than she'd been in accepting this job. Follow her heart.

But she was scared.

Scared of waking up one day and realising she didn't belong here. Scared that she should have stayed where she was, the place she understood. Scared that one day the past would catch up with her in this cute village and it would all be wrecked again. The nightmare of her dad leaving them had been replaced with the one of him finding them. A city was big. Anonymous.

'Either way, it's only a house, Luce. It's not like some inherited mansion or something,' she paused dramatically, 'is it?'

'No, it's your bog standard semi.' But it was *her* bog standard semi.

'Well then, a place here sounds much better.'

'I know.'

'It just means you've got your security here, not there. And you can always move again. Here, anywhere.' Sally paused, bottle of wine in hand, Lucy must have let her thoughts flitter across her features. 'And you might always fall in love with somebody else.'

She gave a grim smile, ignoring the Charlie remark. 'It's a good source of income.' The bottle of wine was still in Sally's hand. Poised. 'Are you pouring that or is this some weird mannequin challenge I don't know about, Sal?'

But it wasn't just about an income, security now. It was a decision. A step. It was letting go of her anchor.

Sally topped up their glasses. 'Don't stress about it. You'll know, when the time's right, you'll know. Maisie likes you, doesn't she?' She tipped her head on one side and smiled. 'She was in the surgery yesterday, talking about how she wished she could live with you all the time, instead of with Charlie who always says no.'

Lucy smiled back. 'I like her too. She might go off me now I have my teacher hat back on though.' It was hard not to fall in love with Charlie's curly haired daughter, although she wasn't always quite the angel she appeared – with her halo of soft auburn curls. They'd had a good summer, the three of them, but it was hard. She wasn't Maisie's mother, she didn't want to get too close to her. A part of her held back.

'What if Josie doesn't come back? You know, says she can live with Charlie permanently.' Sally was offering the other option.

She wasn't ready to be a mother, she didn't know *how* to be a mother. 'Oh don't be silly, she's Maisie's mum, of course she'll come back.' Then where would that leave her? But worse, what if Josie started laying down the law again, made it hard for Charlie to see his daughter?

Josie had taken Maisie away from Charlie once, she could do it again. And if a DNA test proved that Maisie wasn't his, well, it didn't bear thinking about. A hard lump formed in Lucy's throat at the thought of him having to suffer again. Although she knew he'd fight. But was the law on his side?

Charlie had told her it was over between him and Josie, and she believed him. But who knew what would happen if it came to the crunch? If Josie insisted he had to choose between seeing his daughter, and seeing her? She'd have no choice, she'd do whatever she could to make sure he saw Maisie. No way would she ever want the little girl to grow up without her dad, like she'd had to.

They'd both held back since the start of term, Maisie was the important thing, Charlie's priority now, and however much Lucy had fallen for the gorgeous vet she knew she couldn't jeopardise that.

'Pour the wine Sal, then seeing as it was your idea you can help me wash Pork-chop. He can't go into school smelling of chicken poo.'

\*\*\*

The Ofsted inspector stepped neatly round Pork-chop and squatted down next to Harry, who was clutching a small box.

'Now, young man, who do we have here?'

'Mario.'

Lucy's heart sank, and she looked at Jill in alarm. Harry's hamster Mario had sadly died in the spring and as far as she knew had been buried. Surely not? No, it was impossible, Harry couldn't have dug him up. Could he? She edged closer. He was opening the box, the inspector was peering in. He put his hand in, and pulled out ... a hamster treat, followed by a picture, and a tuft of fluff.

'My dad said we had to bury him, but we made him a mim, mimo, mimor thing to remember him by.'

'A memorial! How wonderful, what a clever boy you are.'

'When the vet came in to school we talked all about him dying, and we drew pictures, and I took this picture home so I could put it in his mimoroyal box.' Harry nodded wisely. 'But I don't look at it much now because I've got a lamb.' He sighed heavily. 'Well he was a lamb and I had to feed him with a bottle and everything cos his mum dropped dead.' He shook his head. 'Sheeps always do that you know. But that lamb is getting real bossy now, we'll be having him with mint sauce soon I reckon.'

The inspector, looking slightly shocked, got to his feet and moved on to study the children's books which had been laid out on a table by the window.

\*\*\*

'Well.' Jill shut the door firmly and leant against it. 'That was an interesting day.'

'Gawd, I thought he was never going to go, I think Sophie producing her nit comb and telling him what her mam had to say about it was what finally convinced him he'd heard enough.' Lucy sat down on one of the tiny chairs. 'Any news on how the rest got on?'

'No, but Liz Potts was singing so that's a good sign. They're in again in the morning, but we should get an update in the afternoon.' Jill grinned. 'I did overhear some comment about it being the first time he's seen a pig in a classroom.'

'And it will be the last time anybody sees one in my classroom, if it has anything to do with me. Roll on Friday.' One thing Lucy was sure of was that tonight she would fall into bed exhausted – but at least she'd done her bit. Now all they could do was wait for the verdict.

# Chapter 5

Charlie couldn't help it. He needed to talk to somebody, or he'd be snapping at Maisie and upsetting the very fragile state of her emotions. When he'd met her from school on Wednesday she had been bubbly, excited to tell him about her day, what Roo had done, and how she wanted a 'pet day' every day. But then she'd wanted to tell Mummy all about it, and Mummy unfortunately was not in an area with Wi-Fi. The skype tone had echoed out until he'd had to admit defeat, and the hope had died from her face.

Then he'd felt guilty. It had been his fault – even though where Josie was and what she was up to was totally out of his control. In fact everything seemed out of his control right now.

The week had gone downhill from there, when he'd had to explain that Roo wasn't allowed in school again, and he'd felt a complete heel when ten minutes after collecting her from school on Friday he'd had to leave her with Sally while he dealt with an emergency.

And he wanted to talk to Lucy, desperately. He wanted to chat to her about the house, about the future, but in-between Maisie's tantrums, his emergency call outs, and her evenings sorting lesson plans they hadn't been able to grab more than a few minutes alone.

He squeezed his eyes together. He was totally knackered. He'd always loved being a parent, but being a single one was a different kettle of fish altogether. Especially when he was trying to run a veterinary surgery almost single-handedly, and his clients seemed to think he was available 24/7. Thank goodness he had the very capable Sally to help out, or he'd be really stuck.

But, keeping his professional life in order was nothing compared to trying to reassure his daughter that she was the most loved, the most wanted child in the whole wide world. That she meant everything to him. That although she felt like her little world had been tipped upside down, it hadn't. That everything would be okay. He'd sort it.

He felt totally inadequate though. It had taken him quite some time to cheer her up when he'd finally finished work for the day, and when he'd tucked her into bed she'd been hanging on to a toy as though it was her only friend. When he'd gone up to check on her before leaving, the toy had been replaced with the

Border terrier Roo.

'Should she have the dog in bed?' Sally who had been called in as emergency babysitter raised an eyebrow when she saw the sleepy child, and Charlie shrugged.

'Maybe not.' He sighed. 'I'm a crap parent, but I know now why so many dads just say yes to everything.' It had been so much easier when it had been the two of them, him and Josie, and to be honest Maisie had seemed so unflappable. She'd always been a happy child who had been easy to distract from her tantrums and was rarely demanding. Even the terrible twos hadn't seemed to have a huge impact.

Now she was frightened; clingy in a way he'd not noticed before, and tearful. Maisie had always been the child with a smile on her face, and it worried him that she seemed to be getting more sensitive as each day passed. He had to work out what to do. He'd always thought he was doing okay as a parent, but now he wasn't sure. Now he was scared he was failing her.

And he had to talk to Lucy about this bloody email.

'I won't be long.'

Sally nodded at his slightly curt tone, and her voice was soft. 'Take your time, Charlie.'

Lucy didn't answer when he knocked, and when he jiggled the door handle it was locked. He felt like sitting down on the step, closing his eyes and blocking out the world and his problems. Instead, with a weary sigh he headed back down the garden path.

She couldn't have gone far, and if he didn't find her, a brisk walk round the village would do him good and maybe clear his head.

The cobbled square was deserted when he strolled across, the shops shut up for the night. Only the sound of his own footsteps broke the stillness of the evening, and as he walked some of the peace leaked into his soul.

By the time he reached the village green he was feeling more positive. He wasn't a bad dad, he wasn't doing *everything* wrong. They just needed a bit more structure in their lives, he needed to reorganise – instead of trying to shoe-horn his daughter into the chaotic and over-busy life he had been leading.

There was a crowd on the benches outside the Taverner's Arms, making the most of the warm September evening, and he soon spotted Lucy sandwiched between Jill and Timothy.

She waved as he walked across the grass.

'We're celebrating. Come and join us.'

'Sit here young man, my supper calls me and it's been a long week.' Timothy stood up, and put a hand on Charlie's shoulder. 'Goodnight all, thank you as always for all your hard work. See you all bright-eyed and bushy-tailed on Monday morning!'

'Good Ofsted report then?' Timothy's upbeat attitude was infectious, and Charlie felt his spirits lift another notch.

'Great.' Lucy had a big grin plastered to her face. 'Well we won't get it in writing for a couple of weeks, but everything was pretty positive.'

'I'll get a drink, another?'

By the time he got back with his pint, Jill had gone. 'Something I said?'

Lucy smiled, and put her hand on his knee. 'She said you looked like a man with the weight of the world on his shoulders.' Her smile slipped. 'What's the matter, Charlie? Nothing's wrong with Maisie, is it?'

'Maisie's fine, I left her with Sal.' He shrugged. 'Well she was fine when I left.' He needed to talk to her about the email, his biggest problem, but then again it was all part and parcel of the same issue. If Maisie wasn't happy with him, if it got to the stage where she didn't want to spend time with him, then he really was in a mess.

'Oh?'

'It's not working out.' He knotted his fingers in his hair in frustration.

'What do you mean?' Lucy looked alarmed. 'You can't ...'

'She's not eating properly, she didn't want her tea, only picks at stuff.'

Lucy shifted closer, so that her shoulder rested against his, and it felt like an anchor. Something stable. 'She eats her lunch at school so she'll be fine. But, maybe saying no to what you give her is her way of showing you she's not happy, it's the only thing she can say no to. The only thing she can control.'

'She says she doesn't like it here, she wants her old friends back, she wants her bedroom.' At the moment the list seemed endless. She wanted everything to be different.

'Well the bedroom bit is tricky, but why don't you invite one of her friends here for lunch, a picnic, just a play in the garden?'

'The surgery doesn't have a garden,' he gazed across the green, not really seeing it, 'and the flat is cramped, that's why I've let her go and visit friends. It's easier. It's not helping her make a home here though if I keep letting her go back there, is it?'

'Nope. She seems more unsettled than unhappy though, she gets on with the kids in her class and once we're past the initial half hour she's fine.'

'She's not fine at home. She doesn't cry, she just looks at me, sad as though I've let her down.'

'You've not let her down, it's just different. The summer was a big adventure, something new, but in her head she probably thought that everything would go back to how it was at the end of the holidays.'

'She was always so happy. That's the worst bit, she was always smiling, giggly, and now she always looks wary, unsure. Unhappy.'

'It's not just the move, Charlie. She's getting older too, she's not that chubby toddler any longer. School is more demanding, she's starting to question things.'

'You're telling me. She asked why Roo couldn't sleep in her room and I couldn't think of an answer, especially when she said she was lonely.'

Lucy grinned. 'You let him?'

'I said he could, in his basket though.'

'And?'

'He was on her bed when I checked on her. They were curled up together, the dog was fast asleep, and she was drowsy but clinging on.'

'She just needs to feel secure, Charlie.'

'And only the dog does that for her.' He gave a wry smile.

'You know that's not true. But Roo's a warm, living, breathing friend to fall asleep with. My dog was my best friend when I was her age.'

'I know.' He took her warm hand in his, threaded his fingers through her slender ones. 'I wish it had been easier for you.' He'd been lucky, the perfect childhood surrounded by animals, fields and two loving parents – unlike Lucy, who he knew had faced disruption and the feeling that she'd been abandoned. She'd got through it, but he didn't want the same for his own daughter. He wanted her to be happy.

'It was fine.' Her tone was light. 'But I get how it feels for Maisie right now.'

'I know.' He looked straight into her clear blue eyes. 'I'm not giving up, but our whole living arrangements, everything, is a mess.' That much at least had occurred to him, and it was something he had the power to change. 'I can't run a busy surgery, and look after a child properly,' he paused and looked at her, 'on my own. I feel so bloody guilty every time I have to rush off.'

Lucy smiled. 'Guilt's an important part of being a parent.'

He shook his head. 'Very funny. It's not fair on either of us though. I don't want her pushed from pillar to post while I'm working, or left to play on her own.'

'No,' she squeezed his hand. 'She's too young. When I was her age I hated it.'

'Is that how it was when you and your mum moved?'

'It is. I was a couple of years older than Maisie, but I'd been used to having Mum around. I felt,' she paused, 'abandoned.'

He stared back bleakly. That was the last thing he wanted Maisie to feel.

'I mean, it is a bit different for Maisie, because Mum had always been at home for me, she didn't work after I was born, until ...'

'You moved?'

She nodded. 'Maisie's used to you and Josie working, isn't she? What did you do before?'

'Her old primary school was part of an academy trust, they had after school clubs, breakfast clubs, it was a big set up. It's different in Langtry Meadows.'

'Back at Starbaston, the last school I taught at, they had much the same. But she's used to doing that, so why not get somebody to help you out? It's not admitting failure, everybody does it. There must be somebody in the village who'd be glad of a few extra pennies. Somebody with kids?'

Why hadn't he thought of that? Why had he decided that looking after Maisie was totally his responsibility, that he owed it to her to try and do it all by himself?

'Oh God, you know what? I've been an idiot haven't I? I've been as guilty as Maisie of treating this as an extension of the holidays, and not looking at this long term. No wonder she's not settled.'

They both stared into their drinks for inspiration.

'What about Becky?'

'Sorry?' The name didn't immediately ring a bell with him.

'Becky, the teacher I took over from. I mean she's not bothered about money, but I'm pretty sure she'd be glad of a break from just looking after her baby, and she'd be brilliant with Maisie, and I bet Maisie would love helping with the baby. Children her age like to help with little ones.'

'But,' he hesitated, 'I don't want it to look like I'm copping out, that I can't cope.' That was still his problem. He'd failed on his own life, failed in his marriage. If he failed on this, he could lose his daughter for ever. 'I need to prove that I can look after her. I got this.' He pulled the copy of the email out of his pocket and handed it over. This was what it came down to. One short email.

Lucy smoothed the paper out, not looking at it. 'But letting people help *is* looking after her Charlie. Nobody is expected to do it on their own, and you're doing your best.'

'I know, but read it. It's from Josie. She wants a divorce.'

Lucy sobered up, and picked up the piece of paper, which from the look of it he'd been folding and unfolding as though he didn't know quite what to do with it.

She'd been feeling on a bit of a high at the end of the school day after the Ofsted team had left and had missed Charlie's agitation when he'd first arrived, but now it was evident. He looked worn out, his face tinged grey. And she was pretty sure it wasn't just the normal ups and downs of being a parent. Whatever he said,

Charlie was made of sterner stuff. He'd never let his daughter down if he could help it.

'I'm worried, Lucy. It's not the actual divorce, that'll be a relief in a way, but she's playing games again over Maisie. I thought we'd got a truce, that we'd worked a solution out. You know, that when she comes back to the UK she'd get a place nearby and Maisie wouldn't have to be uprooted again. We'd share the arrangements.' He ran his fingers through his hair in the agitated way that was so familiar to her. She put a hand over his, but the ache of dread inside her grew. This was what had been worrying her, eating away inside her. But she had to be the calm one here. 'That's what she said. But I don't know, the whole tone of this spells trouble.'

'Are you sure?' Lucy searched his face, but all she could see was worry. Charlie wasn't one to overreact. And Lucy still couldn't quite work out what she thought about Charlie's ex. From what Charlie had told her about their break-up, Josie had seemed pretty callous. There probably wasn't a nice way to tell a man that his daughter probably wasn't biologically his, but doing it as you walk through the door and suggesting he never see her again was bad by anybody's standards. But then when she'd brought Maisie in to Langtry Meadows Primary School in the spring, telling Charlie his daughter missed him, needed him, Lucy thought she was seeing the real Josie. The caring side, the side that was putting her daughter first.

Until she'd announced the real reason – that she wanted Charlie to look after Maisie while she worked abroad, ignoring her responsibilities.

And now this.

Lucy wanted to tear her hair out and scream, but instead took a deep breath.

Either the woman was incredibly selfish, or there was far more to this than Lucy and Charlie realised. Lucy's heart ached for the man and his daughter. She loved both of them, she wanted them to be happy, and as hard as she tried, taking a detached view of this was impossible.

'Read it, tell me what you think.' He touched the very edge of the sheet of paper. 'When she comes back she's going to take Maisie away again.'

'Only if we let her.' Lucy felt her throat dry. She'd seen the state Charlie had been in when he'd thought he'd lost his daughter before – when he'd returned to Langtry Meadows heartbroken. It had taken a long time for him to confide in her, admit what Josie had done, that she'd told him he'd be in the wrong trying to see his daughter.

He'd jumped at the opportunity to see her again, to have her stay with him.

Neither of them had seen this on the horizon. And not so soon.

Lucy scanned the words as he spoke, *we need closure ... I feel we need to formalise arrangements for Maisie and think about what she will want as she gets older ... I miss her ... this was just a temporary solution ... better with her mother ... I've spoken to my solicitor.*

'She's just been using me, Lucy, so she could have six months off gallivanting and living her dream.' His voice was tinged with bitterness. 'She'll come back and try to push me out of their lives again, won't she? Disrupt Maisie, do exactly what she wants.'

Lucy's stomach felt hollow as she looked at him. 'She can't do that to you, or to Maisie.'

'Can't she?'

When Lucy had first met Charlie, he'd spent months struggling to put his life back together. He'd always been prepared to fight for his right to see Maisie – whether she was his or not – but then when Josie had unexpectedly offered an olive branch, his life had picked up. 'But surely any court would see you've been a father to her? That you're looking after her now? She can't just stop you seeing her.' The unspoken question that neither of them knew the answer to hung in the air between them, can she?

He shrugged, looking defeated. 'But what if I'm not her father? Do I have any say at all? What if her ...'

'I don't know.' She squeezed his hand, looked into his eyes and knew they were having the same thought.

What if he really wasn't Maisie's dad, what if her real father came back? 'But we can find out what rights you've got, can't we? You do want her here with you don't you?' She knew he did, but he needed to say it.

'Of course I do.' His eyes were shadowed. 'I really thought Josie was planning on coming back, settling locally so that Maisie had both of us. That's what she said, we agreed. But now ...' He shrugged despondently, the droop of his shoulders saying it all.

'Oh Charlie.' She wrapped her arms round him, and after a moment he put his arm round her shoulders and pulled her in tighter against him. 'We can't think about the worst case right now. We've got to assume the best, make it look like you're expecting her to stay.' She could feel the burn of tears in her eyes. Josie couldn't be allowed to do this again. She wouldn't let her. Swallowing away her upset she forced the tremor out of her voice. 'You're right though, you need a proper home and you need child care.'

'But the surgery needs somebody there all the time. It works, me being in the flat, on hand.'

'But it doesn't work for Maisie.' Lucy pulled away and straightened up. 'Eric didn't live there before, did he?'

'No, it was just used if Sal needed to stay overnight, if we had a dog in.'

'Right, well it sounds like it's time you moved out,

and went back to that arrangement. It was fine for just you, Charlie when you were a locum and weren't even expecting to stay long.'

'True.' Charlie nodded, ran his fingers through his hair in a gesture she knew so well. When he'd moved back to Langtry Meadows, it had been to help Eric out. A temporary position. Eric was now on the road to recovery, and soon he'd be back in the surgery helping out, but he'd already told Charlie he wanted him to stay. That he needed help for the foreseeable future.

'But it's different now, isn't it? In fact,' she paused as a sudden idea popped into her head, 'why not ask Eric if Sal can move in permanently? I know on the wage you pay her,' he raised an eyebrow but she carried on, 'she can't afford anywhere big, and there are hardly any small places up for sale or rent in Langtry Meadows. Oh come on, Charlie, it makes sense, I know she's dying to get away from her parents.'

'Sounds like we need one of your spreadsheets.' There was a glimmer of the old Charlie there, a hint of smile tugging at the corner of his mouth.

'It does. And an estate agent.'

'You're right, it might make Maisie feel more settled as well if I get a place that reminds her of home.' He put a hand on her knee, the warmth seeping in, and she leaned in against him. She couldn't help it. 'Thanks.' He dropped the lightest of kisses on her hair. 'You've got to show me this house that you're after as well, over the weekend. I am interested you know, sorry we've not had time—'

'Neither of us have had a spare moment. I'll show you round, but don't expect much, it needs a lot of work.'

'But you've got time, before Annie comes back?'

'True. But first let's sort your stuff out, that's far more urgent.'

'I'll get Becky's number off Sally tomorrow, she's bound to have it.'

'She is, or I can ask at school. Jill will probably know.'

'Talking of Sal, your little Piper is ready to go home. Shall I bring her round in the morning?'

'Sure.' Lucy frowned. She really wanted the little dog, she'd been thinking about her ever since she'd found her by the garden gate – and she'd popped into the surgery regularly after school to check up on how she was doing. But the thought of taking responsibility for her was a bit daunting, even though she'd been caring for all of Annie's animals. This was different, this was a dog of her own.

'What's up?' Charlie nudged her.

'How can I look after her? I don't often get a chance to pop home at lunch time, and she can't spend all day on her own.' And soon she might have a house-renovation project on her hands as well.

'Well I can soon sort that.'

Lucy jumped at the gruff country burr behind her, then twisted round to find Jim had sneaked up unnoticed. 'Jim!' The school governor, and Annie's brother, had been looking after her since she'd arrived in Langtry Meadows. It was Jim who had introduced her to Annie, found her a place to stay, he kept an eye on things and checked she was coping with the gorgeous but overgrown cottage garden, and now it seemed he was jumping into the breach again.

'Evening!' He grinned, showing a chipped tooth.

'But how ...'

'You've no need to go worrying about that pup while you're in school, I can quite easily take the young 'un a walk for you when I take Molly.'

'You walk Molly?' Lucy was surprised, she'd never realised that Jim helped Elsie out with her dog, and she hadn't realised that her discovering Piper was common knowledge either. But in Langtry Meadows it was hard to keep anything under wraps.

'Oh aye. I offered a while ago, when Elsie was finding she was too,' he paused diplomatically, looking for the right word. Nobody would dare call Elsie old, or suggest she couldn't cope, 'busy. Not been feeling quite herself lately, and she has a lot on some days so I said it was no trouble.'

Lucy frowned. 'Is she okay?' She'd not seen quite as

much of Elsie Harrington as she should since she'd been caught up in the new term, and the old lady had been so kind to her.

'Just old age and a bit of a summer cold, but you know she doesn't like a fuss young Lucy. I'm sure she'd welcome a visit though if you're passing. Aye well, official dog walker, me.' He chuckled. 'It would be good for Molly to have a youngster come along with us, she doesn't run around that much since her own pups went, the lazy old thing.'

'So that's settled then.' Charlie stood up. 'Can I get you a drink, Jim? Lucy?'

Lucy grinned. 'Definitely. Sit down Jim. I reckon you're better than any estate agent, aren't you? Do you know if there are any houses up for rent in the village?'

# Chapter 6

'Oh God, no.' Lucy clutched her head. It wasn't how she liked Saturdays to start. Piper was barking a high pitched 'I didn't know I could do it' kind of bark, and a hen was squawking indignantly.

A hen.

She sat up abruptly. The hens should be in the garden, not in the house. Not even stopping to put her slippers on, she scrambled down the narrow staircase.

'I didn't know you could bark.' Piper flapped her tatty tail sheepishly, but didn't look up. Her chin was on the floor, her gaze fixed on the bottom of the bureau. She wriggled forward a few inches on her tummy, commando style and Lucy tried not to laugh. The hen that she'd nicknamed Squeak wasn't squeaking, for the first time since Lucy had set eyes on her she was flapping her wings and squawking out what sounded like a warning.

The puppy was unperturbed.

Lucy knelt down so that she was at her level, and

peered. Peeping out from the darkness under the bureau was something yellowy-brown and fluffy. A chick. She put her head on the floor so that she could see right under, and another three pairs of eyes stared out from the gloom.

'Oh.' She stood up and frowned at Squeak. 'You're supposed to lay eggs for breakfast, not hide them until they hatch. Now what are we going to do?' What on earth was she supposed to do? Leave the chicks there? Put them somewhere warm? Put them back outside with Squeak and the other hens? 'How did you get in the house anyway?' Squeak ruffled her feathers, deciding that now Lucy was there to protect her she didn't need to scream, and settled down.

Piper sat up, whined then lay down again, nudging her nose in the direction of a fluffy chick.

'I think we're going to have to ring for assistance, aren't we?'

When Sally arrived at the cottage ten minutes later Lucy had made a pot of coffee, but Piper hadn't budged from her position.

'You're lucky that we're quiet in the surgery, can't stay long though, Charlie said he'd call me if the phones got busy. He hates answering calls because he ends up saying yes to everything.' She paused. 'Is he okay, Charlie? I mean, I know it's none of my business, but when he asked me to babysit last night he looked uptight. Though he does seem more cheerful this morning, and Maisie made him laugh because she dressed Roo up in a Batman outfit.'

'He had an email from Josie.' Lucy didn't want to gossip, but Sally knew all about how Josie had ambushed Charlie on May Day and asked him to look after Maisie. Lucy was pretty sure that she didn't know about the fact that Charlie might not be Maisie's biological father. That piece of information hadn't got any further than the staff at the school – she hoped. 'It looks like things might get nasty, and,' she shrugged as she handed Sally a mug of coffee and sat down, 'Maisie's not very settled. I think he's worried, that's all.'

'Hmm.' Sally frowned. 'She's more up and down than she was at the start of the summer. She seems a bit, well ...'

'Sensitive?'

'She's touchy, and she actually refused to do what he asked her to the other day which was a bit out of character. They had a mini stand-off,' she smiled, 'I could see he was itching to tell her to behave, but scared stiff she'd burst into tears and run back to her bedroom. Then her cute little bottom lip wobbled and he was putty. Not that I'd have a clue what to do, I don't know anything about kids.' Sally gave a little shudder. 'Give me a hen any day!'

Lucy smiled. 'All hens get to worry about is an egg getting stuck. Maisie's lost her mother. I know Josie will be heading back soon, but to a six year old a week can seem like a lifetime. Six months, well, she probably feels abandoned, unwanted.' Lucy swallowed the lump in her throat down, this wasn't personal, it wasn't about her. 'Even though Charlie's doing his best to make it up, having your dad isn't always good enough, when you want your mum is it? Especially if you're scared she doesn't want you.'

'I can remember when I was little, I always wanted Mum if I fell over or anything went wrong.' Sally smiled. 'Though my dad is pants at hugs and sticking plasters so it's no wonder, is it?'

'No, dads can be pants.' Major pants, well hers was. Although Charlie definitely wasn't. 'And on top of that she's moved schools, been torn from her friendship group and been dropped into what has to feel like an alien world.'

'You can say that again, Langtry Meadows can definitely have a touch of the alien.'

'And,' Lucy fought the laugh and tried to be serious, 'living in the flat at the surgery can't be good, and Charlie whizzing in and out sorting out emergency calls when he should be sitting down practising spellings. I mean, I know you're there, but—'

'Believe me, I'm no mother substitute, I've told you

– give me a puppy any day.'

Lucy shook her head and battled on. 'She's just not got a routine. Kids like routine, knowing what to expect, it gives them something solid.'

Sally nudged her. 'Which is why you told him to ring Becky?'

'He's done that already? I'm impressed, Mr Efficiency.' Charlie was obviously worried sick about the email he'd had from Josie, about the threats, or he wouldn't have been making phone calls the moment he got up on a Saturday morning.

'It was a brill idea. Becky's jumped at the chance, I think she misses the kids at school, but her husband's already talking about baby number two so she knows she won't be going back. She'll get a chance to natter to the teachers if she's picking Maisie up as well, she told me she's feeling a bit stranded, left out at the moment. It must be strange.' Sally pulled a face. 'I can't imagine being at home all day with a baby. Oh God, puke and nappies and gaga noises all day.'

Lucy laughed. 'Me neither, but I suppose some people love it.'

'She says she can't wait for hers to grow up a bit and start doing things. I told her it was your suggestion and she says the moment she's not on 24/7 feeding duties she'll escape and buy you a drink.' Sally grinned. 'Do I owe you a drink too? Was it you told Charlie to offer me the flat above the surgery?'

'Has he?' Lucy grinned. 'Brilliant,' she paused, 'if you want it that is?'

'Want it? You've got to be kidding me. I knew you would have had something to do with it. I do love you Lucy Jacobs! And he said he's talked to Eric and I can stay for practically free, which is amazing, it means I can still save some money towards, well,' Lucy could swear she saw a blush, 'save a deposit for a house with Jamie.' She changed the conversation before Lucy had a chance to comment. 'So, Charlie's moving in ...' She glanced around.

'No. Oh no, he's not moving in here. And don't thank me, he needs to move out for Maisie's sake, but I did think maybe it would be handy for you.'

'It's fab, and I am thanking you. But, where's he going if ...'

'He can't move in here, Sal. For a start we're not that involved,' Sally raised an eyebrow, which Lucy ignored, 'and he's got to think about Maisie. She needs to know she's the most important person in his life. Being here would complicate things,' and would give Josie all kinds of ammunition for the battle she was sure lay ahead, 'and let's face it what kind of a mother figure would I make?'

'A good one. She loves you. Okay, okay, don't give me the evil eye. It's true, but I get the fact it might not be perfect timing. I suppose if her mum gets back to find you two shacked up she might go off bang.'

Go off bang was probably an understatement. Lucy felt herself go red as she remembered the embarrassment of the last time Josie had knocked on her door to find Charlie there. And that was before Maisie was living with him.

'But where are they going to live?'

'Jim seemed to think he might know a place.' Jim, it seemed, had the answers to everything. He'd sorted out Annie's cottage for her to stay in, and now he'd assured Charlie he'd 'sort something'. His quiet confidence had helped though. Charlie had cheered up knowing he had a plan in place, a way forward.

'Oh?'

'Well apparently Elsie Harrington owns some of the cottages in the village, they've been in her family for years. Jim said he'd check with her, he thought one was coming vacant soon. It'll mean Charlie's got a proper garden for Maisie and Roo.'

Sally giggled. 'I don't know who's worse, Jim or Elsie Harrington, they both seem to have fingers in every pie. So, we're all on the move then.' She studied her feet. 'You don't think me and Jamie are rushing things do you? You know, thinking about a house?'

'Rushing?' Lucy laughed. 'You've got to be kidding, from what I've heard everybody expected you to start dating ten years ago.'

'Hang on, I'm not that old! But, well, we've only been seeing each other a few months.'

'But you love each other don't you?' Lucy spoke softly. 'You know he's right for you, and you know each other inside out, don't you?'

Sally nodded. Then suddenly smiled. 'Shall we drink to us all moving then?'

Lucy shook her head. 'You'll drink to anything. But first,' she nodded her head in the direction of the bureau, and Squeak who had settled down but was keeping a beady eye on proceedings. 'I did think about just moving them, but I didn't quite know if they'd be okay in the coop with the others.'

'Are you on guard duty Piper?' Sally stroked the puppy, who flapped her tail and cocked an ear in her direction. 'I thought you were picking her up this morning, Lucy?'

'Jim and Charlie persuaded me to take her last night. After two glasses of wine I was in a sentimental, slushy mood. Jim has already taken over midday puppy duties and insisted on meeting her, and Charlie said I need a friend.'

Sally laughed as Lucy pulled a face, put down her mug of coffee then levered herself out of the very deep and comfy armchair. 'I knew I'd gained a dog, but where the hell have this lot come from?'

'You didn't by any chance spend time in the back

garden waiting for Piper to do her business last night, and leave the back door open?'

'Probably.' She felt herself going crimson again. More to the point, they'd let Piper out to explore the garden, and taken the opportunity for a rather long, drawn out, reacquaintance. Time alone had been severely rationed lately. 'But why would they come in?'

'Who knows what goes on in the tiny brain of a chicken.' Sally tilted her head to one side, chicken style. 'She must have hidden some eggs in the garden, these aren't exactly just hatched.'

'Well they can't live in here.'

Sally laughed. 'At a guess she's done it before, and Annie's let her.'

'Well she didn't write that in her book of instructions!' Lucy sighed. Annie had left a folder cram packed with useful information on how to look after the house and animals, how to deal with unexpected broods of chicks was not in there.

'Don't worry, we'll find somewhere safe for them outside, you could even email Annie and find out what she did last time.'

'Why didn't I think of that? Although sometimes I don't hear from her for days.' Lucy picked up her laptop and tapped out a quick message, then took a deep breath and peeped over the top at Sally. 'I've got another confession. Last night, as well as acquiring a dog, a house full of chicks and sorting everybody else's housing requirements out, I did something else.'

'You didn't?' Sally leaned forward.

'I did. I emailed the estate agent in Birmingham,' she'd done lots of things after leaving school on an Ofsted-induced high, 'and,' deep breath, 'said I'd accept the offer on my place.'

'Really?' Sally put her coffee down and jumped up to give her friend a hug, which sent the chicks back under the bureau cheeping in alarm, Piper shot into the kitchen, her tail between her legs, and the hen went back onto full squawking alert.

'Well it is ideal really isn't it?' She crossed her fingers behind her friend's back. 'We've got fab feedback from Ofsted so hopefully the school is secure for a few years, and while I'm here at Annie's I could start to do up the cottage.' She frowned. 'Although if it falls through, I am a bit worried about finding somewhere else in the village, but according to Jim they've not quite finished that new estate and there'll be a few small affordable houses going up. He said they had to include one or two in the plans.'

'Oh yes,' Sally was still smiling, 'and if anybody knows it will be Jim! I'm sure it won't fall through though. Oh I am so pleased, now I feel like you're really going to stay.'

'I am.' Lucy nodded. 'I'm really going to stay.'

# Chapter 7

'You've no idea how good it is to be back in the old saddle.'

Charlie looked in astonishment at the man who was sitting in the chair he normally occupied in the small staffroom at the back of reception. He had a mug of coffee in his hand, their appointment book spread on the table before him, and looked at home. Which he was. Charlie felt a twinge of what felt alarmingly like a territorial feeling and had an irrational desire to snatch the book away.

He'd got used to running the place as though it was his own. And it wasn't. 'I wasn't expecting you back yet, Eric. I didn't realise you were fit yet.'

A wide smile spread over his employer's face. 'Well I'm not, if you believe the doctors. But being locked up in that house with my wife and nothing to do but read the newspaper is driving me nuts.'

'So, you're back at work then.' He eyed the book again.

Eric's management style was flamboyant, to put it politely. Despite Sally's best efforts to keep him in order, it had been apparent to Charlie when he'd started work at the practice that efficiency wasn't a word in the man's vocabulary. Eric liked to freewheel and see what happened. 'Wonderful.' He squinted and tried to see if any of his carefully arranged appointments had been rearranged.

Eric pushed the book away. 'Very rigid this is, not that you've not been doing a splendid job, but a bit of give and take always works wonders. Fluidity.' He laughed and slapped the table. 'That's the word you need, fluidity.'

It wasn't the word Charlie wanted. He wanted organised, methodical.

'Now I notice you've blocked all this off for surgery, well what if there isn't any?'

'Well we use the time to stock take, cover emergencies, and there's always somebody t—' He was about to say 'turns up' but Eric cut him short.

'Ah well, now there's going to be two of us at it we can change that. Don't you be worrying about it though, lad, we can sort all that later when I'm back on my feet properly. Only reason I'm in is I thought young Sally here,' he winked at her, and rather disturbingly she blushed. 'Deserves a bit of a break. Not had one since I had my accident, have you, dear girl?'

Oh hell, did that mean he was going to lose his efficient receptionist-cum-veterinary nurse, and gain the 'fluid', disorganised Eric? He looked helplessly at Sally, who gave an almost imperceptible shrug of her shoulders and looked guilty.

He was being mean. She deserved some time off, she'd uncomplainingly held this place together since Eric had been trampled by a herd of cows and ended up in hospital. Without her the practice would have sunk.

'Yes, yes, Sally definitely deserves a break.' Please, please don't let it be for long though. 'But I could always get a temp in to cover.'

'Nonsense. I might not be fully fit, but I'm up to chatting to the clients and helping out where's needed with the operations. Can't do the farm visits of course, Charles, but I can hold the fort here for you. Do my bit as receptionist.'

Charlie gave what he knew was a weak smile. 'Great to see you back in action, I know you've been missed by all the clients.' This had to happen sooner or later, Eric easing himself back into work. It was him, Charlie, who was the interloper.

'Don't you worry.' Eric chuckled. 'She's here for a couple of weeks or so to give me a chance to bed in, then we're not losing her for long, just a long weekend isn't it Sally?'

'It is. I'll be back on the Tuesday. Honest.'

Charlie tried to inject some real feeling into the smile that was stuck to his face.

'Wonderful, glad that's settled.' Eric rubbed his hands together. 'Now, settle down with a coffee. I've bunged some extra bookings in for this morning, thought we could just make it open surgery and we'll pick them off in the order they arrive rather than messing around with fixed times.'

Charlie stifled a groan.

'Daddy I've got tummy ache, I don't want to go to school.'

They all turned to look at Maisie, who was stood in the doorway in her pyjamas, clutching a teddy bear.

'Come on Maisie, let's get you up and dressed, Becky's going to do you a special breakfast.' Charlie had popped down, hoping to check up on a dog that had been in overnight, then go back up to the flat to wake Maisie up. He'd been completely thrown by the sight of Eric.

'I feel sick.'

He felt a bit queasy himself.

'I've got a special medicine we give to dogs that feel sick, makes them very sick, gets it out of their tummy.' The little girl stared in alarm at Eric. 'Would you like some?'

She took a step back, panic on her face, and Charlie scooped her up. It was going to be a long day. 'Let's get you to Becky's and see how you feel. Then we can go and look at this new home later, can't we? Although,' he paused, 'if you're too poorly I suppose we'll just have to stay here until ...'

She bit her lip. 'I'll try and be brave, I'll go to school.'

'Good girl.'

By the time he'd got her dressed, persuaded her that Roo was too busy to attend lessons, and decided which toy she had to put in her bag, they were running late. 'We can go in the car to Becky's, or run?'

'Run, Daddy. It might make my tummy hurt go away.' She scrambled down the stairs and gazed up at him, her big brown eyes wide. 'If we move to a nicer house, will Mummy come back?'

'Mummy is doing some very important work,' his voice came out rough-edged, all he wanted to do was gather her to him, make her promises, 'but she loves you lots and she'll be back as soon as she can. And it doesn't matter where we live, but I'm sure she's dying to see your new room, wherever it is.' He checked his watch. 'Come on piggy back time.'

By the time they stopped outside Becky's, he was exhausted but Maisie was giggling and had forgotten all about her stomach ache and worries about when Josie would come back.

'See you later, be good for Becky and for Lucy.'

'She's Miss Jacobs in school, not Lucy. Honestly

Daddy.' Maisie shook her head in disapproval and grabbed hold of Becky's hand. 'I thought you would know that.'

\*\*\*

By the time Charlie got back to the surgery, the waiting room was full. News had soon spread round Langtry Meadows that Eric was back in action, and they'd all flocked there to find out for themselves if the rumours that he'd lost a leg and developed a lifelong fear of running animals in the accident were true.

Serena Stevens, blonde hair immaculate, low cut top flaunting her cleavage and pink high heels matching the tote bag on her knee was first in the queue. Inside the bag was Twinkle, her Chihuahua, who raised a lip in a warning snarl the moment she spied Charlie, before ducking back into the safety of the rather posh tote.

Serena turned the colour of her shoes. 'Oh Charlie, I feel terrible, but I've somehow managed to book in to see Eric. You know what I'm like, too much going on in my head.'

'It's no problem at all, Miss Stevens.' Charlie hoped the huge sigh of relief hadn't escaped. 'I'm sure Eric will be delighted to see you and Twinkle, he deserves it after all he's been through.' And after what he'd done to the appointment book. 'He'll have you sorted in a jiffy.'

He didn't deserve it, he didn't deserve the tiny bad-tempered dog at all. He glanced up at Sally, who'd made a funny explosive little noise, which turned into a cough and a splutter.

'I'll just go through and get ready for surgery, I do hope it's nothing serious with Twinkle.'

Sally was staring fixedly at her computer screen as he passed, and he bent to whisper in her ear. 'You're laughing. Tut, so unprofessional. I don't know about having a weekend off, we should sack you.'

She grinned, then span round on her seat and followed him through to the back. 'See, there are benefits to Eric being back, like not having to deal with the lady in red.'

'By the look of it they all want to see him.'

'So you can have a quiet morning.' She paused, her tone softened. 'You'll love working with him once you get used to his ways.'

He raised an eyebrow. 'I know, he's a great vet and a nice man.' But so disorganised. Right now he didn't know if he could cope with that on top of all his other problems. 'And we've got half the inhabitants of Langtry Meadows crammed into the waiting room.' Eric loved to chat, they'd be there all day. 'Plus he's managed to fit two more farm visits in for me this afternoon, oh no,' he groaned, 'not alpaca castrations again, and,' he peered at Eric's scribbled note that had been pinned to a cupboard, 'what does this say? *Charlie – initiate Judas*! Is there a hidden meaning in that message?'

Sally giggled. 'Student not Judas you idiot. There's a student asked if he can come and see the practice before he applies for veterinary college, Eric said you'd have a chat to him.'

'How can you leave me? The place will be chaos by the time you get back.'

'I'll sort it.' She patted his arm reassuringly. 'Now go and get in your consulting room, first off is a dog that can't stop grinning, unlike you Mr Grumpy.' He raised an eyebrow. 'Got a stick stuck between its teeth.' She did a remarkably good impression. 'Now shoo.' She pushed him in the direction of the room and went back to her desk.

Eric's open surgery was more successful than Charlie had expected, although with two vets handling the list of clients it was bound to move things along more quickly. The rumble of Eric's deep-throated chuckle reached him from time to time through the thin walls of the surgery making him smile, and it was also nice to be able to seek a second opinion from the more experienced vet, if he wanted it. He actually found himself whistling by the time the waiting room was empty and his stomach was rumbling for some lunch.

'Quite a team aren't we young man? Now if you two

will excuse me I'm going to get off home and have a rest, taken it out of me a bit being on my feet all morning. I'll be up to a full day by next Friday though, and I'll be fine when Sally's off on her travels.'

'Going away are you Sal?' Sally blushed at Charlie's question, which was a bit out of character, but there again she'd been acting a bit strangely since Eric's reappearance anyway. Maybe she was a bit in awe of him. They were obviously fond of each other, but she no doubt had a different relationship with Eric to the one she had with him.

'Well I need to do something with my four days of freedom, don't I?' She didn't look up from the pills she was counting out, and Charlie had a distinct feeling she was avoiding giving him a straight answer.

After working his way through the afternoon visit list, Charlie headed back to the surgery to find Sally tidying up the visit and operations books, which were now littered with Eric's illegible scrawls, and a few crossings-out.

'Well I'm glad you can read his handwriting.'

'I've had plenty of practice.' She smiled. 'Looks like you can finish early and pick Maisie up from school.'

'What do you mean? I've still got one cat to neuter, and one that needs its teeth cleaning.' He checked his watch. 'It's going to be a bit of a push.' They normally did all the operations in the morning, to give the animal's time to recover and return home late afternoon, but these cats had been taken in by a busy rescue centre and the owner had been relieved when Charlie had said he'd fit them in late and drop them back in the evening.

'Oh Eric popped back and did them. He said after some lunch and a power nap he felt much perkier.'

'Did he?' Charlie looked at her in surprise. 'That was good of him.'

'He asked about Maisie, after seeing her this morning, I mean I didn't say anything I shouldn't, or gossip.'

'Really?' Charlie raised an eyebrow, and laughed. 'You? Not gossip?'

'I'm going to ignore that. But he did say that maybe with him being round it would mean your hours could be a bit more flexible.' She smiled. 'I told you, he's kind.'

'I know.' Charlie sighed, feeling guilty about his earlier uncharitable thought that having Eric back could cause disruption. 'Dad was always very fond of him.'

'Oh, and he also left something for you in your consulting room, told me to make sure you saw it. Right, well I'll make us a coffee, you can catch up on your notes.'

'Thanks, Miss.'

'Then you can go and pick Maisie up. I'll give Becky a ring and tell her not to bother today, shall I?'

\*\*\*

Lucy couldn't miss the tall figure of Charlie as he hovered just inside the school gate. Maisie spotted him instantly as well, and squealed with excitement.

'Are you heading home?' He'd hung on until the rest of her class had dispersed, then made his way over to where she was standing in the doorway.

'I am actually.' Lucy smiled. 'Let me just gather my books together, I've got a load of marking to do tonight, and I'll be right with you.'

'Can we have cake?' Maisie ducked her head under Charlie's arm and grinned.

'Piper might have eaten it all.'

'Oo I can see Piper!' She clapped her hands, then ran across the playground, launching herself at the hopscotch squares that had been painted along one side.

'Maisie seems happier today. She seems to like Becky?'

'She does. She played up a bit this morning, phantom tummy pains.'

'I can sympathise.' Lucy grinned. 'There are days when I don't want to come to school either.'

'I bribed her I'm afraid.'

'Nothing wrong with a bit of bribery now and again, but I'd call it reward not bribe if I was you.'

'Teacher speak?'

'Well if you give a dog a treat when they do what

you want, you call it a reward, don't you?'

'True. And the reward was nothing sugary, it was the promise of going to look at a place Jim has found for us tonight.'

'Wow, he's moved fast! Where is it?'

'He wouldn't say.' He gave a wry grin. 'I don't know whether that's good or bad. But he did say it had two bedrooms and a nice garden. He told Maisie it was fit for a princess, so I hope she's not going to be disappointed.'

Lucy laughed. 'He might be thinking more Rapunzel's tower than the pink and pretty Maisie has in mind.'

'Exactly.'

'Right, hang on while I get my stuff, I won't be a minute.'

Lucy hadn't seen Charlie for a few days, and in fact she'd been so busy with school work, talking to the estate agent, arranging solicitors and looking after Piper she would have found it impossible to get out of the house for more than a couple of hours anyway. But it looked like he and Maisie had thrived in her absence. He was coping, it looked like he was finding a way to deal with Maisie's insecurity, and the two of them were happy together. So maybe she was better keeping her distance. Letting them find their own way without her interference. But just seeing him made her want to forget about being sensible, to just be selfish and dive in there.

'Eric's come back to help out at the surgery.' Charlie took the cup of tea and sat down on the garden bench, making room for Lucy beside him. The soft dregs of September sun were just strong enough to bathe them in a gentle heat, and it suddenly hit him just how lucky he was as he watched Maisie plonk herself down on the grass in the garden. Piper lay at her feet watching her every move as she ate a cake, and crawling forward on her belly to collect crumbs.

They might have their ups and downs, but moments like this made it all worthwhile.

'Oh has he? What's he like? I've not met him yet.'

'Oh he's lovely. He says Sally deserves a few days off, which I've got to admit I'd not really thought about. She's worked non-stop looking after the place since his accident. I think after I spoke to him about letting her have the flat above the surgery he had a chat to her.'

'That's kind. She must be dying for a few days away from the place, I mean she ends up working nearly as long hours as you, doesn't she?'

'Not far off. But it's more than that. I think he wants to ease himself back in, see how he feels, see if he can cope.'

'Which is good?'

'Brilliant, as long as he doesn't get his hands on the appointment book. I need Sal, she's my last defence, our only hope of avoiding Eric style chaos.' He grinned.

'He's only been back five minutes and caused mayhem in the waiting room this morning with his new free for all scheme.' Lucy raised an eyebrow. 'No appointments, just turn up.'

She grinned. 'Really?' She knew that went against every one of Charlie's instincts, as it would have with her. 'It's what they all do anyway isn't it? Turn up when they like.'

'True, they do tend to ignore my carefully planned appointment system. But to be fair, strangely enough it worked okay, and it meant I could knock off early and pick Maisie up myself. But it is a bit odd, not being boss any more after running the show on my own for so long. It could be bad though when Sally isn't in to keep an eye on him, he's already started scribbling in appointments where we'd normally do surgery, and I can't read his writing. He could be booking me in to provide a new leg for a hamster for all I know.'

'Can you do that?'

'No!' He shook his head. 'He is a great chap. I really wish he wouldn't let people leave without paying though because the cash flow is horrendous. It is his business though at the end of the day.'

'And?'

'And,' he paused, 'he's offered me a permanent job. He says it's obvious he'll never get back to doing the farm visits, or heavy stuff. It's the perfect opportunity really, with two of us spreading the load I can afford to cut back on the hours, I'll have more time for Maisie.'

'I can sense a but.'

'Well I did swear I'd never return to the family practice.'

The rueful smile tugged at her heart. She'd sworn never to return to village life, so when she'd arrived in Langtry Meadows earlier in the year they'd been in the same boat. Reluctant, the outsiders. She had a good idea how he felt. 'But you actually quite like it, don't you?' He'd told her that after university he'd been determined to move onto bigger and better things – a modern town-centre practice with cutting edge technology. But although it was circumstances that had brought him back here, he was popular, and he did seem happy.

'Yes, I do.' He put his hand over hers, his voice soft. 'But that might be more to do with the company than anything.' The air hung heavy between them. They were both conscious of Maisie, of the fact that their future together seemed to be balanced precariously. Lucy made an effort to move the conversation on.

'But?' Gosh, there were a lot of 'buts', but she was sure there was more on his mind.

'Josie's latest email hinted about settling abroad, and that if I want to carry on seeing Maisie I need to think about it.'

'Going abroad?' Lucy knew the shock had registered

in her voice, on her face, as a solid weight settled in the base of her stomach and she pulled her hand away without thinking. Putting their lives on hold for Maisie was one thing, but if he went abroad, if Josie wanted them out there as a family...

'It's all bollocks Lucy.' His touch was firm as he placed his hand over hers again. 'She's filing for divorce, and she's not even got a permanent job out there. It's not the solution at all, it's just her trying to control what I do, she's just proving she can wind me up, mess with my head.' He ruffled his hair with long fingers, and Lucy resisted the urge to hug him. 'I've got to fight to be able to see Maisie here, either part of the time like most divorced couples do, or just for holidays if Josie does move. Haven't I?'

Lucy nodded, suddenly sad. She didn't want Maisie to have to go through a childhood of being shifted between parents, or even worse, of being without her father. 'Taking the job might be a good start.'

'That's what I thought. And finding a home is the next step. Sal is already trying to move into the surgery flat before I've had a chance to move out.' The corner of his mouth lifted into a rueful smile.

'I told you she'd be keen. Is she moving her stuff in on her weekend off?'

'Nope. She seems to have plans to go away, but she never goes away, does she?'

Lucy watched as Piper made a lunge for the rest of Maisie's cake. Charlie was right, she'd never known Sally to go anywhere, was she planning her first weekend break with Jamie?

# Chapter 8

'Well, what do you think, lad?'

Charlie looked around. There was no doubt that Jim had come up trumps, but not in the way he'd expected, and it gave him an unexpected lift.

This was no cute cottage on the green where all the neighbours could watch his every move, or a tidy house on the new estate where they might have felt cooped up. This was perfect.

'I don't know what to say Jim.' He looked up at the high ceiling, and glass fronted mezzanine floor that ran from one end of the building to the other, then turned to gaze out of the enormous window that gave views over the fields and beyond, all the way to his surgery.

'Say yes, say yes, Daddy.' Maisie was more animated than he'd seen her in a long time, jumping up and down as she tugged at his hand, and he was glad that he'd gone along with the impulse to bring her. 'Look, look there's a proper kitchen, and everything.' He grinned, her enthusiasm would have been catching, if he hadn't already been smitten with the place. She ran over to the other side of the lounge, and into the bright open plan kitchen —which meant he would never be far from Maisie even if he was doing his best to cook an edible meal. 'And a proper TV.' She dashed past them, and into the cosy lounge area, with its wood burning stove and large television. And he felt a sudden sharp pain in his chest. In their small flat at the surgery, which they'd spent the summer in, Maisie had missed out on all this. *Normal* living. It was no wonder she was unhappy, longing for something familiar. 'And Ted from school lives here so I'd have a friend even though he isn't a girl.'

With a grin, she was off again, up the spiral staircase to the mezzanine floor, where she stopped to wave at them, before disappearing into a room at the end of it. They'd already both been up there and he knew she'd fallen in love with the spacious bedroom with its fairy-tale skylights. Within seconds she reappeared and stood on the open area that overlooked the ground floor. She could play there whenever she wanted, and watch him at the same time.

For an insecure little girl, who needed the comfort of always knowing somebody was there, and a blundering parent who was doing as many things wrong as right, it was perfect.

'I was expecting an old cottage.'

'Ah well, I asked around and there's none free, and Elsie Harrington wasn't much use. Then I thought of this place. Ed's old mum used to live here. When he took over the farm she said she had no place in the house any more, didn't want to be in the way. He wasn't for having her move away so he got this place turned into a granny flat.' Jim chuckled, 'well, granny house. Independent old bird she was, bit like Elsie Harrington, so she wanted her own driveway, own bit of garden, but he felt reassured like, happy that he was close by if she needed any help.'

'It doesn't look like any granny flat I've ever seen before.' Charlie wandered back up the short corridor that led to the master bedroom, bathroom, and a small study that could also be used as a bedroom. If Maisie was really unhappy he could always put a mattress in there for her, and she'd be almost within touching distance, but still with her own room.

'He's used it as a holiday let,' Jim tapped the side of his nose, as they wandered back outside, 'on the quiet like, since she passed away.'

Charlie nodded as they wandered out of the front door and gazed over at the nearby farm buildings.

He was no stranger to Wright's farm, but he had never known this place existed. It was close enough to walk into the village even for Maisie. The barn conversion was simply furnished, but felt homely enough and although it was a far cry from the town centre home they'd once shared as a family, he couldn't have wanted anywhere better for his daughter to grow up. If he got the chance to see her grow up. He tried to push the ever present worry to the back of his mind. 'It's perfect Jim.'

'Good.' Jim Stafford puffed his chest out in obvious delight. 'I thought it might suit the young 'un. Nothing like fields, a kid their own age, and a bit of fresh air to cheer them up.'

Charlie tried not to frown. It was that obvious was it, that his daughter was unhappy? They watched her for a while, peering into the barn at the calves.

'She'll be missing her mum no doubt, not that you aren't doing a grand job, Charlie boy.' Jim patted him on the arm. 'I'll be off then, leave you to sort it with Edward, shall I?'

'That's great, thanks, Jim, fantastic. Thanks for your help.'

Five minutes later, Charlie had the keys in his hand and an agreement on what he needed to pay. 'You stay as long as you want, be a weight off my mind knowing there's somebody in it, especially with autumn on its way. Get damp it will if it's not being used.' The farmer had said. 'Don't be asking me to help you move your stuff in though.' He winked.

'Maisie?' She turned round expectantly. 'Do you want another look at your new room before we go and start packing your stuff into boxes?'

Charlie read through the document one last time. He hadn't wanted to come back to Langtry Meadows, take a backwards step from his modern town centre referral practice, this was only meant to be a stop-gap. A favour for one of his father's oldest friends.

At first he'd resisted because it meant coming back with his tail between his legs, admitting he'd failed. Now he was worried he'd fail again. If Josie got her way and took Maisie from him, then the villagers would witness it all. Which was why he'd hung on to his temporary, and very unsuitable flat above the surgery. And why he'd resisted Eric's job offer.

Now though, things were different. He wanted to stay because of Lucy, and he wanted to stay because there was the slightest glimmer of hope that if he put roots down he might be able to prove he was a good father. A father who deserved to spend time with his child.

He picked up his pen, and with a sigh scrawled his signature along the bottom of the contract of employment. He'd always said he wanted nothing to do with his father's practice, he'd been happy to see Eric buy it when his father had retired, but now by a roundabout route he'd done it. Become part of the family firm.

The other sheet of paper on his desk was more of a problem.

The words glared out at him boldly. Home Paternity Test. The result, it declared, would offer peace of mind. He gave a short laugh. It could give him peace of mind that he had a fair chance in any battle Josie wanted to enter into, or it could shatter the shred of hope he was hanging on to.

If he truly wasn't Maisie's father, as Josie had suggested, where would that leave him?

He'd spent many a sleepless night trying to work out dates in his mind, but it was impossible. At the time she was conceived, he and Josie were still on good terms, in what he thought was a happy marriage. Having sex. Okay, maybe not as often as they had when they'd first got hitched, but they'd been busy. Building up a business. There were late nights, emergencies to deal with. But it wasn't like they were sleeping in separate rooms, or no longer got the urge. It was just a bit more ... well, a bit less.

And unfortunately, she'd also been sharing her time with another man.

He swallowed down the bile. The thought still made him feel sick, even after all this time. Even though he no longer loved her.

Charlie pushed the sheet of paper to one side, turned

to his laptop, and pulled up the email address of the firm of solicitors the family had always used. He needed advice.

He'd just hit the send button when the whimpers reached him.

'Daddy, daddy ... scared ... Roo's left me. Want Roo.'

He was scared too. He covered the short distance from the lounge area of the flat to the bedroom, but Maisie was asleep. Her long lashes fluttered against sleep-flushed cheeks. Her auburn curls clung damply to her face. He brushed a lock of hair gently away and eased a wriggling Roo from her grasp.

She gave a little moan, then settled again, her thumb in her mouth. Tip toeing out of the room, the dog at his heels, he grabbed a can of beer and settled down on the sofa again, just as his phone vibrated to signal an email.

It was brief and to the point.

*Don't do anything, and whatever you do, don't do any kind of DNA test – legal or otherwise. If it comes up negative you won't have a leg to stand on. Talk tomorrow. Malcolm.*

# Chapter 9

Lucy watched the last of the children leave the playground, and then on impulse set off across the green to join Elsie Harrington, who was sitting on the bench by the pond. Molly, her dog, at her feet.

'I bet you've watched a lot of the village children grow up.'

'I have, dear.' She patted Lucy's hand. 'It's so wonderful to watch them on their little journeys; so wary on their first day, so excited and ready to challenge the world by the time they leave.' She sighed and sat back. 'Time passes so quickly, it's over in the blink of an eye, although by the time you reach my age the pace of everything in life is far too fast.'

'Have you always watched them come out?' Lucy hadn't really thought about it until now, but ever since she'd first joined the teaching staff at Easter, Elsie had been a constant presence. If the weather was fine, she could be seen sat on the small bench that overlooked the village pond. As the last of the children rejoined their parents she'd make her way past the school and head down towards the cobbled square, and her home.

'It's one of my little rituals. At first it was something I had to do, and then it became something I wanted to do. I've watched them every day for so many years.' Her voice had softened and Lucy glanced at her.

It was something she'd had to do.

Elsie had always seemed tinged with sadness, despite her spirit and obvious intention to make the best of life. Lucy had bonded with her from their first meeting, a few minutes' chat with the elderly lady had often helped her solve problems that she'd been chasing round in her head for what seemed like forever. Elsie was good at solving other people's problems, even better at avoiding her own, and had only reluctantly admitted what gnawed at her heart and left her sad. She had a secret, a secret she'd told Lucy that had to be kept. A wrong that it was too late to put right.

All she'd told Lucy was that she'd lost a child, and although she didn't want to pry, inside she was sure it was too important to ignore. Something told her that Elsie's child hadn't died, but that she'd had to give him or her up. And now she was surer than ever that she was right. 'Did you watch your own child, Elsie?' She didn't want to intrude, but somehow she just wanted to find a way to make things better.

Elsie had told her some time ago that to dig up the past would be altering somebody's life, opening a can of worms, that it wouldn't be fair. She seemed to have made up her mind that it was too late to put right the mistakes of her past – she'd made a choice and had to stick to it. But Lucy wasn't so sure. Getting to the bottom of the secrets in her own life had helped her move on. Be happy. Be who she wanted to be, not the person life was dictating she should be.

'Yes dear.' The old lady sighed, a sigh that turned to a cough. She waved away Lucy's concern. 'That was when it started.' Elsie stirred up the grass at her feet with the tip of her walking stick. 'There was no other way of watching him grow up, no other way without people asking questions. I wanted to see his first day, check that he was happy, to watch him grow from a toddler into a bold child. And so I watched them all, I came down here each day and waited for the school bell to ring, for his mother to arrive and collect him. And then, even when he grew up and left the school, I kept on coming. It became a habit. But some days now,' she stroked Molly's head, 'I feel like a silly old woman, the weather gets into my bones if I sit too long. Watching the children doesn't make me feel young like it used to.'

'Oh Elsie, don't say that.' Lucy blinked, knowing the last thing the independent Elsie wanted was her sympathy. But she just couldn't imagine what it must have been like for the young Elsie to watch her child from a distance, knowing she could never hug, never hold. Watch and have to keep her secret. And now she was still watching, her heart still aching, because she felt she had to.

'They make me feel like some ancient relic, a fool who has spent her life on the side-lines.'

'Nobody would ever say you were a fool Elsie, and you've always been the centre of village life. Langtry Meadows wouldn't be the same without you.'

'They wouldn't call me one to my face maybe.' Her tone was dry, a little bit of her normal sparkle returning. 'But what kind of a fool is somebody who is the centre of everything but her own child's life? A woman who can't forget the past, but can't find a way to repair it?'

'A kind-hearted one, one who cares. Didn't you ever have the,' Lucy paused, looking for the right word, 'opportunity to have another child?'

'No dear.' The sadness in the old lady's eyes brought a lump to Lucy's throat and she felt a pang of guilt. She'd been so busy since the start of term, she'd hardly popped in to see Elsie. 'There was only one love in my life, and that wasn't meant to be. When he left he took a part of me with him.'

They sat in silence for a moment, watching the ducks, and Lucy knew that if Charlie had to leave, it would do the same to her.

'Jim tells me that Charles is settling in Wright's place?' It was as though Elsie could read her mind, and wanted to divert the conversation from herself. 'A child shouldn't be without its father, it's impossible to understand what is going through the head of that ex-wife of his.'

'It seems perfect for them, Maisie was so excited about moving in, she's much more settled now.'

'And Charles?'

'Charlie's worried.'

'And is the child his?'

If anybody else had asked, Lucy would have hesitated. But Elsie seemed to know everything, but didn't actually gossip. She just discussed things with the people concerned. 'He doesn't know. He doesn't actually care, he thinks of her as his, but knowing she definitely was his daughter would help his case, but ...'

'Knowing she isn't could damage it?'

'Exactly. He's been told not to risk the possibility. Make it Josie's responsibility to prove he isn't Maisie's father.'

'All he can do is his best, and we have to trust that common sense and kindness will prevail.' She looked down at Molly, who had her chin resting on the old lady's knee and was gazing up at her adoringly. 'We're getting old, aren't we Molly? One day soon I might not be able to come and watch, I might get shunted off to some home full of old dears.' She looked at Lucy, but didn't smile. 'And then my secret will die with me, won't it? Is it right? Did I do the right thing?'

'I think maybe he needs to know, your child, as long as it won't hurt anybody. I mean, it's important to know where you belong, isn't it? Who you are.' Lucy tried to keep her tone measured and steady. So this was Elsie's secret, a son, a child she'd had to give up. She didn't really care why, it didn't matter, but what did matter was that it came out in the open, that there were no regrets.

'It is important dear, but he does know who he is. He has his family, the people that have nurtured him and made him who he is.' She paused. 'Would it make me a bad parent, a selfish parent, to shake the foundations? It could be argued, and I'm sure it will be, that Maisie should know where she belongs. But who is to make that judgement? Maybe it is up to this other man to prove he is her father, rather than for Charles's parentage to be questioned. He's been a good father to the child.' She frowned. 'He is the only father she's known. And my child, my child had a mother, the only mother he's ever known.'

'But what about you, Elsie?'

Elsie sighed and shook her head. 'What makes a good parent, a true parent? A good parent puts the child first, my dear, just as yours did for you. Always first, and if

I couldn't put all my faith in that belief, then it would destroy me. It is what has kept me going.'

'And what does his mother think?'

'Oh she died some time ago, which is when I started to wonder.'

'Do you think she'd have minded?'

'To be honest, dear, I don't think she would. She was a good woman. We never talked about it, after it was done, and I would never have done anything to upset her. But when I last saw her she did say, he's yours again now Miss Harrington. Take care of him.'

Lucy patted the old gnarled hand, which was curled over, clutching the top of her stick. 'Then I think you know the answer. You need some time with him. You're not allowed to die for years, Elsie, we all need you too much, but you've told me to be brave ...'

'And now it's my turn, dear? Maybe. Maybe. Oh well, enough of my moaning.' She sighed. 'Come on Molly, time to head home and give you your tea.' She struggled to her feet, coughing again as she did so, a dry cough that left her out of breath.

'Are you okay?' Lucy frowned. Jim had mentioned that she was a bit under the weather.

'I'm fine dear, one of those dratted summer colds. Don't ever get old if you can avoid it, that's my advice. Now,' she waved a hand to dismiss Lucy's concerns, 'I do hope you're going to invite me round to Jasmine

Cottage when you get it how you want it, dear girl.'

'Of course I will, you'll be the first guest.' Lucy hesitated. 'Was that anything to do with you?' The estate agent had mentioned that Elsie had suggested they give her first option on the property. But was there more to it than that?

'Now, now dear, don't quiz me. An old lady has to have the opportunity to make amends, to do some things right in life. And you,' she patted Lucy's hand, 'need to make sure that you're there for Charlie. Or you'll regret it one day, mark my words, we never wish we'd spent less time with somebody, we always wish we'd had longer.'

Lucy watched as she made her way slowly across the green, and wondered exactly who it was she wished she'd had the chance to spend more time with. Elsie seemed to have lost some of her zest for life, acknowledged that the years were passing, and Lucy hoped that she could persuade her to let go of her secrets.

It wouldn't happen these days, when all births were carefully recorded, and children had a right to know who their parents were if they'd been fostered or adopted. But Elsie had given birth in a different time. Her son might not even know that he'd been given up. The shock might alter his life for ever, and what if he rebuffed Elsie? Could Lucy's interfering do more harm than good?

'You look like you're up to no good!'

Lucy jumped; she'd been so deep in thought that she hadn't heard Sally sneak up behind her. 'I was just having five minutes' peace actually,' she frowned at Sally, who knew she was joking and laughed. 'I've been chatting to Elsie. Do you think she's okay? She doesn't seem herself, and she's got a terrible cough.' She didn't know what bothered her most, the cough, or the air of regret that seemed to hang round the subdued Elsie.

'I haven't seen her out and about as much lately, and well, now you mention it she is a bit subdued, not quite her normal self. She's usually quizzing me about everybody, if you know what I mean?'

'Oh yes, I know.' Lucy smiled, then sobered up. 'She seems sad, old.'

'She is old, Lucy.' Sally sat down beside her.

'But I never think of her as old. Jim said the other day she was under the weather and she'd got a bit of a summer cold, you know what she's like though, she's not going to admit she feels ill is she?'

'Nope, not our Elsie.'

'Jim's the only one who knows how to handle her, she seems to accept help from him, he's brilliant at making everything look like it's no bother.' She really should find time to check in on Elsie herself though. 'It's not just her cold though, I'm sure that whatever secret she's hiding she did with good intentions, but she's beginning to regret it.' If it hadn't been on her mind so much, she wouldn't have answered Lucy's questions, she was sure of that.

'Well you'll have to find out what it is. She likes you.'

'I think she wants to tell somebody.'

'Well I don't know how anybody can keep a secret all that time, and not tell anybody at all. I'd burst. In fact,' there was a long pause, and Lucy looked up at Sally, 'can I tell you my secret?'

'Secret?'

'There's only one other person knows, but if I don't tell you I'll explode, but you've got to promise not to breathe a word, not to anybody.'

'O-kay.'

'Not even Charlie.'

'Well I can't lie to him.'

'You won't have to lie, he won't ask because he hasn't got a clue.'

'He said you were acting a bit strangely, he thought maybe it was because Eric was back.'

Sally giggled. 'Eric is in on the secret as well, I forgot about him. So that's me and two other people, but you're the last person I'm telling.'

'Are you sure it's safe to tell me, if it's such a big secret?'

'I have GOT to tell you.' Sally put her hand on Lucy's arm.

'Go on then.' Lucy grinned, and had barely finished talking when her friend leaned in closer.

'You know I said we were saving a deposit for a house?'

'Yes.'

'And I mean, well, using the flat at the vets for now is brilliant and ...'

'And?'

'Well ...' Sally was fidgeting, and had turned pink, even though from the smile on her face it was obvious that this was something she was happy about.

'Well?'

'And I asked you if you thought we were rushing things?'

'Yes.' She'd never known Sally not get to the point within seconds. 'Spit it out, Sal, the suspense is killing me.'

'And you honestly don't?'

'Don't what?' She frowned, wondering what this was leading to. Maybe Sal was having second thoughts. Maybe Jamie had done something to upset her, though she certainly didn't look upset. Just nervous, in the same over-excited way the kids at school could be when they knew the bell was about to ring. But worse.

'Think we're mad, you know, rushing?'

'I don't. Honestly. You've got a lot of lost time to make up for, and everybody knows you two were made for each other.'

'Well.' Sally glanced round again, to be sure nobody was within hearing range, but Lucy was sure her loud whisper could have been heard all the way across the green. 'We're getting married!' She ended on a squeak.

'You're ...?' She stared open mouthed at her friend – she hadn't expected that. 'Really? Wow!' It sank in, and Lucy knew she was grinning. It was perfect. 'Congratulations,' she hugged Sally, then looked round guiltily as she realised she'd been screeching. 'Oh I'm so pleased for you Sal.' She dropped her voice to a whisper. 'To Jamie?'

'Of course to Jamie.' Sally bounced on the bench. 'I nearly told you the other day, after I'd asked you if you thought I was rushing things, I really wanted to tell you, and I know everybody will say it's quick, but I don't really care, I mean, we shouldn't, should we?'

'No!' Lucy laughed again at the rush of words. 'You definitely shouldn't, though honestly, nobody will think you're rushing. And it's how you feel that's important, and you know you're sure.'

'Oh yes, I'm sure, really sure, more sure than anything ever. I just knew he was the one for me, when I was nine and he rescued me after his horrid brother Matt had pinned me down and was trying to make me eat worms.' She shuddered, then sighed melodramatically. 'He was so big and strong, and he chased Matt right to the end of the field.'

Lucy laughed. Everybody in the village loved Matt Harwood, Jamie's brother. He was cheeky, good-natured and always up for a laugh. As outgoing as his brother was quiet. For years he'd set himself up as the village Lothario, whilst Jamie had eyes only for his childhood sweetheart Sally. But now Lucy had a feeling Matt had fallen, and fallen hard, for Jill her kind-hearted classroom assistant. Both brothers it seemed, had fallen in love.

'Oh Sal, it's brilliant news. I'm really pleased for you. But,' she paused, 'how can you get married in secret?' Then frowned. 'And I don't get it, why?'

Sally smiled, a little secret smile as she clutched Lucy's hands. 'That's what the weekend off work is all about, we're going to Gretna Green.' The last two words came out as an excited squeak.

Lucy stared, knowing her jaw had dropped. Sally and Jamie getting married wasn't a huge surprise, but at Gretna Green, and so soon? 'You're kidding? You're eloping, in a few weeks' time?'

'Nope, no joke.' Her grin had broadened, if that was possible. 'Doesn't that sound so romantic? Eloping.'

'But why not here? Your parents, everybody, I mean, well,' it was her turn to stutter, 'everybody will want to be at the wedding, and well ...'

'Exactly.' Sally sighed and dropped her hands back

into her lap. 'It would just get so complicated if we got married here. You have no idea. I mean, I know Mum will be cross, but she'd take over, and the whole village would be involved, and I don't want a load of fuss. I just want to get married, all I care about is me and Jamie. When we told them all in the summer that we were getting engaged, Mum went into overdrive.'

'We did have a great party.' The landlord at the Taverner's Arms had been as delighted as everybody else – they all loved Jamie and Sally, and had waited years for the couple to get together. The fact that when they finally had, things had moved at speed, had not been totally unexpected. The bunting had been put up, a hog roast set up and the fun had gone on way past normal closing time.

'Exactly, it was a great party. But Mum had planned a marquee on the green, guest of honour, flowers, the Bishop of Whatchamacallit.'

'A real bishop?'

'No I'm kidding, but she did want to invite the vicar, and that was just because we'd got engaged. Imagine what she'd be like planning a wedding.' She rolled her eyes.

'You don't want a white dress, the dream wedding?'

Sally sighed. 'I don't want a big fuss, and I know it would be impossible to keep it low key. All we'd want is a simple service followed by a cold buffet in the pub, but we'd end up with a two hour session in church followed by the full works, all formal and everything. And I know it sounds daft, but it just isn't us. I just want it to be fun.'

'So you're really eloping! Crumbs, my mum would kill me if I did that.'

'Mine might.' Sally giggled. 'And Jamie's family might be a bit put out; his dad thought a barn dance was a good idea when we got engaged. God, can you imagine trying to stage manage a wedding? With my mum wanting everybody in posh frocks and fascinators, and Jamie's family wanting bales of hay, do-si-do's and cowboy hats?'

'Well when you put it like that!' Lucy grinned. 'I always thought the main problem was the seating plan.'

'I know Mum will come round, eventually.' She paused. 'She'll just start planning a big christening instead.'

'You're not ...?' Lucy glanced down at Sally's flat stomach.

'No I'm bloody not.' She shuddered. 'If we have pattering feet it'll be a puppy not a baby.'

'Oh Sal.' Lucy reached out and hugged her friend again. 'I'm so pleased for you. Both of you. And thanks for letting me in on the secret.'

'Well I do have an ulterior motive, I want help with my hair and make-up.'

'You're on.'

'And somewhere to hide my suitcase.'

'So when is the big day? Charlie told me you were having a weekend off, but that's really close.'

'Nope, that's the date. Half term hols.'

'Gosh, that's not long off.' Lucy realised with a jolt that a good part of the half-term was already over. September was drawing to a close, it was already autumn and soon the green would be draped with the soft golds and ambers of the leaves. Soon the classroom walls would be decorated with the colourful pumpkins that the children had been painting, and they'd be talking about bonfires and fireworks. 'That's practically tomorrow.'

'Well not tomorrow.' Sally giggled. 'But it's very soon, isn't it? But I've picked an outfit, and Jamie's got a suit, he's going to look so sexy. I mean he does anyway, but he's always in his farm gear, and we've got rings.' She frowned. 'Though once we get home they'll be spotted straight away, well we did think we might take all the parents for lunch at the Taverner's, then they can't kick up a fuss.' She paused. 'Do you think Eric and Charlie will be okay without me? Charlie is panicking already.'

'I'm sure they will.' Lucy nodded reassuringly. 'And now Charlie's taken up a permanent post it might do them good,' she grinned, 'they can do some male bonding.'

'Not sure bonding is the word, but it's funny you know. They are so totally different, but they kind of rub along together alright, like an old married couple. Charlie tidies up after Eric, and finishes his sentences off. They're hilarious, and Eric is so pleased to be back. He said he feels useless stuck at home, but I'm sure he's even more vague and forgetful than he used to be. I caught him chatting to a parrot he'd booked in the other day, couldn't remember what it was there for and he'd crossed the entry out of the appointment log to make room for some notes.'

'That sounds a bit, well, serious.' No wonder Charlie was worried. 'Did the parrot tell him?'

'Oh no, all it can say is "*off for a pint again, are you, Albert?*" in a sarcastic voice. It belongs to Mrs Graham, but every so often Albert drops it off with us on the pretence of some strange imaginary illness. He's hoping that one day there will actually be something wrong with it. Eric's always doing stuff like that though, says he'll remember and of course doesn't. But I have backups.'

'I hope you've told Charlie.'

'Oh I have a plan, Charlie will be fine. Quite honestly though, as long as they don't castrate anything they shouldn't, then it can't be that bad, can it? I mean it is only a few days. Oh gosh, is that the time? I've been going on and on, it's just it's so nice to talk about it, and I know you won't tell anybody. I'm supposed to be meeting Jamie. He'll be so pleased you're in on the secret,' she kissed Lucy on the cheek and gave her another hug, 'I really better go, see you later.'

'I'm pleased too, are we allowed a secret bottle of wine the night before you go?'

'Only if we can watch *Love Actually* on DVD.'

'You've got a deal.'

# Chapter 10

Charlie squinted as the low autumn rays of sun sneaked over the top of the school roof. Things had certainly changed since Eric had decided he was ready to return to work.

He still wasn't entirely sure about the go-with-the-flow attitude to appointments, and he definitely didn't approve of the 'drop the payment in any time' strategy. But it was nice to have a bit more flexibility as far as his days went. Now, if he was called out at 5 a.m. to deal with an emergency, some days he'd be away for 3 p.m. and be able to pick Maisie up from school.

Not that she was as bothered now; she was more interested in discussing worms with Ted. Or guinea pigs. They were apparently going to train his as a showjumper. Charlie suspected that the nearest the guinea pigs would get to completing a show-jumping round would be to eat it.

Maisie spotted him the moment he stepped into the

playground (fashionably late compared to most of the other parents) and he couldn't help but smile. Seeing her happy made him happy.

She flew into his arms managing to simultaneously kick him in the groin and nearly give him a black eye. He glanced up, knowing Lucy would be laughing at his mock groans. She wasn't.

She was pressed hip to hip with Matt Harwood, who had a possessive arm resting across her shoulders, his dirty blond-brown hair brushing against her head.

He leaned in, his lips inches from her ear, and she laughed as he whispered something. Then Archie, his tiny Chinese crested dog licked her chin and made her laugh more.

Charlie shook his head; Matt Harwood had to be the only farmer in the country who'd decided a small, bald dog was preferable to a collie or terrier.

'Daddy. Daddy.' Maisie wriggled. 'Stop squeezing me so hard, I want to tell you about the story we had today, and the pumpkin I painted.'

Charlie gently put her down on the floor and turned away, trying to ignore the irrational twinge of annoyance. He knew he could trust Lucy, knew she loved him – despite all the complications – and he really couldn't blame Matt for ladling the charm on. After all, who wouldn't want to chat to Lucy? And Matt was charming, the man was popular with most of the girls in the village. Charlie reckoned he was one of those men that just couldn't help himself. He just had to flirt.

Lucy had told him more than once that Matt was like a loveable big brother. But he still didn't like it. Every time he saw her close to another guy it made something tighten in his stomach. Love had obviously brought out a possessive streak in him he hadn't known he had.

But he knew why he was disgruntled. In a way, these moments when he was able to meet Maisie from school were shared moments, he'd look and she'd be watching them from the school doorway and they'd swap a look. A little raised eyebrow from her, if Maisie had had a tough day, a thumbs up or wink if things were going well. The shake of a hand if he needed to be careful how he handled things.

He sighed. It was as intimate as it got some days.

But irrational disappointment flooded him when he missed out.

'Come on Daddy.' Maisie tugged at his hand. 'Home time.' He let her guide him, weaving between the parents who were still waiting for the older children to emerge from the small school building.

Maisie was happy. They were getting there. Slowly. So why wasn't he?

'Can I go?' He nodded, letting his daughter run ahead to catch up with Ted.

The brutal truth of the matter was, he'd been running away since Maisie had come back into his life.

He'd told himself he'd been facing up to his responsibilities, but he hadn't, not really. He'd been doing what he thought was the right thing, not what his gut was telling him. And if he didn't own up to what he really wanted, and fight for it, then he risked losing the lot.

'Are you listening, Daddy?' His daughter was back, and he wasn't even giving her the few minutes of time she needed. 'I'm going to tell you about the pumpkin painting.'

'I'm listening, Maisie. If you draw me a picture of your pumpkin, then I'll make sure we make one for real, exactly the same.'

'Out of a real pumpkin?' Her brown eyes opened wide. 'Not tissue paper? With eyes, and teeth.' She bared her own and he laughed.

'A real pumpkin, but after the holidays.'

'I know that. I'm not silly. Hallowe-en is just before we go back to school. Will you make pumpkin soup?'

'You might be pushing it a bit there.'

'Well we can ask Lu—I mean Miss Jacobs. She knows how to make pumpkin soup. She told us so. You need bacon and other spicy stuff. Come on, let's go and tell Roo, then you can ask her to come and show you.'

\*\*\*

'Ted says summat nasty might happen to it if you don't say yes.'

'Something.' Charlie corrected Maisie then glanced up from the laptop and frowned. 'Something nasty will happen to what?'

Maisie gave a heavy sigh and folded her arms. 'The guinea pig of course.'

'Sorry?'

'Daddy you haven't heard a word I've said, have you?'

Lucy gave a muffled squeak, then put her hand over her mouth apologetically. He loved the way she switched from professional, but caring, school teacher to relaxed funny person. He loved lots of things about her.

'I thought you were talking to Lucy, not me.'

'I was talking to everybody, but she said I've got to ask you.'

'Ask me what?' He'd been studying some case notes when Lucy had arrived, and she'd smilingly told him to finish off while Maisie gave her a tour of their new home.

'It's called Treacle.'

He raised an eyebrow at Lucy, who grinned. 'Ted's guinea pig has had babies, and he asked Maisie if she wanted one of them.'

'There's two left. Ted is keeping Peanut, but said I can have Treacle, and Treacle's the best anyway. They can carry on seeing each other then and be friends, like me and Ted. I might not always want to be his friend, cos he is a boy and he doesn't know how to make daisy chains,' she glanced at Lucy, 'Daddy can't either, so I don't think Ted will, do you?' She didn't wait for a response. 'But he told me he can climb really big trees instead. So it would be mean not to have Treacle, wouldn't it, Daddy?' She ended on a hopeful high.

'We haven't got a hutch.'

'You can make one. Ted's dad made theirs and it's big.' She held out her hands as far apart as she could. 'It likes sprouts, which will be very useful at Christmas because I don't. So it could eat them for me, couldn't it? You said you don't like waste.'

'I don't.'

'I'm going to go and have another look at it. You can have a think, but I think you should say yes quickly.'

With a wave she was off, diving out of the door, Roo at her heels.

'Well she seems happier.' Lucy was laughing as he fought to keep his face straight.

'She is, it's been good for us moving here. You were right, as normal. What would I do without you?' He spoke lightly, but he meant every word.

'Well you'd have a pizza all to yourself for a start.' She smiled back and for a moment everything was perfect in Charlie's world. 'What are you doing?'

'Research into alpacas. Poor Maria's been plagued

with bald spots, well the animals not Maria herself.' He folded down the lid of the laptop. 'It's been bugging me for ages, but Eric suggested a zinc deficiency. I've checked for mange, ringworm, you name it. I even thought they might just be plain bored and rubbing on the fences. Then Eric pops up with the answer, just like that. He comes across all vague and forgetful, but he's brilliant, sharp as anything underneath. Sorry, this must be boring.'

'Not at all.' She shook her head. 'Obviously not as funny as watching you try and wriggle out of taking on a guinea pig, but still interesting.'

'Do you think I should let her?'

'Well she might have a point about the sprouts.'

'Thanks for those words of wisdom.'

'Pleasure.'

'So what's the half term hols got in store? I was hoping we could go for a day out, if you fancied it? Although with Sally buggering off for a few days, it might be a bit mad at the surgery.'

'A day out sounds good. I can help out with Maisie as well if you like? Mum said she'd pop over one day, and I've got marking to do, and some quotes to arrange for work on the cottage before I put an offer in.'

'Time for a pizza one night?' He sat down beside her on the sofa, and pulled her in close to his side.

'I'd like that.'

'So would I, I've missed you, we've both been far too busy.' She smelled far too good, looked far too good.

'True.'

He slipped his fingers under her hair, ran his thumb over her slender jawline. 'We should find time. I know I've been a bit preoccupied with Maisie, but I want you. I've decided that I can't just ignore us, Lucy. You're too important to me.' He rested his forehead against hers, looked into her clear blue eyes. 'That's if you're happy to put up with a single dad who's also a workaholic?'

'What if Josie, you know, if it gets nasty ...?'

'If it's going to get nasty I'd rather have you by my side than be on my own.'

'But it might annoy her, make it worse.'

'She's already shown me the worst, Lucy. I'm not going to let her dictate to me how I live my life any longer.' He hadn't thought this through, he was just saying it as it came into his head. The words that mattered. Life without Lucy was lonely. 'I know we can't throw ourselves into this like teenagers, but we can make sure we don't lose it, can't we?'

The words hung between them. It mattered what she said, how she reacted. He didn't want her to be with somebody else, he wanted to give them a chance.

She nodded, blonde waves cascading around her face. He wanted to kiss her, but he wouldn't. There was time; he was old enough to be patient. But not too patient.

'Stay for dinner?'

'Don't you have an itchy alpaca to sort out?'

'Tomorrow. This is supposed to be my afternoon off. We can make pizza with Maisie?'

'You make pizza?'

'Well.' He shrugged self-consciously. It had been a 'thing' since Maisie had been about four years old; she made cupcakes with Josie and pizza with him. 'It involves a lot of flour and mess. I can manage a basic dough, and she makes faces out of pepperoni, sweetcorn, mushroom and pepper.'

'I'm impressed, a man of hidden talents.'

'I'll be impressed when you make us that pumpkin soup.'

The door suddenly swung open and distracted both of them from all thoughts of cooking. Roo hurtled in and launched himself at Charlie, Maisie following more slowly.

She was staring intently at the animal in her arms.

'I've got to be very careful not to drop him.'

Charlie looked from his daughter to Lucy. This looked a bit of a mission accomplished.

'This is Treacle.'

'Sorry about this.' Mrs Wright dressed in her normal overalls and muddy wellingtons, a collie at her feet, waved cheerily from the doorway. 'I won't come in duck, what with my wellies and the mess.' There was a broad smile on her round face, and there could never be any doubt that she was related to Ted. 'The kiddies told me you were happy to have one of these, but I thought I better check myself.' She winked. 'I know how it is.'

'Well I ...'

'Now you've not been having me on young Ted, and Maisie, have you now?'

'Daddy,' Maisie edged closer and hissed, 'you don't want anything bad to happen to him, do you?' He looked down at the dark whiskery face, then carefully extracted the animal from her arms and looked more closely.

'I'd say it's a boy from the way it's been behaving. Had to separate them from their mother we have, haven't we Ted?'

Ted nodded, his face solemn. 'They play naughty games, they're a pain.'

'I'd say you're right Mrs Wright. Well, you'd have to feed him Maisie.'

She nodded, her auburn curls bobbing.

'And help keep his cage clean.'

Another nod.

'But,' he glanced up at Mrs Wright, 'we'll have to sort a cage and run out.'

'That's no problem, lad. We've got a spare. I'll pop the little one back for now, then get our Ed to bring him over with all the stuff later, shall I?' She held out her hands for the guinea pig, and Charlie gladly relinquished it. 'The kiddies will help, won't you?' Ted and Maisie nodded in unison. 'Right then, I'll leave you two in peace. Come on Maisie, we'll put Treacle back for now, and you can help me feed the calves. If that's all right with you, Charlie?'

'If you're sure?'

'Oh she's no trouble, are you love? I'll get her a pair of Ted's wellies.'

'I've got my own.' Patting the guinea pig on its head, she raced upstairs and came back with flowery pink boots. Charlie wasn't sure they'd ever be that colour again.

'You can see my chicks too.' Ted grinned. 'You can have one if you want.'

Charlie shook his head, and held a hand up. 'No chickens. No more pets.' He shared a look with Lucy as the children followed Mrs Wright across the yard. 'Was it really such a good idea to live on a farm?'

'She's happy.'

'She is. I just hope we're not going to turn her life upside down again.'

'Stop worrying.' She put a hand over his. 'Let's concentrate on happy for now.'

'True. Talking of which, I'll be glad when Sal is back.'

Lucy laughed. 'She's only just gone.'

'Yes, but I'm imagining how bad it can get in four

days. Although she did show me her alternative online appointment book, that Eric hasn't got a clue about.'

'Sneaky.'

'Necessary. Castrate the wrong animal and we're up that creek without a paddle. If he didn't have a habit of crossing stuff out we'd be okay.'

She giggled.

'Any idea where she's gone?'

She shrugged. 'Not exactly.'

Charlie frowned, the way she said it came across all wrong. 'Do you know something I don't?'

'I don't know.'

'You're rubbish at lying.' Deceit didn't sit happily with Lucy, she was far too open and direct. Now there was a look of mild panic on her face.

'It's probably better if you don't ask. Please?'

'Girlie secret?'

'Something like that.'

He shook his head. 'Well, whatever she's up to, she better be back on Tuesday.'

# Chapter 11

'Oh, Lucy.'

Lucy braced herself. She'd known that her mum would think she'd completely lost her marbles. Ever since she'd left home Lucy had been a complete stickler for order, tidiness, everything in its place. For *clean*. It had been a backlash against the total disarray that her mother had brought her up in. Too many magazines overflowing from the tables, too many books in teetering stacks on the bookshelves, cushions overcrowding the settee. Piles of clothes begging to be ironed. Dirty dishes taking over the work-surfaces. An overgrown garden that was a fly-tipper's dream.

She'd compensated in her own way, tried to bring some order back into her own life. Until she'd discovered, earlier in the summer, exactly why her mother had brought her up the way she had. To prove her independence, to celebrate her release from a cruel, controlling husband. Lucy's dad.

Up until then, she'd never known why they'd fled home, leaving everything but their clothes behind. But it all made sense now. And in a strange way finding out had given her a release, permission to let go a little. Live how she wanted to, not how she thought she should.

But this was probably a step too far in her mother's eyes. She thought Lucy had lost her mind. Buying a cottage that needed a major overhaul. 'I know what it looks like Mum, but if I just—' She loved it already, she had to persuade her mum that it was perfect.

'Well I know what it looks like as well Lucy Jacobs.' Trish shook her head. 'It looks amazing, it looks just like the type of home I'd been dreaming of when,' she hesitated, 'he, your, when he said we were moving to a village.' She turned to look at Lucy and her eyes were awash with unshed tears. 'Oh, come here, darling.'

Lucy felt her own eyes burn as she was wrapped in her mother's strong embrace. Her mum had always been strong, it ran through her, right from the tone of her voice through her slim body. Lucy had never noticed that it had only appeared when they ran away from her dad, that the only time it had crumbled was when she'd explained to Lucy why she'd done what she had. Why they'd run away, and she'd lost all her friends, her home, her dog. Her dad.

Trish pulled back a little, tucked Lucy's hair behind

her ear. 'I am so proud of you, Lucy. How on earth did you find such a wonderful place?'

'I think Elsie Harrington had a lot to do with it. You know, the old lady I introduced you to? She was standing at her gate, near the church.'

'Ah yes, the elegant lady. I always wished I could have been that type of person, you know perfectly groomed.' There was a wistful note in her voice that made Lucy smile.

'It's far too much effort, Mum. Just think about all the colour co-ordination, all the time you'd have to spend on your nails.'

Trish grinned. 'It does suit her though, doesn't it? She's very refined,' she paused, as though working out the best way to say what she was thinking, 'but she's got this air about her, she's sad. If that doesn't sound odd?'

Lucy shook her head. 'Not odd at all, Mum. She's definitely sad. I wish she'd talk, tell me the whole story, or tell somebody, anybody. She's just told me little bits at a time, but I'm pretty sure she had to give her baby up when she was younger, when it was born.' She looked at her mother, who nodded. 'I don't think she's ever told anybody, but I think she'd really like to have things out in the open before it's too late.'

'Surely this day and age it's possible to track somebody down? Although I suppose records weren't as good back then.'

'Oh she knows who it is, she's watched him grow up. I bumped into her not long ago and she was sat here, on the green, watching all the kids coming out of school.' A pang of sadness bit at her, making her eyes burn. 'She's done that for years, all the time he, her son, was at school, and then ever since.' How hard must it have been, to sit all alone, just watch?

'He doesn't know?' Her mother raised an eyebrow.

'She left it and left it, not wanting to mess up his life, and then it felt like it was too late. But the woman who looked after him is dead now, and maybe it's the right time.' Lucy shrugged. 'What do you think? I mean he'd be better knowing wouldn't he? If he found out after she died, that would be terrible.' If Josie had taken Maisie away, and she'd not seen her father again, not known how much he'd loved her, until after he died. She shuddered. It didn't bear thinking about.

'Well I'm sure you can guess what I think, Lucy. I put off telling you about why we'd moved for far too long, I regret that. But you do know why I was so frightened to tell you?' Trish walked up the narrow, overgrown garden path and pushed open the cottage door before turning round. 'I was scared of rejection, Lucy. That's what we're all most afraid of, isn't it? Poor Elsie.' She paused. 'Well isn't this lovely? You could polish these floorboards up a treat.'

They stood side by side and looked out of the dusty window towards the green. Maisie and Charlie were playing with Roo and Piper.

'This is what I wanted for you before you were even born, Lucy. It's been a winding route to get here. And that,' she nodded at Charlie and his daughter, 'is what I've wanted for you since you've grown up.'

'But we aren't a family, Mum. Even Charlie doesn't ...'

'It's not the legalities, love, they don't matter in the end. It's what is in your heart, it's love.'

'I think in her heart, Elsie wants to risk telling her son.'

'Then that's what she needs to do, isn't it?'

'But it's different for Charlie.'

'He'll never lose her completely, love, not if he doesn't want to.'

'And we're not a proper couple, we can't be, not with ...'

'Tell the world whatever you want, but,' she smiled, 'inside you know exactly what you are. Now, the kitchen must be through here, is it?'

Trish smiled broadly at the big bright kitchen and its old Aga, then frowned at the mishmash of old-fashioned cupboards (which Lucy thought would look wonderful after they'd had some TLC), before exclaiming with delight at the quarry tiles. She declared the back garden 'wonderful, though an industrial digger might come in handy'; she laughed at the bathroom, but agreed that removing the olive tiles and avocado suite and installing a claw foot bath and new basin and toilet would transform the place (although the plumbing might need more serious surgery).

'You're really settled here in Langtry Meadows, aren't you?'

'I am.' Lucy ran a hand over the old, worn wood of the stair banister and smiled. 'I feel like I've come home.'

'I'm pleased.' Trish's tone was soft. 'I never thought living in a city was right for you.' She pulled the front door shut and they walked down the path arm in arm, then stood next to the rickety little gate, which hung bravely on one hinge.

Lucy turned back to gaze up at the cottage. The place that, fingers crossed, would soon be hers and it seemed to wink back at her as the last dregs of sunlight splintered off the old panes of glass.

The summer white of the jasmine that gave the cottage its name had all but disappeared now, giving way to the more autumnal oranges and golds of the marigolds, roses and gerbera. There was the slightest October nip in the air, and the chimney of the cottage at the end of the terrace was already puffing out smoke.

'Oh my goodness look at that!'

Lucy glanced over at Charlie in alarm as her mother headed back up the path, then veered off towards the corner of the house. What on earth had Trish spotted? Was it something structural, something terrible that would throw all her plans into disarray?

Her heart in her mouth, Lucy rushed after her mum, Charlie and Maisie at her heels.

'Blackberries!' Trish held a fat, juicy blackberry up in the air triumphantly. 'I've never seen so many so late in the season, look.' Her eyes glowed with excitement and Lucy started to laugh with relief. 'We can make crumble, come on, let's all get picking.' She paused for a second, doubt suddenly hitting her. 'We are allowed I suppose? It isn't stealing?'

'No Trish.' Charlie was laughing too. 'I'm sure nobody will mind at all. Hang on, I'll go to the Taverner's and get some bowls to put them in.'

Half an hour later they had several tubs full of fruit, Maisie's fingers and mouth were smeared with juice, and Trish had declared she had enough to keep them in pies and crumbles for quite some time.

She brushed her hands together with contentment. 'Now then, I don't know about you two, but I could murder a nice cup of tea and a biscuit.'

Charlie scooped up Piper, who had been racing round and round a giggling Maisie. 'I'll have to leave you to it I'm afraid. We better get off, hadn't we Maisie?'

Maisie pouted and stared at the ground. 'But I want to make crumble.'

'Sorry darling.' Charlie ruffled her hair. 'Maybe another day? We really do have to get home. I'm expecting a call.'

Lucy could see the flash of tension that caught his features as he spoke. No doubt Josie had promised one of her intermittent calls, and Charlie dreaded them. He'd given up on telling Maisie in advance, because all too often the call didn't materialise and he'd get a message the next day with excuses about lack of Wi-Fi, or emergency situations. It was bad when they didn't happen, but in a way worse when they did. Maisie was pleased to see her mum, but all she wanted to know was when she would be back. Why she wasn't here. When she was going back to her old bedroom and friends.

Moving to the farm had made a big difference to their lives already, but every mention of Josie raised questions. And Charlie couldn't answer them.

'You sure it's okay if Maisie comes to see you in the morning, while I'm in surgery?'

'Of course it is. She can tell Mum all about Treacle, and,' Lucy paused, 'we could make crumble maybe?'

Trish nodded and Maisie grinned, good humour restored. She bounced on the spot, rather like Roo did, and Lucy had to smile. 'Yes, yes, blackberry crumble.'

'That would be brilliant, thanks.' Charlie raised one eyebrow. 'And what do you say, Maisie?'

'Thank you.' With a squeal she launched herself at Trish, who blushed bright red and hugged her close as though she never wanted to let go.

'You're welcome.' Lucy stood on tiptoe and kissed Charlie's cheek. 'Call me later?'

He nodded, smiled and handed over the wriggling cockerpoo. 'I'll be fine.'

'I know you will be.' She moved closer to whisper in his ear. 'But will I? Mum seems to have planned a mother-daughter bonding session, which sounds a bit dangerous to me.'

'You'll be fine.' He chuckled, the broad, deep chuckle that never failed to send a shiver down her arms.

'Mum?' Lucy put a cup of tea down in front of Trish, who smiled.

'Lucy?'

'I'm worried about Elsie.'

'I know you are darling.' Trish rested her hand lightly on top of her daughter's.

'It's not just the baby thing, she's got this cough, and she just doesn't seem herself at the moment.' She ran her hands over her face. 'I feel guilty because she's been so good to me, and I've hardly been round to see her at all lately.'

'You've been busy, love.'

'But I only need to pop in for five minutes, don't I?

On the way home from school. And I haven't.'

'Well they say actions speak louder than words, so I think once we've finished this drink we'll make a nice pot of soup.'

'Soup?' Lucy couldn't help herself, she smiled. There was one very good thing she'd never forgotten about her childhood, and that was the smell of soup. Trish had worked two jobs to make ends meet when Lucy was at school, and often after she'd gone to bed she'd hear her mother start to chop vegetables. Make a cheap but nourishing pan of soup, so that there'd be something waiting for her when she got in from school.

She'd doze off to the steady chop, chop, and when she woke up next morning the house would be full of the smell of chicken soup.

'Well I know your Elsie doesn't like charity, but she can't say no if we turn up with a good pot of soup can she? And it works wonders if you've got flu. Right, get a pen and paper love and I'll tell you the recipe, then when I've gone back home you'll be able to make another pot in the week. Oh, and while we're at it we can make her a nice blackberry crumble. Nobody can turn down one of those, can they? We'll soon have her feeling chirpier and back on her feet, though I'm sure,' she patted Lucy's hand, 'you're right. Persuading her to come out into the open will be a weight off her mind, there's no saying how much damage secrets do to your state of mind, darling. No saying at all. A burden they are.' She shook her head, and her own regrets were clear. 'There'd be a lot less stress in our lives if we didn't hide things. Now, come on, where's that notepad of yours?'

Lucy had just started to root through the drawers for a notepad, when there was a rap on the back door. She glanced up to see Maisie's smiling face, and Charlie's slightly apologetic one.

She raised a questioning eyebrow as she opened the door, and he shrugged. 'My phone call has been put off until later, so we wondered if maybe you could let us have that recipe so Maisie can bake me a crumble for tea? If we don't make it soon she'll have eaten her share of the blackberries, they're going fast.'

Trish chuckled, and turned on the tap. 'No time like the present, is there Maisie? You come over here and wash those hands of yours, we can all make blackberry crumble together. You too Charlie, that table is big enough for all of us to work at.'

Lucy couldn't help but laugh at the expression on his face.

'I might be better just watching.'

'Nonsense.' Trish handed him an apron. She winked at Lucy. 'There's nothing sexier than a man elbow deep in flour!'

Ten minutes later Lucy had to admit her mum might have a point, as she chuckled at Maisie and Charlie.

'Daddy, that's wrong, that's too big.' Maisie sighed, her little fingers working on mixing the hard, cold chunks of butter into the flour, oat and sugar mix. 'Look, this is right, isn't it Trish?' Trish nodded, but Lucy could see she was fighting to keep the smile off her face. 'Perfect.'

'You need crumbs for crumble, Daddy.' She was frowning, the tip of her tongue peeking between her lips as she concentrated hard.

'Well I think my hands must be doing it wrong, maybe you should do mine as well?'

'You shouldn't give up, should he Lucy? You have to do your best,' she gave her bowl a little shake as Trish had told her to, so that the large lumps rose to the surface, 'and if you do your best then that's good enough.' She peered over the edge of Charlie's mixing bowl and shook her head. 'I'm not sure that is actually good enough though, is it?' Leaning over she gave his bowl a slightly more vigorous shake than was needed, and showered the table with flour.

'Hands off, Missy! Honestly,' he rolled his eyes, 'can't a man be left in peace to make his own crumble?'

Maisie grinned, and cheeky little dimples appeared at the side of her mouth. 'Yours would go all wrong if I did leave you in peace.'

'She's got a point, Charlie.' Lucy chuckled as she rubbed away the last chunks of fat in her own mix. She felt like hugging them both. Seeing them here together, laughing and joking, covered in flour had to be the best end to a lovely day. She glanced over to her mum, who was watching them. For a moment, as the scent of cinnamon tantalised her nostrils, she was a little girl again, helping her mum bake in a different kitchen.

Trish smiled and held her gaze for a moment and Lucy knew that they were there together. Sharing memories, the good bits.

'Is mine crumbly enough?' Maisie's words broke the silence.

'Perfect.' She nodded approval then held up a tub of fruit. 'Right, Miss Maisie, come and help me mix these blackberries of yours with some apple and sugar, and we'll let your dad have a rest. He looks worn out.'

Lucy sat down next to Charlie, and he reached out and squeezed her hand as he watched his daughter carefully mix the fruit together, and sprinkle in the cinnamon.

She copied Trish, slowly spooning the fruit into oven dishes, then layered the crumble mix on top. 'That one's yours, Daddy.' Maisie pointed and giggled. 'It's got big bits in.'

'Well I'm sure it will still taste delicious, and that's what counts.' Trish slid the dishes into the oven. 'I think you've all done a wonderful job. Right, I'll put the kettle on for a nice cup of tea, and before you know it we'll be eating the best blackberry crumble in Langtry Meadows.'

The smells of the warm fruit, tinged with the sweetness of cinnamon flooded the kitchen as they drank their tea and Maisie played with Piper in the garden.

'I'll have to go.' Charlie looked regretfully at his watch. 'She should be ringing soon. We'll pop back later and pick up the crumble.'

'We can walk round with it if you like? If that's okay, Mum?'

Trish smiled and nodded. 'Lovely, an evening walk seeing a bit more of this village sounds a good way to end the day.'

As they waved Charlie and Maisie off, Lucy slipped her arm round her mother's waist. 'Thanks, Mum.'

'Whatever for, darling?'

'Being here, being you.'

Trish dropped a light kiss on the top of her daughter's head. 'I really wouldn't want to be anywhere else, Lucy.'

# Chapter 12

'She's filed for divorce.' Charlie said it as he buttered the toast, thinking that somehow it was easier that way. More normal.

Not the blow that it really was.

He'd known it was coming, in fact, in a way he welcomed it. They needed that closure. But even so, it still was a mark of failure. Confirmation that he'd cocked up, that his view of his marriage and family life had been a million miles from the truth. Whether Josie had duped him, or he'd been as un-present in their relationship as she'd accused him of being, it still added up to one thing. The image in his head had been wrong. It had all been an illusion.

He'd been living a lie. And this was the final, damning confirmation.

'Letter on the table.' He nodded towards the envelope as he pushed a mug of coffee towards Lucy, regretting that he'd gone for instant. He needed a real caffeine hit.

Half term had gone far too smoothly, which should have set off warning bells. Josie had skyped once, and gone into such raptures about the new guinea pig and Maisie's art work, until the connection had been unceremoniously curtailed, the little girl hadn't had a chance to ask when she was coming home. When he'd tucked her in bed, he'd managed to distract her, by talking about the pumpkin they were going to carve, the new hutch they were building, all the things she could tell Mummy about next time.

Josie had been politeness and jollity itself, but he hadn't realised until now what that glint in her eye had been. It had been determination. A decision made. In fact, he had a sneaking suspicion that seeing them so happy together, hearing about the life they were making, had made it all worse.

She was jealous.

'I'm going over to chat to my solicitor, he's an old family friend.' He made a conscious effort to snap out of the negative thoughts. 'Will you come?'

'What about Maisie?'

'She's at Becky's today, and Eric is covering the surgery.'

'Well of course I will, if you want me to.'

'I do, I need you to.' He sat down opposite her and tried to smile, but it hurt his cheeks. 'Malcolm, the solicitor, said it could be a bumpy ride.'

'Well as long as the trip over to his isn't, you can count me in.' She smiled, but it was tinged with apprehension. Which was exactly how he felt.

***

Malcolm Taylor lived in what could be called a des. res. Situated in a small market town a twenty minute drive from Langtry Meadows it didn't reek family money as Lucy had expected though. It was ultra-modern.

'So this is the payback for handling other people's divorces is it?' Charlie eyed up the acres of glass, and Lucy knew her jaw had dropped. It wasn't to her taste, but she could certainly admire the place.

'The house came with the wife.' Noticing the admiring looks as he answered the door, Malcolm winked at Charlie, then gave Lucy an assessing look that made her blush. 'Come in, come in,' and led the way down the bright hallway to a surprisingly old-fashioned study. 'But as you can see, the furniture in here came with me, old fuddy-duddy that I am.'

He didn't look that much of a fuddy-duddy to Lucy. His hair was greying, but she only noticed that now that he'd directed his attention in Charlie's direction, when he'd been looking at her all she'd been aware of was the piercing gaze which wasn't unkind, but was definitely unsettling.

'Right.' He got straight down to business, glancing through the papers on his desk. 'Let's cover the easy bit first. Your previous business, the joint practice you had, isn't a concern, I take it?'

'No.' Charlie shook his head. 'We sold that soon after we separated, split the proceeds. She carried on working there for a bit, for the new owner. She's moved on now.'

'Any other shared assets?'

'Nope. We both had a car. She was independent, the business was a partnership, equal shares.'

'And you have one child?'

Lucy was sure he blanched.

'Yes, Maisie.'

'Did she stop work when she was pregnant, when the child was born?'

'No, well only for a couple of months. She liked working, we were similar in that respect. Ambitious. Well I thought we were.' Charlie's lips had tightened, and Lucy wanted to reach out and reassure him. 'But apparently I got that wrong.'

Malcolm made a note. 'And she has nothing to stop her working?'

'No, look Malcolm, I don't think any of this is an issue.'

'I need to establish all the facts, Charlie.' His tone was low, soothing.

'But it comes down to our, to Maisie.'

'Who she claims here might not be yours?' Malcolm peered over his glasses, then tapped his pen on the pad in front of him.

'She looks like you.' Lucy spoke without thinking, then decided she'd be better keeping out of it, when Malcolm shot her a glance.

'And you haven't taken a DNA test?'

'No.'

He leaned forward. 'Positive? No kind of paternity test, not even a kit off the internet?'

'I was this close.' Charlie held forefinger and thumb close together. 'The form was printed out, on my desk. But then I decided to ask your advice first.'

Malcolm sat back, his fingers steepled together. 'If a test proved you were the child's biological father, then obviously that would work in our favour. But,' he sat forward again, 'taking one risks a negative result, which could, only *could* mind you, leave you in a very vulnerable position, depending on the mother's stance,' he glanced at the sheet of paper on his desk, 'although she does appear rather confrontational. You were having sexual relations at the time she fell pregnant?'

'Yes, we were married for God's sake, I just assumed she was mine. Okay maybe it didn't happen that often, but it happened. We slept together.'

'And you say,' he paused, 'you didn't see your daughter for a while?'

'Josie said it would be confusing for Maisie if I wasn't her dad. It wasn't my choice.'

'But you didn't challenge her?'

'I wanted what was best for Maisie, I was in shock, I'd just been told ...'

'And the child is now living with you?' He looked from Charlie to Lucy and back again, and she felt her cheeks burn once more.

Charlie glanced at Lucy himself, then at Malcolm. 'We don't live together. Maisie is with me, yes. She came in July, and has stayed. I'm renting a place in Langtry Meadows.'

'You're?' Malcolm fixed his eagle-eyed gaze on Lucy.

'I work at the school, we're well, dating.' She swallowed, feeling like she was guilty of something. 'I'm her teacher.'

'And was your wife aware of this when she left Maisie with you?'

'She bumped into Lucy one day and wasn't amused.' Charlie shrugged his shoulders. 'But we aren't living together, we thought Maisie had enough change to take on-board.'

'But your wife was aware that Lucy was in your life, when she asked you to look after her?' Charlie nodded and the solicitor made a note, a frown on his brow. 'And does she have another man in her life?'

'Not that I know of.'

'She hasn't made any claims that another man is the father?'

Charlie shook his head.

'Well that is a positive.' He sat back. 'Child arrangement orders can be a bit of a minefield if I'm honest. If she was in a relationship with the man she claims is Maisie's father, and they could prove it then you'd be on shaky ground. But,' he paused, 'it really is up to her to prove you're not. The courts will tend to assume that as you were married at the time then you are the father.'

'But what about the fact that Charlie's brought her up, assumed she's his, surely ...' Malcolm shot Lucy another of his piercing looks then turned his attention back to Charlie.

'Any judgement is made based on what is best for the child. In your case, I'd say what works against you,' he glanced down at the letter on his desk that Charlie had given him, 'is your daughter's age. If she was older, say twelve years or more, then it could be argued that you have a stronger bond. That if the child wished to continue a relationship with you, then it would be in their best interests.'

'But?'

'At her age the court could decide she isn't old enough to have a valid opinion, and it could be argued that the truth is the important thing. That Maisie at some point will have to know the truth.'

'So a DNA test?'

'Yes.'

Charlie rifled his fingers through his hair, then covered his face with his hands before looking up at the solicitor. 'So you're telling me this is largely in Josie's hands, unless I prove Maisie is mine?' He gave a short laugh.

'At this stage I wouldn't gamble on testing that out.'

'She looks like me, she talks like me.' He threw his hands in the air.

'Maybe your wife's,' he paused, his tone softer, 'taste in men is why Maisie looks like you.'

'Oh great, thanks for that Malcolm.'

'I'm only saying what her solicitor might.'

'I've brought her up.'

'Her mother has brought her up as well.'

'And now she's buggered off for six months to a foreign country.'

'Which might well play out in our favour. She obviously looks on you as Maisie's father, or she wouldn't entrust her to you. She's also abandoned,' he held up a hand as Charlie went to speak, 'her child and left the country.'

'That sounds ...'

'Harsh? Wasn't it harsh when she said you might not be Maisie's father? This will get harsh Charlie, it will get nasty, they'll be digging for dirt, but if you want a joint residence order then that is what will happen. And,' he leaned forward, 'you don't want to give her any ammunition.' He gave Lucy a pointed look and she shrank back in her seat.

'Hang on, Malcolm. Lucy's been helping me, I've had a distraught child who's been torn from her home and friends, she's six years old for God's sake. Without Lucy's help and support I'd have been floundering.'

'Speaking as a friend, Charlie, I wouldn't go down that route. You're a capable, intelligent man, a father.'

Charlie gritted his teeth. 'Her mother left her.'

'And now she's changed her mind.' Malcolm's voice was dangerously soft. 'And she is indisputably her mother. But, there are all kinds of arguments to bear in mind. We could for example claim bad parenting on her part – if she suspected Maisie wasn't yours then she should have disclosed this around the time she was born. You also seem to agree on the way she is brought up, and there are no disputes concerning her upbringing, are there?'

Charlie shook his head.

'Another positive. You are meeting her needs, and a court will favour a residence order where a child has a father *and* a mother figure in their life.' He folded the letter up, tapped it on the desk. 'I can't make any promises, Charlie, you know I can't, all I can stress is that any court will consider what is in Maisie's best interests, and that will carry more weight than what you, or your wife, want.' He looked from Charlie to Lucy. 'Now, you've been served a divorce petition. I assume you want me to handle things?'

'I want a divorce, if that's the question.'

'I'll acknowledge service. She's claiming unreasonable behaviour, mainly it appears that you have devoted too much time to your career.'

'Fine. Well at least she hasn't accused me of adultery I suppose.' His lips twisted into something resembling a smile. 'That would have been a bit rich.'

'I'll contact her solicitor and we can look at child arrangements. Mediation is always the preferred route, but I suspect an amicable agreement might escape us.' He stood up. 'Leave it with me, and I'll be in touch. Coffee before you go?'

They didn't speak until he'd eased the car onto the dual carriageway. Charlie was deep in thought, his fingers beating a tattoo on the steering wheel, his jaw set.

'He's a bit scary.' She spoke to break the silence, the tension.

'He's nice when he's not in work mode.' He paused, then the words tumbled out as though now he'd started to speak, he couldn't stop them. 'What if she isn't mine, Lucy?'

'It sounds like it's better not to ask that question at

the moment.'

'But Josie can, what if she does?' He went back to beating his fingers against the leather.

'But if you're not Maisie's dad, then who is? Josie can't deprive her of a father just to have a go at you.'

'Maybe not, but,' he took a deep breath, 'am I being a selfish git in all this? I think of her as mine, but what about Maisie in all this? What about when she's older, surely she needs to know for sure, deserves to know? Malcolm said that the courts are interested in what's best for the child, well I think if I was a kid I'd feel cheated if I suddenly discovered in my teens that the guy I'd been calling Dad wasn't my father, and he knew all along. That he'd lied to me.'

'Charlie, look, I'm my father's daughter, but he's no dad to me.' His fingers stilled. 'He lost that right a long time ago. He could have tried to find me, but he didn't. He never has, he got married and started again. Not that I care,' she'd told herself she didn't care, but sometimes she wondered if she needed to see him one last time. Have closure. Even if he was a cruel and nasty git who'd made their lives hell. Even if her mum was still scared he'd manipulate her, persuade her none of it was true. 'Charlie he was a horrible, rubbish father and you're the opposite. Even if you're not her biological father, you're still her dad.'

'But she still deserves to know.'

169

'Elsie's son doesn't know, but she had no choice when she gave him up. My mum had a choice and she took me away from mine, Josie had a choice when she decided to let you believe her unborn child was yours. There's no easy answer Charlie, you can't judge anybody else's decision, but you can decide what works for you, your conscience.' Her voice softened. 'She's too young right now, I was too young when we left my dad so Mum made the decision. Look, I know you like to be in control, but I think you've got to let Josie make the decision right now. If she makes you have a test then she'd be mad, she'd be leaving Maisie without a dad.'

'Unless she's got him hidden away in the country.' His tone was acid dry.

'And if she hasn't then we've got to hope a judge can see you're a good parent, that Maisie needs to grow up knowing you, spending time with you. Then after all this is settled, maybe then is the time for you to find out. Then you'll know, and if the news is,' she hesitated, 'not what you want to hear, well you can tell her when she's old enough to understand.'

'I know you're right.' He rested a warm hand on her knee. 'It's just not how I want things. It's shit.'

'It is shit. But Malcolm did say a child needs both its parents, and surely if Josie had another man lined up she'd have told you? Why bring Maisie to Langtry Meadows if she didn't know in her heart that your daughter needs you?' She paused, looked down at her hands in her lap and acknowledged the words she didn't really want to say. 'I think he was also warning us to be careful, not to be too involved.'

'That's one area I decided the other day I wasn't prepared to compromise on. Josie knew about us when she made the decision to leave her here, so as far as I'm concerned she accepted it. I'll be damned if I'll let her ruin our relationship. We'll do what it takes, but I'm not letting you go, Lucy.'

Lucy gazed out of the window, her stomach hollow as she blinked away the hot, prickling tears. They were the words she wanted to hear, but she was scared. Would they have any choice?

# Chapter 13

'Why can't they move Hallowe'en and Bonfire Night further apart?' Lucy clambered on to a chair in front of the classroom display, and ducking to avoid a dangling rocket made out of a toilet roll and orange and red tissue paper, she peeled a colourful pumpkin off the wall. 'It's like Piccadilly Circus, pumpkins up, pumpkins down, fireworks up ...'

'Fireworks down.' Jill grinned. 'I think you need to go back in time and have a word with Mr Fawkes, see if he can postpone?'

Lucy shook her head.

'And then it will be Christmas next, we'll be ripping them down and making room for Santa and his sleigh.'

'Don't! I'm already worn out.'

The new half term had started with a bang, when two boys from Year 6 had decided that smuggling cap guns into school was a good idea. Their argument that it was '*so them silly little babies in Class 1 can get used to noise before firework night*' didn't hold sway with Timothy Parry, who had given them his most intimidating stare before suggesting they clean out the chicken coop and '*get used to hard work before they go up to big school*'.

'Well I'm afraid I've got bad news for you, Luce. His Lordship has called a staff meeting, and it's all about feeling festive. Come on, stick the witches' hats in the bin, or we'll be late.'

'I just can't start to think about Christmas when we've not even got past Bonfire Night.' Lucy clambered down and rolled her eyes at Jill as they made their way to the staffroom for a meeting. 'You are winding me up?'

'Nope.' Jill laughed. 'Believe me, Christmas is big in Langtry Meadows. You'll soon be wondering why we didn't start earlier. Come on.'

Worrying exactly what was going to get added to her to-do list today, Lucy pulled the classroom door shut and followed Jill to the already crowded staffroom.

'Now then ladies and gentlemen, are we all here? Splendid. Now to our plan.' Timothy Parry rubbed his hands together. 'Liz has put together a little reminder of the responsibilities.' He nodded in her direction and Liz Potts busied about handing out a frighteningly long list. 'Now, Lucy, I rather thought you were the ideal person, given the fact that you are in charge of several of our animal stars ...'

The squeak escaped from Lucy before she could stop it, and she looked in alarm at Jill, who whispered in her ear. 'Annie's menagerie always get roped in.'

'And you have a rather good,' he coughed, 'relationship with our veterinary surgeon. The donkey has been our undoing in the past, but maybe an alpaca could stand in?'

'I really don't ...'

'The nativity will take place in the church as normal,' he ignored the interruption and carried on regardless, 'with festivities continuing in the square afterwards.' He glanced up at Liz. 'Jim Stafford I presume will don the red coat and white beard as normal? Splendid. Jill will co-ordinate our mulled wine and roast chestnuts, then ...'

Lucy stopped listening. She was too busy reading the small print – and the suggestion that an alpaca or Annie's pony Mischief stand in for the donkey, as it ruined proceedings last year by braying loudly throughout the carol singing.

'You'll be fine.' Jill patted her hand in a gesture of solidarity. 'It's the goats I worry about, they always try and eat baby Jesus.'

'Back to the coal face everybody, and don't forget that posh George, sorry the Right Honourable George

Cambourne will be switching our lights on, so any suggestion on how best to curtail his speech will be welcome.' He shook his head. 'Life is just too short, I rather think I might confiscate those cap guns and use them myself.'

Lucy opened her eyes in alarm and nudged Jill as they made their way out of the staffroom. 'You don't think he'd dare, do you?'

'Wouldn't put it past him, from the rumours I heard, him and posh George didn't get on at all at school, and boys will be boys.'

'Old boys.'

'Could be as entertaining as last year when the lights exploded, the cow took off and the Christmas tree toppled over on top of the bell ringers.'

One word stood out. 'Cow?'

'Oh yes, cattle are lowing and all that. We like to be authentic.' Jill giggled. 'Oh you should see your face. Oh, don't worry, there's plenty of time to sort things. You are coming to the bonfire on Friday night I take it? Apple bobbing, barbecue, beer.'

'And fireworks?'

'Briefly. You can't have missed the bonfire they've built on the cricket pitch? You've got to come, it's compulsory.' Jill slipped her hand through Lucy's arm. 'And it's perfect cover for a rendezvous.'

Lucy frowned. 'Rendezvous?'

'With Matt.' Jill's hand tightened and she slowed her pace. 'He's not told you, has he?' A flush of red tinged her cheekbones. She sighed and shook her head. 'I cornered him after he'd been chatting to you in the playground and asked him what he was up to, and well, you know what Matt is like.'

Lucy knew what Matt was like; fun, flirty, friendly, a gossip, and with an enormous crush on the woman stood next to her.

On the last day of school before the half-term holiday, Matt had cornered her, which had been slightly annoying as she'd missed her opportunity to talk to Charlie when he'd picked Maisie up. It was daft really, she saw quite a bit of him, but there was something extra lovely about seeing him in his role of dad. Having a shared interest over how Maisie's day had gone, watching the delight on the little girl's face as she showed him the pictures she'd painted. And instead Matt had accosted her – and by the time she'd glanced up, Charlie and Maisie had gone. It was hard to be cross with Jamie's big brother, loveable rogue that he was, though.

It was even harder, after he'd got the flirting and hello's over, when he'd explained why he was there. He was a man on a mission.

It appeared she wasn't the only one to know about Sally and Jamie's elopement – Jamie had confided in his brother. He'd also asked him a favour. A big favour.

Lucy raised an eyebrow at Jill, she was beginning to wonder just how many people knew about this secret wedding.

'He told you about Jamie, and ...?'

'Yep, he told me about Jamie and ...'

'The whole thing?' Lucy had dropped her voice, but she really didn't want to say anything that might be overheard, if there wasn't anybody that didn't already know every single detail that was. 'And the surprise Jamie's trying to plan for ...?' She didn't want to say Sally's name, just in case.

Jill nodded. 'But he swore me to secrecy. He's crap at keeping things quiet isn't he?'

'Well he is, I really hope she doesn't get wind of this though, Jamie will be gutted if she does.' Lucy had thought that Jamie's surprise for his new wife was ambitious, but incredibly romantic, and when Matt had outlined it and asked for her help there was no way she would have said no. Now she was beginning to wonder if Jamie had picked the right person when he'd asked Matt to help.

'I don't think she will.' Jill glanced round, to double check nobody was listening. 'Everybody likes to gossip and know what everybody else is up to, but they really will be careful not to spoil the surprise. Nobody will dare breathe a word to Sal, or they'll have the whole Harwood clan to answer to.'

Lucy nodded. 'And four of us do stand more chance of organising this than three, and you know much more about this place than I do, I'm not going to be much use at all.'

'Oh yes you are, Lucy Jacobs. We're relying on you and your spreadsheets to make this work. Come on,' she inclined her head towards the classroom, 'the little horrors will be coming in any second. Firework pictures using straws and paint is it?'

'It is, and let's hope the Hargreave twins don't try and suck the paint up their noses again. I mean why? They looked like they'd had a Jackson Pollock style nose-bleed.'

'You're funny.'

'I'm not the one with a green and purple spider in her hair,' said Lucy drolly as she propped open the classroom door and Jill fought with laughter, and a pipe-cleaner spider that had somehow attached itself to her head.

\*\*\*

Lucy hugged her jacket round her as she strolled across the cobbled square, clutching her bag of books to her chest. Her steps slowed as she approached Elsie Harrington's house. In the spring and summer the old lady could often be seen pottering about in her garden, and keeping an eye on proceedings, but with the arrival of the colder, damper weather Lucy had hardly seen her. The damp got into her bones she'd said, and the flu bug certainly seemed to have left her feeling frail. She'd even accepted Trish's offering of soup and crumble with only a murmur of objection, and when Lucy had popped in with her own (inferior) versions a few days later Elsie had welcomed her in and actually admitted that it seemed to be doing her good – she'd then insisted on a copy of the soup recipe saying she was more than capable of making it herself. Lucy wasn't quite sure whether to take this as a sign she was feeling more her normal self, or a gentle rebuke and reminder that she didn't need help.

Her mum had told Lucy not to worry. She'd popped in to chat to Elsie a couple of times in the holiday when she was staying with Lucy, and then said she'd got the old lady's phone number. '*Don't you worry, love, I'll keep an eye on her and ring every week. I told her I wanted to check up on you, but I didn't want to be too obvious*', Trish had told Lucy with a wink and hug, before she'd got back into her little car at the end of the week and set off back to her home.

Lucy pushed the gate slowly open. She missed her mum, it had been nice to have her stay, they'd spent far too little time together since she'd graduated and started work, and she knew that she was to blame. She'd almost shut her mother out in her bid to escape her old life, and only realised when she'd come here. Slowed down, taken Elsie's advice.

The old lady was wise, but now she suspected there was more to Elsie's frailty than a winter cold, that there was another reason she felt so down at this time of year.

Planning for the Christmas festivities gave her an ideal excuse to pop in, not that she should really need a reason. But Elsie wasn't keen on charity, and would be highly suspicious of visitors who were obviously just checking up on the state of her health, especially now she was so obviously slowly getting better.

'Checking I'm still alive?' Elsie answered the door before Lucy had even reached it, with a raised eyebrow and dry tone that made her grin.

'I am, so that's mission accomplished.'

'I suppose you're here to sample some parkin?'

'I wouldn't say no.' All of Elsie's cakes were delicious, and she seemed to cook to match the seasons. Parkin was perfect for this time of year, and Lucy was sure it would be as dark, rich and sticky as it should be. 'Although I'm sure I've put weight on since moving here.'

They were soon both settled in Elsie's immaculate room, with Molly the Labrador at Lucy's feet and a large slice of cake in her hand.

'I assume you're here to pick my brains about the Christmas nativity?'

'How on earth did you know that?' Lucy knew she shouldn't be surprised, Elsie knew everything.

'Well Timothy is a man of habit. Whilst the rest of the village is still planning the bonfire, he is already thinking about mistletoe and mince pies.' Elsie levered herself up and walked over to the bookcase, then picked out a faded photo album, before settling herself down again.

'I thought it would be nice to find out what it was all about before I launched myself into finding donkeys and cows.' Lucy grinned, already feeling a bit more positive about the challenge ahead. 'I knew you'd be the best person to ask.'

'The oldest person, you mean.' Elsie raised an eyebrow, and a little bit of her mischievous air re-emerged. 'Now, you know the pictures of the summer picnic that I showed you earlier in the year?'

Lucy nodded. Elsie's photographs had played a major part in saving the school from closure. Without her, Lucy would have never realised how many influential people had attended the small primary school. People like posh George, who was a councillor.

Nostalgia was a valuable tool to add to her box of tricks Lucy had found. Resurrecting the summer picnic on the green, and inviting past attendees to journey down memory lane had made it hard for them to consider cold logic and figures at all. The picnic had shifted the balance in their favour.

'These are the photographs of the Christmas nativity, taken at around the same time.' Elsie ran a slightly shaky hand over the photograph on the first page and Lucy studied it. Wondering.

Elsie had kept careful records, all covering the same period of time, all no doubt showing her son growing up.

She studied the by now familiar faces of Timothy Parry, Jim Stafford, George Cambourne and many others that Jim had put names to for her. Young boys with clean shiny faces and tidy haircuts, and she searched their faces, looking for familiar features. Trying to see things that she might have missed before.

'You may borrow these if you like, my dear.' Elsie closed the book, as though she'd looked at it too long, as though she was frightened of giving something away. 'I rather think we should ask the vicar to set the church bells off if George drones on for too long, don't you?'

'Well Timothy is a bit worried, he did go on a bit at the picnic.'

'He did indeed, he always did like the sound of his own voice that boy. One year they made the mistake of letting him play the innkeeper, you cannot imagine how difficult it was for poor Mary to find out if there was a room at the inn.'

Lucy grinned. She'd spotted a chubby Annie on the photographs, standing over the crib as though she was guarding it with her life. 'I'm sure Annie found a way to get a word in.'

'She kicked him, from what I remember.' Elsie smiled. 'But that child was only six or seven at the time, and he was already an attention seeker. Born like that.' She paused. 'Now, do remember to organise some fencing around the stable my dear, one year it was rather unstable and we had animals all over the square, we nearly lost the mulled wine. But I'm sure Liz Potts has that in hand. Now I'm sure you have enough to go on with. Tell me about Charles and that terrible woman of his.'

Lucy sighed. 'There's not much to tell to be honest, but we did go and talk to his solicitor.'

'Young Malcolm? Now he was another one with a mind of his own.'

'He went to Langtry Meadows Primary School?'

'Oh yes, for a short while, until his parents inherited the family pile and business. He could be quite intimidating, an answer for everything even though he often made it up on the spot. But I suppose that's what some of these legal types do isn't it? Think on their feet. Although he did tell a lot of little fibs back then.'

'He still is quite intimidating.'

'But reassuring?'

'We-ll.' Lucy drew the word out, not quite sure of the answer. 'It wasn't exactly what Charlie wanted to hear, but he seems very capable. Josie got in touch demanding a divorce.'

'But it is the childcare arrangements that are in dispute?'

'I'm sure they will be.' She sighed. 'He's such a good dad, even though he doesn't think he is. He loves Maisie.'

'And that is half the battle my dear.' Elsie leant forward and patted her hand. 'Have faith. And now you had better get back to that puppy of yours, Jim tells me she gives old Molly quite the run around.'

'I'm sure she does.'

'Which is jolly good, the old girl is getting lazy, aren't you?' Molly flapped her tail and smiled apologetically.

Feeling she'd been dismissed, Lucy stood up and added the photograph album to her bag of school books.

'I've given what you said some thought.'

'Oh?' The softly spoken words stopped Lucy in her tracks.

'I think maybe every person should know their true origins, and that announcing it in my will would be cowardly on my part and leave him with unanswered questions. Which would be cruel.'

'I'm sure you're right. Charlie thinks Maisie should know the truth, too.'

184

'Well that day will come, but I think it's rather closer for me.'

Lucy went to object, but Elsie lifted her hand in a warning, then let it drop back into her lap. 'Oh I know I'm an old lady, my dear. I'm feeling much more myself now, your mother has been so kind, so nice to have company. And it has made me stop and think.' She paused, and had that faraway look on her face that Lucy had seen more and more often recently. 'I suppose one never considers that one won't,' her voice was so soft Lucy could barely hear the words, but they still carried in the quiet air of her house, 'live for ever. I've never felt old, I've always had so much energy. But this autumn has been different. I'm as human as the rest of you, aren't I?' A small smile lifted the corners of her thin lips, then faded as her gaze met Lucy's. 'I will tell him, Lucy. I'll tell him.' She closed her eyes. 'When the time is right.'

'Good.' Lucy wasn't sure Elsie had even heard the word, but she was pleased. Elsie had carried a burden for far too long, and it was starting to weigh heavy on her slight frame. It seemed that Sally had been right. Her mum *had* been the ideal person to chat to Elsie; the women did have common ground. They'd both held onto secrets, both tried to protect the children they loved.

Saying a soft goodbye Lucy sneaked out, pulling the

door shut gently behind her.

# Chapter 14

After a tiring week at school all Lucy wanted was a long soak in the bath, followed by a night curled up on the sofa with a glass of wine and a good film, or book, or preferably Charlie. What she'd actually got was a quick bath, which was interrupted by a phone call from Matt.

She stared at his name flashing out on her mobile phone. She could ignore it, but then he'd probably be knocking on the door in half an hour. And he wouldn't be ringing her unless it was something important. Why, oh why hadn't she left her phone downstairs?

'What are you up to?'

'I'm not telling you.' She froze, hoping the swish of the water in the bath wasn't as loud as it sounded.

'You're in the bath, aren't you?' Fail. It obviously was loud, and unmistakeable. The deep chuckle brought her out in goosebumps.

'I'm washing up.'

He ignored the diversionary tactics. 'If you want me to pop over and scrub your back, just say the word, I'm all yours, darling.'

'No I don't!' She tried not to grin, knowing the smile would show in her voice.

'I can hand you a towel?'

'I'm quite capable of reaching my own towels thank you Matt Harwood.'

'Only trying to help, you know me.'

'I do know you.' She did laugh then, she couldn't help herself. 'The best help you can be is telling me why you're disturbing the first proper bath I've had in ages.'

'And I had you down as a clean girl, not a bad, dirty …'

'Matt! Stop!' She was laughing properly now. 'Tell me why you're ringing, or go away.'

'You're such a spoilsport, isn't she Archie? Actually, I was just checking that you're coming down to the fireworks tonight?'

'Well …' Hell, she'd forgotten about that.

'You've got to, this is the main event.'

'I thought the Christmas nativity was the main event?' Langtry Meadows seemed to have a lot of 'main events', and the fact that the school played a part in most of them was a bit scary. At least she had absolutely no responsibility for tonight's fireworks, bonfire or barbecue.

In fact, it was nothing to do with her. She could stay in and eat chocolate. As planned.

'Christmas is for kids, this is the big one.'

'I might.' She sank down further into the still warm water until it covered her shoulders, and poked a toe up out of the bubbles. It would be freezing cold outside, in here was all cosy.

'Didn't Jill tell you we've got a date?'

Lucy sat upright abruptly, and the water sploshed out. He had to have heard that. But, it didn't matter. A date. Him and Jill. At last. And she hadn't told her. 'Oh my God no, she didn't.' She'd probably felt embarrassed. 'You've got a date? That's fantas—'

'Not me and Jill.' His voice had a strained edge. Ahh, she'd put her foot in it. Her toes emerged from the water again as she sank down guiltily. 'We, as in you and me,' he paused, 'and Jill of course. I thought it would be good to rope her in, it's a lot for the two of us to sort out, a party this size.'

'Yeah, brilliant idea, yes Jill's great, so organised.' She was waffling. She pulled herself together. 'Date, yes, tonight.' Crumbs, she'd forgotten all about that. 'She did mention it, but I thought this was a secret, top secret, you, Jamie and me? Have you told him?'

'Yeah I've told him, he's cool.' Jamie was cool about most things, laid back and gentle, nothing like his brother who was nearly always centre stage in the pub.

'Jill's the last, I'm not telling anybody else or it'll get round, and Jamie says he'll kill me if it does. So, what time are you coming? The bonfire's being lit in a bit then I might get a bit busy, although there's always the Taverner's after, but people will earwig. Although I reckon old Jamie and Sal are thinking it's a good time to break the news that they've just got hitched to their parents, you know in the pub after a couple of pints, surrounded by people. Not even Sal's mum would dare kick off.'

'They've not even told your or Sally's parents yet?' Lucy sat up again in astonishment. Jamie's plans were all about a surprise for Sally, but she'd really thought that they'd have told at least family about their sudden decision to run off to Gretna Green and tie the knot.

'Nope. I told Jamie I'd do it myself if he didn't get on with it soon, our mum will be real put out if she thinks she's the last to find out.' There was a pause. 'So you'll be there when we light the bonfire?'

'You could tell Jill, under cover of the firework bangs,' she tried not to smile, 'then she could tell me?'

'I need you, Luce. If you don't come I'm in deep shit. We need you to help come up with a plan.'

'Oh you're so melodramatic Matt Harwood, you'd be better on the stage than that farm. I feel sorry for your cows.' But she knew she was being a bit mean, she really was. He'd done loads for her since she'd moved in, and now he was asking for just a bit of support in return. 'I'll be there.' She sighed, and pulled the plug out with her toe. 'Give me half an hour.' Life would be a lot easier if he'd admit to the massive crush he had on Jill, and actually ask her out, instead of using Lucy as a chaperone. She was sure that it was mutual. She was also pretty sure that Jill hadn't had a relationship since her husband had died. And from the way she blushed whenever Matt came over for a chat, she was ready to enter the dating scene again.

Lucy towelled her hair. She needed to go, and it wasn't just to help Matt out with his secret project. She was going to find a way to play cupid if it killed her.

Putting on jeans, a thick jumper, gloves and a woolly hat she locked Piper securely in the kitchen, and made sure that all the other animals were safe. 'You wouldn't like the bangs poppet, you're much better off here.' She kissed the puppy on her nose, and she slunk back into her basket looking mournful. 'Don't look at me like that; it's for your own good.' Her tail flapped listlessly and Lucy couldn't help but smile. Little Piper had three main interests in life, eating, cuddling up with Lucy, and going for walks. The second Lucy put her shoes on, or picked up the lead she was there – at the door, her tail wagging so hard her whole body did a wriggle.

It was the perfect night as Lucy strolled down the

garden path. Most of the morning cloud had disappeared, to leave an infinite inky blackness that was sprinkled with sequins of stars.

She hugged her coat to her as she walked back down the lane, past Elsie's house which was shrouded in darkness and across the square. She could hear the buzz of voices as she drew nearer to the cricket pitch, where the crowds were already gathering.

There was a winter chill in the air, but around her everybody was wrapped up warmly in thick coats and scarves, and the children were running around excitedly.

'Miss, Miss.' Sophie, one of the children from her class, slid to a breathless halt in front of her. Clutched in her mitten-clad hand was a sparkler, which she was waving about far too wildly. 'My mam says I can write my name with this, look.'

'That's brilliant, Sophie.'

'I can do it better.' Joe had joined them and was doing a very slow and deliberate wave of his own sparkler, which she had to admit she preferred even if it wasn't very effective.

'Got to go, my mam said I had to be quick or all the apples would be gone.'

Lucy shook her head and grinned as the two children ran off.

'Hey.' She glanced up as the deep voice echoed across, to see Matt and Jill. They were stood side by side, but at a very respectable distance from each other, near to the barbecue – which had already drawn a good crowd.

'Am I glad to see you.' Jill grinned. 'I thought you weren't coming, and I'd be stuck with this loony on my own.'

'Miss *the* event of the year?' She raised an eyebrow at Matt, who shrugged good-naturedly.

'It is, I told you, it's the main event. Everything else is child's play. You wait until you see the fireworks, and if Jim and his cronies don't let us down we'll have music.'

'Jim's here?' Lucy looked around, she hadn't spotted him yet.

'Everybody is here, Lucy. He's behind the apple-bobbing tent, setting up his music with Timothy, and Elsie is overseeing it.'

'Elsie?' She looked at Jill with a worried frown. 'Isn't it a bit damp and cold for her?'

'It's tradition.' Jill shrugged helplessly. 'You know what she's like, she doesn't trust the men to get it right, and she's always been involved. I think really she wants to make sure they don't replace Handel with some "modern tosh" as she puts it.'

'Ahh.'

'They do the music, and I,' Matt did a flourish and bow, 'I'm in charge of the fireworks.' He grinned, and waved what Lucy took to be the stick he was going to light them with.

Jill pulled a face at Lucy. 'Thank God you're here. Tell me it isn't true. That's like putting Billy in charge of tidying away the skipping ropes.'

Lucy cringed at the unwelcome memories that crowded her head. During the May Day rehearsals, Billy had used the ribbons to tie more than one child to the maypole with the type of knots that a sailor would have been proud of. He was master of the knot that could never be undone.

Matt shook his head. 'Most upsetting.' But he didn't look upset. 'Now then we need a conflab.' He put one arm round Jill's shoulder, and draped the other over Lucy, drawing them in close. 'I'll bugger this up if you leave me to my own devices, and I've been told that if I bugger it up then I'm dead.'

Jill put her head on one side. 'At least life would be quieter in Langtry Meadows then.'

'I'm wounded.' He put a hand over his heart, and Lucy wondered if she really needed to be there. Maybe she could sneak off? 'Uh, oh, don't look now, it's Sally and the grumpy super vet.'

They looked. Sally was bouncing across the grass towards them, in her flowery wellies, and Charlie was following at a more sedate pace.

'What am I missing out on?' Sally hugged Lucy, and pulled a face at Matt. 'Sorry we're so late.'

'We're just wondering if letting Matt set the fireworks off is a good idea.'

'I doubt it, he's like a big kid. You will never believe the day we've had, will they Charlie?' Charlie, who had followed her over smiled at Lucy, and narrowed his eyes at Matt, who very gracefully let his arm fall to his side, as though he'd no idea how it came to be wrapped round Lucy. 'We've only just finished, well we had to leave Eric in charge. We've been dishing out tranquilisers to the adults and pheromones to the cats and dogs, tablets, plug-ins, you name it.'

'You haven't?' Lucy was pretty sure there was some kind of law about vets administering drugs to people. She glanced from Sally to Charlie, and back again.

'Oh God we have. It's always the same, they all come in last minute and want them doping up.'

'People?'

'Animals you noddle, cats and dogs. Honestly.' She shook her head. 'You're so gullible; I'm surprised you cope with those kids.'

'She's different at school.' Jill chipped in supportively.

'Just leaves her brain there.' Matt added unhelpfully, and received a kick on the shin from Sally.

'That's nasty Matt Harwood!'

'Or leaves it in the bath with all those lovely bubbles.' He winked at Lucy, who blushed, she just couldn't help it. Now what was she supposed to say? If she told

Charlie that Matt had called while she was in the bath, then he'd want to know why he was ringing, and she couldn't exactly explain, because one, the person they wanted to surprise was stood in front of her, and two, Jamie had told them not to tell anybody at all.

'Haven't you got a rocket to go off and light, or something?' Luckily, Sally didn't seem to have noticed her dilemma.

Matt shook his head. 'Honestly, I don't know how Jamie puts up with the abuse. Where's he got to by the way?'

'Helping guard the bonfire.' They all glanced over towards the recently lit bonfire. Jamie and a couple of the other farmers were doing their best to keep the tape around it up, and the children back. Sparklers in hands, the small army of children were pressing against the tape, mesmerised by the flames which had only just started to flicker at the feet of the guy on top. 'Which is what I assume you're supposed to be doing, instead of gassing.'

'It'll be alright once it gets going properly, the heat will drive the little buggers back. Anyway, what do you mean, gassing? Me?'

'You look like you're plotting, Harwood. I know that look.'

Matt plastered a look of injured innocence across his features. 'You've got such a suspicious mind Sally. I was just asking if Lucy wanted to be part of my dog walking club, now she's got that pup.'

'Dog walking club?' Sally raised a suspicious eyebrow. 'There's no dog walking club in Langtry Meadows.'

'Well I thought we should have one, a very small club. Lucy and me.' He winked at Jill. 'And Jill if she wants, but not you Sal cos you're far too busy,' he paused, 'and you haven't got a dog.'

'Nor has Jill.' Sally folded her arms, obviously convinced he was up to something.

'She can borrow one of Jamie's whippets.'

Jill laughed. 'I'm not sure I want to be part of your dog walking club Matt, I have enough trouble keeping kids in order.'

He shrugged. 'Please yourself. Right, I'm off, I've got fuses to light. Back in a bit.'

'That man is up to no good.' Sally shook her head, then looked at Jill and Lucy. 'You wouldn't know what he's plotting?' They shook their heads.

'Not a clue. Blowing something up? After all it is Bonfire Night.'

'Hmm. He's acting just like he used to at school, all smug and self-satisfied, just before a bucket of water drops on a teacher's head.'

'Well it better not be my head!' Lucy laughed, and was pretty sure the moment had passed. She glanced at Charlie, who seemed to have visibly relaxed the moment Matt had walked off.

'Is it safe to put him in charge of explosive devices?' His voice was dry, but there was a hint of a smile playing at the corner of his mouth.

'Probably not.' Lucy shrugged. 'Not our problem. Where's Maisie?' She'd suddenly realised his daughter wasn't with him.

'She's over by the fire with some of the other kids, Becky brought her down a bit earlier seeing as we were tied up at the surgery. She said she'd keep an eye on her, she's obsessed with watching flames.'

'Sounds a dangerous hobby.' Jill grinned. 'Oh well, I better get off, I said I'd help Matt. Or rather I'd keep an eye on him, he promised me ear muffs and a hard hat. I'll, er, fill you in later, Lucy.'

'Fill you in?' Charlie and Sally stared at her.

'School stuff.' She knew she'd gone pink, but maybe they could put that down to the heat of the fire, that was already well alight. 'We've got to plan the Christmas stuff and er, I think she's asking about the stable, or something.' She had a vague memory that Jill had said something about Matt providing the stable, so she wasn't exactly lying.

Jill gave her the thumbs up. 'Baby in a manger and all that.'

Lucy gave a sigh of relief and hoped nobody had noticed.

'Boring! I'm going to find Jamie.' Sally winked at Lucy, her left hand stuffed deep in her pocket.

'Are you sure you're not all up to something?' Charlie's deep voice was so close to her ear she could feel his warm breath, and it sent a shiver of anticipation straight through her body. It would be so good when everything was settled with Maisie, when they could go back to being, well, more hands on again. She missed the touch of his hand, the heat of his body against hers. Even if she'd only experienced it a few times. Before Josie and Maisie had arrived on the scene. 'You looked thick as thieves.'

'Are you calling me a thief?' She laughed, trying to joke it off, and ignore the tingle of her body.

He didn't move away, and she didn't want him to. 'I know your secret.' The words were so soft, nobody else could have heard them, but Lucy felt a shiver of alarm. How could he know? How could anybody know apart from her, Jill and the Harwood brothers? They hadn't even actually managed to make any progress with plans yet, and she was fairly sure that Matt wouldn't have told anybody else. He'd only told Jill because he was mad about her, and it was an excuse to spend more time together – even if he wouldn't admit it to anybody.

'You ...'

'She thinks I haven't noticed.' Charlie's voice was dry, and when she glanced up he was watching Sally as she got nearer to Jamie. A skip still in her step. He put an arm round Lucy's shoulder and pulled her even closer. 'So that's what the weekend off was about.'

Lucy felt a sudden wave of relief. She looked up, half expecting him to be cross, but although his face was serious, his eyes were sparkling. *That* was what he knew. Which was good, but bad, because really she was dying to let him in on Jamie's secret plan. But she shouldn't, but if he'd pushed...

'You know?'

'I spotted the wedding ring, I mean, have you ever seen a veterinary nurse trying to keep one hand stuffed in her pocket?' He grinned. 'It's hilarious when she's trying to book appointments in on the computer, and as for when she's counting pills out.' He shook his head. 'And she's completely out of it, on cloud nine. She didn't even notice when Eric double booked today's surgery which is why we were so bloody late finishing. That dreamy look doesn't come from a weekend walking round the shops.' He chuckled. 'She's been walking round whistling all week, very disconcerting. She even kissed Maisie when she came over to look at our new home, I've only ever seen her kiss furry things before.'

'And Jamie.'

'He's a bit furry too.'

'And you haven't told her you know?'

'No way, I'm having far too much fun.' He paused. 'I

suppose Eric wasn't in on this?'

'I think he was.'

He shook his head. 'No wonder I left this place, a load of old schemers.'

'She only told me right at the last minute, she wanted a girlie night, somebody to be excited with her.' She slipped her arm through his. 'I'm sorry, I didn't want to hide anything from you, I hate secrets.' She'd vowed never to have any secrets ever again, most of her young life had been based on secrets her mother had kept with the best of intentions.

He put an arm round her shoulder, pulled her in against his warm, safe body. 'I know, don't worry. I knew there was something going on, and Eric doesn't quite fit that bill of girlie friend I suppose.'

'Not really.'

'So this was to avoid her mum throwing a big bash and going completely overboard?'

'It was.'

'She's going to have to own up soon, I mean if I noticed the ring, me, a mere unobservant man, then her mum will.'

'You're no mere man.' She reached up and kissed his cheek. 'But you're right. I wonder if her mum has already realised, but is waiting to be told?'

'Probably. I can understand why she did it though.'

'You know her family?'

'Oh yes, her mother would have been booking a cathedral and a bishop.'

'You can't blame them then. Matt thinks they're going to break the news in the pub tonight, after they've all had a drink.' Lucy could just make out the huddle of Sally and Jamie. She was pleased for them, but the rate she was going she'd never have any type of wedding herself, let alone one with big hats and a fanfare. 'Did you have a big wedding?'

She couldn't help herself, the words just came out.

'Me and Josie? Yeah, the works. Extravagant was not the word, I felt a right dick in top hat and tails.' He kissed the top of her head. 'I should have realised then that we had different agendas. Come on, looks like the fireworks are about to start, let's go and find Maisie.'

Matt managed to let the fireworks off without setting himself, or anything else that wasn't scheduled, on fire. The finale of the music was a good two minutes in advance of the end, which made everybody (apart from Elsie) laugh, and the bonfire – once it got going – was so hot it drove everybody well back, which relieved Jamie and Sally of their fire-guarding duties.

'Maisie's tired, I think it's past her bed time. Fancy a stroll back?'

Lucy looked over towards the barbecue. From the gesturing, Jill and Matt seemed engrossed in a conversation about beef burgers. Over by the dying embers of the fire, Sally and Jamie were sat on the grass, oblivious to the damp, hand in hand. She had promised to stay and have a chat to Jill, but now was not the right time.

'Sure. Matt and Jill look happy together, don't they?'

'They certainly do.' Charlie lifted Maisie onto his shoulders. 'That man needs removing from the eligible bachelors list.'

'Do I detect a hint of jealousy Charlie Davenport?'

'You certainly do Miss Jacobs.' He smiled at her. A warm, cuddly type of smile that crinkled the corners of his eyes and brought a dimple to his chin, then his voice softened. A hint of seriousness crept into his face. 'We'll get through this, won't we?'

'We will.' She slipped her hand in his.

'I can't let her destroy us.'

'She won't Charlie. And we'll make sure Maisie's okay.'

He smiled, the smile lighting up his features. 'I like the sound of that.'

The damp, downtrodden grass leaked into their shoes as they walked across it, and something clutched at Lucy's chest. She wanted to feel positive, optimistic, but something told her life was going to get trickier before it got better.

# Chapter 15

Lucy looked up in surprise as Maisie folded her arms and stared down at her desk, bottom lip trembling, her voice a barely discernible whisper. 'I don't want to be a dancing lady.'

She'd thought this would be the easy part of the Christmas festivities – assigning parts for the twelve days of Christmas, it was the actual execution of it that was supposed to be tricky. It had all seemed to be going okay, until the children had gone back to their desks to draw a picture and write a story about the part they were going to play.

'Why not Maisie?' She crouched down at the side of the little girl. 'You're a very good dancer and our class are all going to be ladies dancing, or lords a-leaping.'

'Mummy used to take me to dancing, and now she doesn't, she doesn't take me anywhere. I hate dancing.' She didn't look in Lucy's direction, just pressed her crayon harder against the paper, leaving a harsh red gash. Lucy knew how it felt, losing the things you used to do, little things that nobody else would have noticed.

'Maybe we can tell Daddy, and he can take you dancing again?' But she knew it wouldn't be the same for Maisie. Dancing had been something her mother had done with her. Something she felt had been lost forever.

'Dancing's for cissies.' Ted was busy drawing a tractor, which didn't quite fit into any of the festive scenarios Lucy had in her head.

'Dancing is for everybody Ted. Is that a Christmas tractor?'

He looked up at Lucy. 'Santa should have a tractor, not a sleigh cos we don't get enough snow. Ask anybody.' He took the red crayon from Maisie's hand and proceeded to colour the new mode of transport in. 'He'd get stuck in the mud here, most years. That's what my dad says.'

'My mam says,' Sophie who was sat on the opposite side of the table stared at Ted indignantly, 'it's too early to talk about Christmas.'

'Well that's cos you don't keep turkeys, do you?'

'I think that we'll stick all the pictures that get finished today on the wall, what do you think Miss Jacobs?'

Lucy nodded at Jill's intervention. 'Definitely, they can be the first part of our Christmas display, and,' she paused, 'whoever finishes first can help Jill take the fireworks down.'

There was a sudden rush of activity, apart from Maisie.

'I hate my room too, and I want to go home.'

'I know you want to go home, Maisie. But your new room is very pretty, isn't it?'

'It's wrong.'

Things were only right when there was enough of the same in them. When you had your mum and dad, your friends, all the things that made up normal life.

'I want Mummy, but Mummy doesn't want me.'

'Oh she does, Mummy and Daddy both want you. But where Mummy is isn't a good place for children is it?'

'The school takes an hour to walk to.' Maisie looked up, her tearful eyes wide. 'A whole hour of walking.' She blinked. 'That's ages isn't it?'

'It's a long way. So that wouldn't be nice would it? And in Langtry Meadows there's lots to do, and all your new friends to play with until Mummy comes back. And you've got Treacle.'

'Treacle is nice, Treacle loves me. He makes snuffle noises and squeaks.' She nodded. 'I don't think they have guinea pigs where Mummy is, and the cows are thin.'

She sniffed, and wiped the back of her hand across her eyes, and Lucy was relieved to see there were no fresh tears.

'What are you drawing now?' Lucy watched as Maisie drew a perfect arc of blue, then picked up a yellow crayon.

'A rainbow.' She carried on drawing, her tongue between her lips. 'Mummy is at the end and I'm never going to see her cos it's so far away.'

'You will see her, Maisie.'

'She's so far away she might be dead. Heaven is a long way, isn't it?'

'My hamster's deaded. He's in heaven, or in the back garden, but I think that's the same.' Harry who had been quietly watching them frowned. 'His soles went to heaven anyway.'

'She's not dead, Maisie. Look,' Lucy slid a new fresh sheet of paper over. 'Why don't we draw her a lovely picture of what Christmas will be like here, and then you can ask her to draw you a picture of what it will be like where she is? You can bring it into school and we can talk about it.'

'Maybe. But she is dead.' She added a stick figure at the end of the rainbow. 'She told Daddy she might as well be, so if she is then she doesn't care about us anymore. She can't come back if she's going to be dead, can she?'

'She cares, and she isn't dead Maisie. I'll talk to Daddy, we'll find out when she's coming to see you shall we?'

'Shall I draw a dancing lady now?' She pushed the rainbow away. 'I'll draw Sally.'

When the end of day school bell rang, Lucy was glad to see Charlie had come to pick Maisie up. She gave a beckoning wave and he lingered until the rest of her class had joined their parents and were making their way out of the school grounds.

'She thinks Josie isn't coming back.' Lucy watched as Maisie hopscotched across the playground, her curls bouncing. Roo ran alongside her, barking with excitement.

'But why would she think that? I've never suggested ...' Charlie ruffled a hand through his hair, and gave her a look of total confusion.

'She thinks Josie wants to be dead, she overheard something, her telling you she might as well be? Charlie, kids hear everything.'

'Oh God.' He sighed. 'I thought she was in bed.'

'The conversations you overhear when you're in bed are the ones you listen hardest to, even when you're only six.'

'I know.' He frowned. 'She'd had a talk to Josie, shown her the guinea pig and gone up. She seemed tired, so as soon as I got her into bed I went down. I skyped Josie back on impulse. How could I have been so stupid?'

'It's not stupid, Charlie.'

'I just thought it was a good opportunity to try and thrash stuff out. Again. She can just avoid me whenever she likes, blame a lousy Wi-Fi connection. It's doing my head in, Lucy.'

'I know.' She put her hand briefly on his arm. She did understand, but right now she couldn't hug him, she had to be professional.

'I was trying to make her see some sense about what's going to happen, at the moment she's all over the place. She's gone back on her word. When she first brought Maisie here she said we could work this out, it was all supposed to be amicable, everything in Maisie's best interests, not her dictating what happened and dragging me through the courts if I wouldn't walk away quietly.' He looked totally dejected, and Lucy knew that the sense of foreboding that had been growing in her since they'd chatted on Bonfire Night wasn't just her imagination.

'One minute she's saying she's moving abroad and taking Maisie with her, the next she's coming back here. One day she accepts I'm Maisie's dad, the next she's telling me I have no rights at all, that it's confusing for her. She went off on a rant, saying she was sure I'd rather she was dead, then that would solve all my problems.'

'Ah.' Lucy flinched. 'That would explain what Maisie

picked up on.'

'Look, Luce, I know this hasn't been easy.' He took a deep breath. 'But I think Malcolm's right. This is going to get really nasty.' His gaze dropped to his feet, then back up to meet hers. 'I had a chat to him earlier and he says so far she doesn't seem willing to negotiate at all. She's told her solicitor that now she's had some time to think, she reckons it would be fairer for Maisie to settle with her and just maybe see me occasionally.' He gave a pained smile. 'A Christmas and birthday dad.' She made a move to interrupt, but he waved the words away. 'I told her I'd fight it, and she came back saying I was unsuitable. Your name was mentioned.'

'As part of the rant?'

'As part of the rant. You can see her react every time Maisie mentions your name. It winds her up.'

'But we haven't ...'

'I've told her it's not about you, about me or even her, it's about Maisie. But Maisie mentioned your new house to her, and was chatting on about Piper, and your mum. She was just spoiling for a fight by the end of it.'

'Charlie, if we want a hope in hell of keeping this civil, then we're going to have to ...' It was hard enough as it was, they hardly saw each other and most of their snatched moments together had been at weekends, doing things together. Like a family. There was a lump blocking her throat, and she had a head full of tears that might explode if she said the words that were on the tip of her tongue. And she couldn't break down out here, not at school, but she could stop this right now. Stop them. If they did it now, stopped seeing each other then there would be one less thing, one very major issue gone as far as Josie was concerned. She swallowed hard, blinked. She could do this. It didn't have to be forever. They just had to not see each other now. Keep it simple for Maisie. She had to do this. But he didn't give her a chance.

'Lucy I'm afraid,' he seemed to be fighting to hold it together, 'I think she's coming home over Christmas.'

Lucy couldn't help it, she felt sick at the thought of Josie being here. Watching the festivities, joining in with Charlie and Maisie. He seemed to realise, let his hand rest briefly over hers. 'Don't worry, we'll meet at my parents'. But I'm afraid she'll take Maisie away again, take her back with her. And I'll never see her again. If she gets her on a plane I won't stand a chance in hell.'

The guilt hit her, she was worried about having to see the family reunited; Charlie was worried about seeing it torn apart. 'She can't ... I mean, the courts ...' Losing Maisie again would kill him.

'She probably could, and if she does,' his smile was rueful, 'she's got the upper hand, hasn't she? It makes it harder.'

Lucy folded her arms, tried to stay in professional mode and put her personal feelings to one side. It was easier here, at school. This was for Maisie, about Maisie. 'Do you want me to chat to Josie? Explain as a professional about how Maisie's taking this and what she can do to help? It might focus her on the idea that I'm just the teacher. I mean, last summer when she came into school she did seem to care.'

'I'm sure she does, which is why she went off the rails at me. It's almost like she's got this urge to run away and be completely irresponsible, but knows it's wrong and so she can't stay away.'

'She probably feels guilty, she seemed very close to Maisie.'

'She was. That's why all of this is crazy. What kind of mother does this? I just, well I just would have never thought she could.' He shrugged. 'But what do I know?'

'Let's do this one step at a time.' It was up to her to be calm, logical, face the immediate problem that was how upset Maisie was. Worry about the threat of Charlie losing her separately. 'You need to get Josie to give Maisie some kind of explanation, some reassurance that she's coming back. Think about it Charlie, if you want me, or even Timothy to have a chat to her then we can. Maybe if it was somebody neutral, like Timothy then it would be better, or I can get somebody from social services involved.'

'Not social services.' He shook his head. 'She'd think I was trying to undermine her. But maybe you or Tim.' He sighed. 'Or maybe not. I better let you go, looks like you're in demand.' He inclined his head towards Jane Smith, who was approaching with a look of determination on her face, holding Sophie with one hand, and brandishing a piece of paper in the other.

Lucy put a hand on his arm. 'Charlie, I know this is impossible, but you really need to try and wipe this from your mind when you're with Maisie. Kids her age are so sensitive, she'll read the tension, how anxious you are even if she doesn't understand it, and it'll put her on edge.'

'I am careful not to let her hear the rows normally, I didn't realise ...'

'It's not just the rows Charlie.' She wanted to squeeze him tight. 'It's the atmosphere, it will put her on edge and then she'll be awkward because she's scared.'

'And refuse to do what I ask her.'

She nodded.

'Now then Miss Jacobs, Charlie.' Jane elbowed her way between them, her stout figure killing all hope of further discussion dead. She shot a brief glance in Charlie's direction, before turning her full attention back to Lucy. 'What's all this about?' She waved the letter in Lucy's face. 'This isn't how we normally do things round—'

213

Lucy inwardly braced. 'Not how we normally do things' were words she'd heard several times in the first term she'd been at Langtry Meadows Primary School (well if she was honest, every time she tried to introduce anything that was the slightest bit new), but they'd been directed at her less recently, and she really thought that they trusted her now.

Jane stabbed the words with her stubby finger.

'I'm sorry Mrs Smith, but the PTA decided that our little stock of costumes were getting a bit tatty.' She glanced over at Charlie, but he'd already turned away. She wanted to help so much, to be there for him, but maybe being there was the worst thing she could do.

'Well they did fine last year.'

She reluctantly turned her attention back to Jane Smith, and nativity costumes. 'The goat did eat a couple though from what I'm told?'

'Well it did, but ...'

'And even the best stain remover in the world hasn't got our whites white again after the accident with the cow pat.' She paused, wondering if she was overdoing this. 'We just thought it would be really fabulous to put on a good show for the councillor this year.'

'Well ...'

'We really don't want the school closing down do we?'

'Well no, but ...'

'We need to show George Cambourne that we still all pull together, like we did in his day.'

Jane frowned, her lips pursed. 'Well I'm all for pulling together, but this is a bit of a tall order. I'm quite happy to tie a tea towel round her head and a sheet round her waist, and call her a shepherd, love, but I don't mind telling you that an angel is a step too far.' She shook her head. 'In the days I had them wire coat hangers I could knock up a mean pair of wings, but you can't get them these days can you? Health and safety, love, health and safety. Them plastic hangers aren't going to cut the mustard are they?' She gave a resigned sigh. 'But I expect I'll do my best out of a bad job.' And tapping the side of her nose she strode off out of the playground. 'And as for 'alos, you can forget them.' Her parting words were shot over her shoulder as her little angel, Sophie stopped dead.

'But I got to have an 'alo, Mam.' She folded her arms. 'Angels have to, don't they, Miss?'

Lucy nodded. 'I'm sure we can sort a halo out, Sophie.'

Jill looked up as Lucy walked back into the classroom. 'Everything okay?'

'I think we might be hearing "my mam says" a lot tomorrow.'

Jill grinned. 'They'll all have a bit of a mutter, then the race will be on to outdo each other.'

'I hope so.'

Jill's smile dropped. 'I didn't mean that though, I meant Charlie.'

'Oh I could wring that woman's neck, but who knows what's going through her mind? And it's none of my business.'

'Well it is, isn't it? On two fronts. First you care as her teacher, and I think on those grounds alone we can talk to her, has she never heard of safeguarding issues?' She raised an eyebrow, then went back to tidying up the paint pots. 'And, then there's Charlie and you.'

'I think we should be trying not to be a *Charlie and me* at the moment. We tried not to over the summer, then he decided that we couldn't pretend but should just not rush, then his solicitor warned me off.'

'Actually warned you off?'

'Not in so many words. He gave me a look.' She pulled a rueful face. 'But he did say that Charlie had to be careful to be seen in the best light.'

'But surely he's allowed to have a girlfriend?'

'I suppose so, but it's all about what's best for Maisie, and at the moment she needs security, she needs to be number one doesn't she?'

'That doesn't stop you being number two, Lucy.'

'It does in Josie's eyes. Charlie's scared stiff of losing her again, Jill, and I'll do whatever I can, anything, to make sure that doesn't happen.'

Even if it meant walking away and never seeing them again.

***

Lucy pushed the untouched cup of coffee to one side. She had to do it, she had to go and talk to Charlie. Loving him was easy, loving him enough to push him away was so much harder. But they couldn't carry on as they had been, it was confusing for Maisie, and ammunition for Josie.

Clipping Piper's lead on, she slipped her feet into wellingtons and pulled her thickest jacket on.

The square was dark and deserted as they made their way across it, but she felt safe here in this village. It was actually quite nice to go out in the early morning, or late evening when only the farmers and animals seemed to be awake.

Now it was only early evening, but the cloak of winter was already draped around Langtry Meadows, the cloudy sky signalling that there was more likely to be rain than frost in the morning. It was cold though, even with the heavy sky, and Lucy walked briskly barely glancing at the cottages they passed as she went through what she was going to say in her head. If she had it all prepared it would be easier.

'Hi, stranger.' Charlie had damp hands and a tea

towel over his shoulder as he dropped a light kiss on her lips and ushered her in. He always made her heart jump, but seeing this relaxed, at home side of him made this all the harder. 'Just finished tea, you didn't want anything?'

She shook her head, and unhooked Piper so that she could say hello to Roo properly.

'Maisie's upstairs, shall I?'

'No, no, Charlie,' this was harder than she'd thought. 'We need to talk.'

'That sounds ominous. Josie?'

'Josie.'

'I don't want her to alter things between us, Luce.' He stepped closer, cupped her face in his hands and those big brown eyes were nearly the finish of her. Those big brown eyes that were so like Maisie's.

'I know.' She knew her voice was barely more than a whisper, partly because she didn't want to say the words, partly because she didn't want Maisie to hear. 'But she has done. Charlie,' she shook her head as he opened his mouth to speak, 'we've got the rest of our lives to sort this out. You and Maisie have only got now, right now.' Hard tears prickled at her eyes, and when he opened his arms she threw herself against him to hide the hurt. She wrapped her arms round the firm, familiar body and forced herself to finish off her little speech. 'If we're not seeing each other all the time, then

Maisie won't be talking to her mum about what we've been doing.'

'But she loves you, Lucy, I love you.'

'She'll see me at school, Charlie. I'm sorry, I really don't ... Malcolm was right, we're only going to make this worse and it's already bad enough. I'm sorry, I ...' She pushed herself away from his chest and made for the door, her sight blurry, a sharp pain in her chest. They'd sort this out after, they'd work it out when it was all sorted, she had to believe that. Piper was at her heels as she burst out of the door, and the cold air made her face smart. Then she was running, down the farm track, down the lane, ignoring Charlie's shout. If she turned round now, if she looked into his face, she'd change her mind.

By the time she'd got home Lucy was totally drained, and was really tempted to ignore her ringing phone, climb into bed and bury her head under the covers. Instead she picked it up, because if she had one person in the world that she wanted to talk to right now, it was her mum.

'Hi Mum.'

'Everything okay, darling?' She could almost hear the frown in her mother's voice.

'Fine.'

'Lucy!'

'It's Charlie.' There was a crack in her voice as she said his name. She swallowed. She had to pull herself together. This was temporary. They were good together, they loved each other. Things would work out. 'We, well we thought we better have a break.'

'Is this to do with that Josie? It is, isn't it? Oh Lucy.'

'It seems best.' She gulped back the tears. 'Just until things are sorted.'

'Well you have to do what seems best, love, but you can't let that woman ruin ...'

'I won't, Mum.'

There was a long silence, and for a moment she thought the connection had been broken. 'I'm coming over.'

'But ...'

'I was thinking about coming over anyway. I spoke to Elsie yesterday.'

'Did you?' Lucy jumped on the chance to talk about something other than her and Charlie.

'I've been calling her once a week since I came over, it gives her something to look forward to. I mean I know you call in, and Jim does, her conversation is all about the two of you, and I know a lot of the other villagers keep an eye out, but there's no harm in one more, is there? And I'm worried about her. She seems breathless, wheezy.'

'It probably didn't do her any good being at the

bonfire, but you know what she's like, nobody could tell her not to.'

'And they shouldn't. It's her whole life, Lucy, Langtry Meadows is her home, her family and she needs to be involved. But I really think she needs to see a doctor and make sure that she's not developed pneumonia. In fact, I've got a few days leave owed me, so I was thinking of coming down there tomorrow. I know it's a busy time for you at school so I can help with the animals, I do love that little pig of yours, Pork-chop isn't it? And the chucks, I used to want some hens of our own, but your dad wouldn't have the mess ...'

Trish's voice tailed off, and brought a rush of memories back for Lucy, setting her resolve. No way would she let Maisie have the childhood she'd had.

'Then we didn't have space at the new house, or the time, but it's nice to do it now.' She paused for breath. 'You know I'm here for you darling, don't you?'

Lucy nodded, then realised her mother couldn't see it. 'I do.'

'Right love, well I won't get in your way, I know you're busy, but I've bought these little cushions for your cottage, I know it isn't all signed and sealed yet, but I couldn't resist.'

Lucy smiled, and rubbed her smarting eyes. 'Thanks, Mum.' Whatever happened, she had moving in to Jasmine Cottage to look forward to.

'Well that's sorted then, lovely, I can't wait. I'll give Elsie a quick ring and tell her she'll be having a visitor in the next few days. Oh, you have cheered me up, love. And don't you worry, you and Charlie will sort things out and the little mite will be fine.'

# Chapter 16

'We need a donkey, a cow and some chickens.' Lucy topped up Sally's glass with white wine and sank back down into the chair, which promptly swallowed her. Once you were in the very worn seat it was useless to argue. It wrapped itself around you, and you just submitted and stayed there. Right now though its soft embrace was very welcome.

It had been a long week, with the initial rehearsals for the Christmas nativity performance taking up a big part of each day, but it felt like the days were slipping by far too fast.

'You look knackered.'

'I am.' Maybe she'd just stay in this chair for ever. Well at least until after Christmas. 'There's just so much more to do. All the kids are getting hyper now, which doesn't help when you're trying to get them all to sing *Away in a Manger* at roughly the same time and vaguely in time to the music.'

She'd actually been reluctant when Jamie had asked if she could 'get Sal out of our way for the evening'. It wasn't actually a hardship drinking wine with her friend, but she'd quite like to be in her pyjamas, in bed. She stifled the yawn, and tried to be entertaining. If she wasn't careful, Sally would be dashing off to find her new husband, and she'd be in trouble. 'I had Poppy just opening and closing her mouth like a goldfish, Sophie bellowing because her mam told her she had to sing loudly, and Harry improvising with his own words.' She sighed. 'He's always seemed so sweet and cute, but he's morphed into a real cheeky monkey since he went into Class 2, who knew that the real words were *Away in a manger, no crisps for a bed?*'

Sally giggled.

'And Jill swore that *the little Lord Jesus* became *the little Malteser* at one stage, I blame the twins for that one.'

'Nothing like a bit of improv. That old stuff is over-rated anyway.'

'That's what they reckoned at Starbaston.' Lucy knew she was rolling her eyes, the school she'd taught at in Birmingham had a totally different take on what Christmas was all about.

'No chickens and cows I bet either?'

'Oh God no, it was totally different, the whole traditional nativity thing was a complete no-no.'

'So you didn't have one?'

'I wish. We had to do something politically correct that had nothing at all to do with Christmas.'

'No baby in a manger then?'

'There was more chance of getting rap dancing Daleks than any reference to baby Jesus, it was usually something so bloody weird it confused the teachers as well as the kids. But the music was always loud and monotonous enough to keep a lot of the kids entertained, though the quiet ones would end up quivering at the back.'

'Rap?'

'Rap.' She nodded. 'Or some kind of street-dancing stuff.'

'That would be so cool to do here, can you imagine what the parents would say? Oh you should do it, Luce, you should so do it. I dare you!'

She giggled. 'I'm sure Sophie's mam would tell me that's not the way they do things round here. Elsie thinks the Morris Dancers are a bit too noisy, can you imagine what she'd have to say about it? There was one big plus though – I didn't have to worry about flaming costumes, they're already starting to give me a headache.'

'I thought they always dug out the same old stuff?'

'They did. Until Liz Potts decided the moths had been at them, and it would be a bit unfortunate if posh George recognised anything from when he was at school.'

'Ah. So you've got them making their own?'

'You've got it.'

'Should be interesting, you'll probably get some of them dressed in feed sacks and the others in curtains.'

Lucy grimaced at Sally. 'I've already got visions of having to stay up all night making the flaming costumes myself. Although Jill reckons once they get used to the idea they'll get all competitive.'

'They're bound to. Just think what it's like at the village show now, nobody just makes plain strawberry jam, it has to have jalapenos and a hint of chocolate in it now.'

'That banana and marshmallow cake I had at the summer fete was interesting.' Piper jumped onto her knee and licked her nose.

'Exactly. Well the animals won't be a problem, you've got chickens, more than enough.' Sally grinned. 'What did Annie think when you told her the brood was bigger than when she left?'

'She laughed. Apparently Squeak does it most years, well she's not called Squeak, she's called Emily Bronte. The one I call Bubble is in fact Charlotte, and Anne came to a nasty end last year.'

'I think Bubble and Squeak suits them better. The cow isn't a problem, Matt or Jamie can soon sort that one, but the donkey has always been a bit of a pain.'

'So I've heard.'

'They did try goats and sheep one year, but the sheep wouldn't stop baa-ing, it drowned everything else out. And the goats climbed the pews. Then Daisy decided to tell them off, which was pretty hilarious before they high-tailed it off down the aisle knocking the crib over and trampling poor baby Jesus. Half the kids were wailing cos Jesus had died prematurely, Poppy was hysterical because it was her doll and Timothy downed his hidden hip flask in one and promptly keeled over nearly ending up in the font.'

'You're really selling this to me,' Lucy said drily.

Sally giggled. 'You'll love it. The cow usually manages to drool all over the decorations.'

'Why on earth do they have it *in* the church?'

'Only chance the vicar has of a full house. Then we all go into the square for the rest.' Her mouth twisted. 'It's a bit of a pain really, Jamie and Matt seem to have got roped into sorting the lights and all sorts out so he's going to be no fun, and you and Jill will be busy with the kids.'

'But we'll all be finished by, I dunno 7 or 8 p.m.? Then it's up to Santa Claus Jim to entertain the kids, and Timothy and Elsie will be looking after George, so we can have fun, can't we?' Lucy decided distraction tactics were in order. She knew Sally accepted that being married to a farmer meant life wasn't always easy, but she'd obviously been looking forward to the Christmas festivities and was now not at all happy that her new husband, and all her friends, were going to be tied up for a fair part of the evening. 'You can keep an eye on my mum,' Lucy grinned, 'you know what she's like after a glass of mulled wine.'

Sally smiled. 'Where is she tonight?'

'Oh, she said she'd go and see Elsie. They get on really well you know, she spends more time there than here. And,' a sudden thought had come to Lucy, 'You can look after the animals!'

'Haha, very funny.'

'No, honestly.'

'I thought Charlie ...'

'Charlie will be acting the part of proud parent, he'll only have eyes for Maisie.'

'I'm sure in Elsie's pictures it was all set up in the square.' She wriggled her way out of the chair, and grabbed the photograph album. 'Look.'

With Elsie Harrington's permission, Lucy had taken some of the photographs from her album and showed them to the children.

One thing she loved about working in the village school was how cleverly Timothy Parry wove together a modern vision, and a willingness to embrace a nostalgic nod to the past. He recognised the importance of the community, of the children knowing their roots, but he didn't let it stop him moving the school and the inhabitants of Langtry Meadows forward at quite a march when it suited him. Lucy loved him, she couldn't imagine what they would do when he retired.

She'd scrutinised the pictures ever since Elsie had lent her the album. Taking in the familiar outlines of the faces that would mature and become the Jim Stafford, George Cambourne, Edward Wright and Timothy Parry she knew today – searching for the familiar features of Elsie in one of their faces and feeling constantly frustrated. It could be any of them, or none of them.

'Aww now isn't he the cute little angel.' Jill had pointed at one of the pictures. 'You can see where Ted Wright gets his looks from can't you?' She'd laughed. 'And I bet his dad had all kinds of wildlife stuffed in his pockets too.'

'Charlie said his dad told him that one day Ed thought he'd got foot and mouth and hid in the fields, the whole village was out searching for him.'

'You're kidding? So Charlie's dad is on here too?'

'That never occurred to me.' Lucy had squinted at the photo, searching for familiar features and failing miserably. 'He must be. Or he could be a bit older than this lot, I think he is actually.'

'You're trying to spot somebody who looks like Elsie, aren't you?'

'I am.' She'd sighed and pushed the photograph away.

'I'm rubbish at it though, I'm just beginning to think everybody could be.'

Jill had laughed. 'Come on, the kids will be in from break in a minute and we've got to walk them down to the church to rehearse.'

Lucy had tried not to groan, she'd been dreading the idea of their first session in the church, with the vicar looking on. 'We'll show them these first.'

Sally leafed through the album. 'Oh God, look at that.' She suddenly stopped and chortled, poking at one of the pictures. 'Timothy looked like a teacher even when he was in short trousers. I wonder if Elsie's got any stuff from when my parents were kids? My mum and dad were childhood sweethearts, they're holding hands in every single photo I've seen of them,' she pulled a face, 'even when they were five years old.'

Lucy smiled. 'Sweet.'

'Soppy more like.'

'So how's married life?'

Sally's grin said it all, as she put the book to one side. 'We even told Mum when we all went in the Taverner's on Bonfire Night, and she wasn't anywhere near as mad as I thought she'd be. Though we had to agree to a first anniversary party next year. But that's way off, I've got plenty of time to plan how to get out of it. We had to tell really cos Eric said Jamie could move into the flat, and you can imagine what people would have said.'

'So, it's all out in the open now?'

'It is.'

'And you're happy you did it that way?'

'Oh God, yes.'

'You didn't miss having a party?'

'Well,' Sally shrugged, but Lucy was sure she detected the very slightest hint of regret, 'we're always celebrating something or other in Langtry Meadows anyway, there'll be a massive piss up after this Christmas thing. You should see Elsie once she's hit the mulled wine, I caught her line-dancing one year although she completely denied it afterwards.'

'Line-dancing?' Lucy tried not to laugh.

'It always turns into a bit of a shindig at the village hall afterwards, when everybody is sick of freezing their fingers off. It's only round the corner so they set up a bar in there.'

'I could be the one asleep in the corner.'

'Rubbish, after a couple of Matt's special mulled wines you'll be up for anything!'

'Matt makes the mulled wine?' Now she was worried.

Sally laughed. 'He doesn't make it, he sneaks half a bottle of brandy in it when nobody is looking. You look like you need one now.'

'I will be *so* glad when this term is over.' She wriggled

her toes, her feet seemed to be permanently aching these days.

'Right, I'm off, you need to go to bed.'

'But it's not late ...' What if Jamie hadn't done everything he needed to? He'd given Lucy strict instructions on keeping Sally occupied until him or Matt gave her the all clear.

Keeping quiet about Sally's wedding had been easy, compared to trying not to spill the beans about Matt and Jamie's top secret surprise. It would be a miracle if Sally didn't discover what her husband was planning for her. This grand romantic gesture could be the death of her, and if she wasn't so fond of Sally she'd never have allowed the brothers to rope her in.

'Jamie just text,' Sally looked apologetic, 'he was asking where I was.'

'Really?' Lucy laughed, hoping she didn't sound too relieved. 'You go, can't get in the way of a pair of newlyweds, can I?'

'You don't mind do you? I know it's still quite early.'

'Of course I don't mind, you noddle. And for a school night this is way past my bedtime. I just hope Mum isn't too late back, honestly she's like a teenager.' Lucy smiled to herself. Her mum was happier than she'd ever seen her, in fact the only long-distant memory she'd got of her this carefree was when she was little, very young. Before things had all gone wrong. 'I think it's doing

Elsie the world of good too, she seems much more her old self even if she still looks slightly older and slightly sadder.'

'Well maybe she'll confide in your mum about this mystery child if they get on so well.'

'Maybe.' Lucy crossed her fingers. 'She did promise me she'd tell him soon.'

'Well she will then.' Sally leaned in and kissed Lucy's cheek. 'Elsie Harrington is old school, she wouldn't dream of breaking her word. Night Lucy.' She pulled the door open. 'And stop worrying about everything, honestly you're getting worse than Charlie!'

# Chapter 17

Charlie read the letter that he'd found in the bottom of Maisie's bag again. 'You need a costume making?' He wished he'd never spotted it, but after missing something important a couple of weeks earlier he'd got in the habit of tipping the contents of her school bag out on a Sunday morning and sifting through the leaves, pebbles, squashed flowers, sweet wrappers (occasionally still full of squashed sweets) and notes that always found their way to the bottom.

Maisie nodded, all her attention fixed on peeling off a string of cheese, so she didn't notice the frown on her father's face. 'I got that letter ages ago.' The dramatic sigh was all Josie. There'd always be a reminder of her here. Once upon a time he'd celebrated the similarities, laughed as they'd said the '*just like you*' type of things new parents say as their newborn screws up its face, as the toddler sticks a tongue out in determination. Now it was bittersweet, but he'd loved Josie so much when they'd first met, and he loved Maisie even more. This bond was different, this ache of love would never go – however much she was frustrating him at the time.

'You only got it this week.' His tone was mild as he took another swig of coffee and wondered how the hell he was going to fulfil this particular challenge of parenting. 'Are you sure I have to actually send one in?'

'Two.' She chewed her way along the string of cheese in much the same way she'd watched her guinea pig devour a strip of carrot.

'Two?' He noticed too late that at the bottom of the printed letter, where there was a small gap for details of the character Maisie would play somebody had helpfully managed to squeeze in several words.

'I'm two things, I'm a dancing lady and I'm a shepherd so I need two costumes. Miss Jacobs said she was very excited to see what we look like.'

He bet she was. 'What kind of dancing lady?' Ballet he might be able to cope with, he was sure he could get a next day delivery on a tutu and tights.

'The song type.'

'Song?' So that was *Swan Lake* out. They were heading into the land of musicals now, but he wasn't sure if he should be thinking, *Mamma Mia* or *Lion King*.

'Class 3 have to pretend to milk cows.' She giggled. 'Ted said they'd do it wrong, he's a leaping lord but he wanted to be a drummer.'

It dawned on him then. 'The twelve days of Christmas? You're nine ladies dancing?'

'That's what I said, but I'm only one, how can I be nine?'

'And the shepherd?'

Maisie rolled her eyes. 'Chases sheep of course. I need a big stick with a curly bit at the end, Rosie said it's like hook-a-duck but for sheep. When's the fair going to come? Does it come here, or do we have to go back to Mummy's house?'

'There's a little fair, with hook-a-duck, but not until the summer when it's sunny again.'

'Oh. Can I have more cheese? I don't want a pink one.'

'No not now. What do you mean, pink? We don't have pink cheese.'

'Not pink cheese, silly. Why can't I have another one? It's good for you, Miss Jacobs said so.'

He was beginning to understand why Josie got niggled at the mention of Miss Jacobs, though for very different reasons. Agreeing to a break had seemed sensible, even if the complete opposite of what he wanted, but the constant reminder of her was like banging your head against a wall when you already had a headache. He fought to keep his tone even. 'Only in reasonable quantities, you won't want your lunch if you have any more. Now, pink?'

'Dress for dancing. It's not really a costume if it's a dress, is it? But a shepherd is.'

'Er, no.' He wasn't sure if this was getting simpler or more complicated, or whether Maisie even had a dress.

'I've got to take it into school soon so we can practise. I'm going to go and play with Roo while you do the costume, Daddy.' She slipped off the kitchen stool and carried her jumper round to him.

Charlie glanced out of the window as he helped her put the top on. Outside it was dull, but still dry. An hour or so running round would do her good, and he knew that she was always drawn to the barns where she'd find Ted, and calves.

The first few days they'd been here he'd watched her constantly, going out with her if she wanted to play – even though he knew that the farm was a pretty secure place. But it was vast, and she was little, but he gradually relaxed.

Ed Wright or his wife were always around, and little Ted had an older brother and sister who mucked in on the farm and kept an eye on their little brother. Ted's sister had been delighted to find out Maisie was moving in, and happily spent hours entertaining her, plaiting her hair and showing her how to feed the calves and collect eggs.

He still watched her like a hawk, but she never went far and the Wrights already treated her as one of the family – glad that their son had a playmate his own age.

Charlie hadn't had any plans on what to do this Sunday morning – his first free time of the week – but he'd have rather been playing out with Maisie and Roo than spend it searching on the internet to find out whether a tea-towel on the head still counted as an acceptable school shepherd costume.

'I might need a hand later, I've never made one before.' From what he could remember, his involvement in the school nativity had always been minimal. All he'd had to do was turn up at the right time to watch. And he was pretty sure that Josie hadn't been involved in any costume making behind the scenes. He was sure he would have heard the swearing.

'I haven't either, so I won't be much use.' Maisie looked at him, her head tilted to one side. 'You've got your cross face on, Daddy.' She frowned in concentration, then suddenly smiled triumphantly. 'We can go and ask Miss Jacobs, cos she must have made lots. She can do everything.'

He was feeling woefully inadequate, but he really didn't want to go and ask Lucy. The last time Maisie had spoken to Josie there had been a definite reduction in the number of times she said '*Lucy said*' and '*Lucy showed me how to*', and he was sure the atmosphere had been less frosty. The '*Mummy you're doing it wrong,*

*Lucy said do it like this*' had been like lighting the touch paper and he didn't want to go there again. Much as he hated creating a distance between them and Lucy, for now it was worth it. It also kept Malcolm happy.

'We could go round and ask Becky? I bet she's made lots of costumes before too.'

'Don't want to ask Becky.' Maisie pouted and took a step backwards, as though she half expected him to pick her up and drag her off to see Becky right there and then. 'She's not a proper teacher any more. I want to go and see Miss Jacobs.'

'I'm sure she's busy, just this once we can ask Becky.' He'd agreed to do this, agreed they'd keep their distance for a while. He'd give anything to be able to see her again, properly not just at the school gate, but he couldn't. If she was prepared to go through this for him and Maisie, then he had to at least play his part.

'No.' Her bottom lip was wobbling. 'I want to see Lucy.' He noticed the switch from Miss Jacobs to Lucy, this wasn't about seeing her teacher, this was about seeing the person she regarded as a friend.

'I know, darling.' So did he. 'But not today, Maisie. She's busy.' Ever since they'd decided to make a conscious effort to make Lucy slightly less important in Maisie's life, he'd been fighting the urge to call in and see her, he'd lurked for far too long by the school gate, and been crushingly disappointed each day when he'd checked the appointment book and found out that she hadn't made an appointment. He'd never wish an animal ill, but surely she needed at least some advice about looking after one of her many pets?

It would be so easy to cave in and ask for her help with the costume, but cold-turkey had seemed the best option. Until he'd tried it.

'You always say she's busy now. Everybody is busy. Mummy is always busy and now so is Lucy. She didn't used to be. She doesn't want to see me.' She was clenching and unclenching her little fists, tears welling in her eyes. Any minute now it would spill over. 'She doesn't love me.'

'Oh Maisie, of course she—'

'I hate you, I just want Roo and Treacle.' She sat down on the kitchen floor and struggled to get her wellingtons on, then clambered onto the chair to get her coat and scarf off the hook.

'Maisie.' Charlie reached out to help her. She always presented herself in front of him, so he'd do the zip up. But this time she didn't. She kept her gaze fixed on the floor, and struggled on her own.

He sighed as she ran outside, the dog at her heels, then he scrunched the school letter up in his hand.

There had been times over the last few weeks that he'd thought maybe Josie was right. Maybe he wasn't cut out to be a parent, and living with him wasn't a good place to be. But lately a new resolve had been growing in him, and it had nothing to do with proving his ex was wrong, and everything to do with giving Maisie the best upbringing she could have in the circumstances.

Good as he was at wielding a needle in the operating theatre though, making a costume for a school nativity was completely outside his experience. And taking Maisie to see Lucy was a no-no. They had to get through this, together. There'd be plenty of time afterwards to make up for seeing less of Lucy now. When Josie had calmed down, when the threat had eased and he knew where he stood, then they could all go back to spending some time together. To building their future.

He flicked the kettle on, to make another cup of coffee. He needed the caffeine. Maybe if he called Lucy after Maisie was asleep in bed tonight? Or, he glanced out of the window to see Maisie and Ted crouched side by side next to the guinea pig run, maybe he could sneak off for half an hour now? Mrs Wright would be more than happy to keep an eye on Maisie, and she need never know where he'd been. After all, the main thing was to avoid his daughter becoming too attached to her teacher – it didn't stop him, did it? Even though it made him feel a bit of a traitor. Maybe it wasn't fair on Lucy or Maisie.

Ten minutes later and Charlie was halfway down his cup of coffee and it still hadn't helped with decision making. His mobile rang and for a second he was tempted to ignore it. He glanced down at the display, and seeing that it was Sally he picked up.

'Sorry to bother you on your day off Charlie.'

'No problem.'

'I just wanted to check if you knew where those puppy food samples are? I can't find them anywhere.'

'Puppy food?'

'You know, those free sachets.'

'I know what you mean, but ... hang on a sec, Sal.' Maisie had flung the back door open and was stomping past him, heading for the stairs in her muddy wellies. 'Maisie.'

She paused, one foot on the spiral staircase.

'Maisie, you know not to wear muddy boots in the house. Be a good girl and put them in the basket. Hang on Sal.' He put the phone down and headed over to her, but she didn't turn round to look at him – just lifted her feet so that he could pull the wellington boots off. He ruffled her hair, but even as he did it she'd slipped below the touch of his fingers and had dashed up the stairs.

She shouted something he didn't catch and he shook his head as he dropped the boots in the big basket by the back door. 'I won't be long Maisie, as soon as I've finished talking to Sal we can have a chat about your costume, yes?' She didn't answer, but he could hear her as she opened and shut drawers in her bedroom.

He really needed to talk to her, as soon as he'd answered this call.

With a sigh he picked up the phone again. 'Hi Sal, still there? ... No, she's fine.' He sat down at the kitchen table. 'So, what's this about puppy food? Why do you need the samples?'

'For the puppy socialisation.'

That was a new one on him. 'What puppy socialisation?'

'The puppy party.' He heard her take a breath. 'Eric didn't tell you about it, did he?'

'No.'

'Oh.' There was a long silence. 'It's starting in ten minutes, he invited everybody with a young pup, I think, er, well he thought we seemed to have a lot of clients with pups and he had one in the other day that was a bit tetchy with the other dogs. We used to do them ages ago, and er, I think he even invited Serena, and I think he rang Lucy.'

'It's okay, fine, not a problem.' He didn't know what felt worse, not having a clue what Eric's latest plan was, or the fact that he didn't even know Lucy was going. Because he hadn't talked to her for days, apart from at the school gate.

'He only arranged it the other day.'

'Fine. But if he planned a bit ahead you'd have some food samples.'

The long sigh travelled down the phone wires.

'I know it's not your fault, Sally.'

'And I know you like planning everything, Charlie.'

'Touché. Look forget it, not a problem, but I don't know where the pouches are. Have you looked in the store cupboard where the mop and cleaning stuff is?'

'Ah, that could be it.' He heard the sound of her opening doors and rummaging. 'You're right, brilliant! Eric will be chuffed, right better go, think I can hear barking at the door. Have a good day, Charlie, see you tomorrow morning.'

The church clock chimed eleven as he put the phone down and sat back in his chair. It wasn't even lunchtime and he already felt like he'd done a full day.

Levering himself up he walked to the bottom of the stairs and shouted Maisie. They both needed a lift, a walk into the village and maybe dropping in to see Miss Harrington might help. Or they could stop by and see what was happening at the puppy party. That would cheer her up.

'Maisie!' He shouted again, but there was no reply, or answering bark – so he headed upstairs.

Her bedroom was empty. She must have come back down while he was on the phone, so with any luck she'd cheered up and found something interesting to do outside with Ted. Whatever it was though, he wanted to join in. Show he was there for her. It was the weekend, and it was supposed to be his day off.

Out in the small patch of garden that bordered the bungalow the guinea pig was busy munching away at the small pile of dandelion leaves that were already wilting in the corner of the cage. Charlie glanced around. There was no sign of Maisie or Roo, but a good chance that she'd gone off in the search for more greenery for Treacle. Or been distracted by Ted.

Charlie popped back into the bungalow and put his wellington boots and coat on, then headed over to the barn where the Wrights kept the young calves. He remembered being drawn to them when he was young, and Maisie was just the same. She'd sit cross-legged in front of them and tell them all about her day. Now there was a good chance she was explaining how rubbish her dad was at making school nativity costumes.

The animals looked up in interest as he walked in, than wandered over, heads low and regarding him warily through big brown eyes. But there was no sign of a little girl, so he walked the length of the building, peering into the corners, expecting to see her mischievous face any moment. Expecting Roo to jump out, to hear the giggles of hiding children.

There was nothing. He stood still, concentrating. But

there was just the sound of the cattle moving around, the munching of hay.

A niggle of doubt started in Charlie's chest. He should have found her by now. He peered across the pen that held the cattle. With Ted she might have dared venture into the pens to see the animals close up, but he was sure that she wouldn't do that on her own. She just wouldn't. His heart quickened, and he forced himself to calm down. It was fine, she'd be here somewhere. She wouldn't have gone far.

Relief suddenly flooded through him, as the obvious occurred. At the back of the building there was a hay store. Why hadn't he thought of it earlier? The children loved to play in there, and it was warm, much more inviting than the cold shed, where only the heat of the calves took the chill off the winter air.

Striding out briskly he soon covered the length of the building, he turned the corner.

It was silent, no sign of any of the children, no answering call or bark when he shouted out first for Maisie, then Roo.

Charlie quickened his pace, his walk breaking into a jog, as he headed back across the yard to where the hens were scratching about in their run. They'd helped collect the eggs together more than once, she'd be there, looking for fresh eggs for lunch.

But there was no sign of Maisie or the dog.

Frowning, Charlie knew he'd broken into a sweat. He wiped his forearm across his brow. He was worrying unnecessarily. She had to be with one of the Wrights, she'd never go far on her own.

He glanced over the fields. There was no sign of the children, no splash of colours from her wellingtons, from her coat. Only green, turning to brown. Only the black and white of the small dairy herd, picking at the late autumn grass which had little nutritional value but gave the animals a chance to stretch their legs and have some fresh air during the last fine days of the year. Soon it would be winter and if it was a wet one they'd be spending long hours in the cosy sheds, picking at hay.

Charlie spun on his heel, and forced his growing panic down. They weren't in a city, this was Langtry Meadows for heaven's sake.

Then he realised exactly where she'd be. Maisie was no doubt in the big farmhouse kitchen, eating newly baked cakes or biscuits, rather than waiting expectantly for him to entertain her. Frustration mingled with worry, putting him more on edge and he fought to plaster a smile on his face as he walked up the path to the farmhouse.

He shouldn't be cross with her. He was in the wrong, he should be glad she was settled here, that she felt at home and could entertain herself while he was taking work phone calls, but the moment he got in the house he knew Ed would be asking his opinion about some aspect of farming, and before he knew it another chunk of his precious time with Maisie would have been eaten away.

The front door opened just as he raised his fist to knock.

'Now then Charlie.' Edward Wright nodded a welcome. 'Not got the little one with you today?' He looked round Charlie as though he half-expected Maisie to be hiding behind him.

Something deep in his stomach twisted. She had to be here. 'Er, no.' The panic was rising again, blocking his throat. His daughter was six years old, and he didn't know where she was. 'I was wondering if she was here?'

'Oh no.' Edward frowned. 'We've not seen her for a couple of hours, she played with Ted and the guinea pigs then he came back here for a drink on his own.' He half turned and shouted. 'Not seen the little one have you, Beth?'

'Little one? Maisie?' Beth Wright appeared from the kitchen, wiping her hands on a tea towel. 'Hello there Charlie. No, I've not seen her. The kiddies played with the guinea pigs for a bit, then Ted wanted to come back to help me make the cakes, I did ask her but she said no. Not that I would have brought her back without asking first, seeing as it's Sunday and you're not working.' She smiled. 'Not in her bedroom or playing with little Treacle?'

'No.' Charlie grimaced. 'And there's no sign of the dog either. She came in while I was on the phone, but had disappeared by the time I put it down. I was only on for a few minutes, I just thought she'd have come over here.'

'I'd check under the bed and in the wardrobe love, they can be little horrors at this age, full of mischief.' She gave Ted, who had followed her from the kitchen, his hands sticky with dough, a quick hug. 'You've not seen Maisie have you love?'

'No. She went in. She wanted to play with Roo not me.' He stared up at Charlie.

'I better go back and have another look.' With a wave, Charlie strode back down to the path and towards their home. It wasn't like Maisie to ignore him when he called her, but she had been upset and acting a bit out of character lately. Maybe he'd got it wrong again, maybe breaking the developing relationship she had with Lucy was the wrong thing to do. He'd talk to her properly when he found her, explain.

The house felt strange when Charlie walked back in and shrugged his jacket off. The uneasy feeling in the pit of his stomach grew. It was too empty, echoingly empty, it didn't feel like his daughter or dog were there hiding.

There would be a welcome. A shout, a bark.

There was nothing.

He shook off the feeling of foreboding. 'Maisie?'

He got on his hands and knees, looked under the bed, from both sides. Flinging the wardrobe doors open, he rooted in the belongings at the bottom, pushing stuff to one side, throwing things out from the bottom, even though it was clear she wasn't there.

'Maisie, you can come out now.' He pulled the drawers open, even though she was too big to fit in them. 'It's not funny now.' The last he muttered roughly under his breath as he wheeled round, spotted the cupboards and yanked the doors open. Even though there was no way she could be in them. Even though she'd never, ever hidden there.

Dragging his fingers through his hair he spun round, then headed back into the bathroom, which he'd already checked. Then he ran back down the stairs, and to his own bedroom, checking under his bed on his hands and knees.

Then he sank back and stared round. Where the hell was she? Where hadn't he looked?

The game had gone on far too long, Maisie couldn't keep hidden and quiet for this long. And even if she had been hiding, Roo would have made a noise.

There was something wrong. Something very wrong.

Her boots had gone from the basket. Her coat wasn't

flung on the chair as it usually was, or abandoned on her bedroom floor.

He looked at the coat pegs again, there was something else wrong, something missing. Then he realised.

The little rucksack that she took to school wasn't there.

He was painfully aware of the hollow feeling in his stomach, the thud of his heartbeat in his ears as he dashed round the house one more time, then scoured the garden and the shrubby bushes that without their summer leaves offered little cover anyway.

Grabbing his car keys he ran out, drove the short distance to the farmhouse and ran back up the path.

Beth Wright was on the doorstep before he reached it. 'No sign, love?'

Her calm tone didn't help. 'She's not there, definitely not there.' He'd already wasted far too much time fruitlessly searching. 'Look I'm going to pop down to Lucy's and check she isn't there.' There was a chance. A remote chance. 'She's obviously missing Lucy like mad, and she knows the way. We've walked it often enough.' It would be easy. He glanced at his phone, surely Lucy would have let him know if she'd turned up alone? 'What if she's had an accident?' He looked blindly at Beth. If she'd walked down the road, anything could have happened. She was small, a car might not have seen her. She could have slipped. Fallen.

'I'm sure she's not, dear.' She put a steadying hand on his arm. 'Now don't you get worked up, I'm sure she's just in one of the sheds, or been picking dandelions for that guinea pig and lost track of time. She'll have just wandered a bit too far.'

'Yes, I'm sure you're right. But she doesn't normally …' She never went anywhere without asking.

'You go down and check with Lucy, love, and we'll check round the farm. Our Helen can go and sit in your house in case she turns up while you're away, don't want her getting upset, do we?'

'No.' He tried to smile, but it wasn't happening. 'Thanks.'

'You take your time, love. We've got your number so we'll call if we see her before you get back.'

Charlie was torn between speeding the short distance into the village centre, and getting there as quickly as he could, or taking his time and making sure he checked out all the hedgerows on the way. As he turned the car out of the entrance to the farm he took a deep breath and eased his foot off the accelerator.

He had to calm down, be logical. Beth had a point, she could have just wandered off further than she meant to, she'd be totally unaware of the scare she was giving him.

But why had she taken her rucksack?

His foot came down heavier on the accelerator.

If she'd headed for Lucy she would be well on her way now. Unless she'd had an accident, was lying injured.

His heart rate increased, clammy perspiration building up on the back of his neck, even though the weather was cold.

Roo wouldn't leave her. He'd keep her warm. He'd bark.

Pulling up outside Lucy's cottage, Charlie was out of the car almost before he'd pulled the handbrake on and with a brief rap on the door he barged in – and almost ran into Jamie Harwood.

Lucy looked at him, eyes open wide in alarm, a flush of guilt on her features as her hand dropped from Jamie's arm. As his arm dropped from round her shoulders.

'For Christ's sake.' The words were out before he could stop them.

'Catch you later.' Jamie raised a hand in apology and was out of the door before Charlie could say another word.

'He's just got married.' He stared at Lucy. 'To your friend.'

'I know.' She glared back. 'You're jumping to conclusions again, and really silly ones. It was a thank you hug.'

'A thank you? For what? No, no, it doesn't matter. It really doesn't matter.' And it didn't, he knew it didn't. Lucy was kind, nice, people liked her. People hugged her. He wanted to hug her.

'Charlie, you're being—'

'Sorry.' He held up a hand to stop her talking, then raked his fingers through his hair. 'Maisie is missing.'

'What?'

'I've lost Maisie. She's gone.' Charlie flung his arms up in the air.

'What do you mean gone?' She was frowning at him, but he didn't want to say the words again – in case they were true. 'Josie's back? But she can't ...'

'Not Josie.' He shook his head in frustration. 'No, she's just gone. She's not in the house. She's missing. I was on the phone talking to Sal about her bloody puppy thing, then I turned round and she was gone, and so was Roo.' He covered his face with his hands, he had to get a grip. 'God, you really don't think ...?' Something twisted in his gut. 'What if Josie has come back, what if she's taken matters into her own hands? She was so bloody worked up last time we talked.' The words rasped in his throat. 'No. She couldn't. Not again. She couldn't just take her.'

'Charlie, no, that doesn't make sense. She wouldn't even be able to find your place without somebody on the farm seeing her, would she?'

He took a deep breath. 'No.' Let the air slowly escape from his lungs. 'No.' He was being ridiculous. He'd spoken to her only the other day, not even Josie could have booked flights and hatched a plan like this.

'Tell me what's happened. Slowly.'

'I thought she might come here to you, we've got to go and—'

'Charlie stop.'

He stopped. Looked straight into that direct blue gaze and stopped.

'Charlie I need to say this now, I'll explain later about why Jamie was here, okay? But right now you need to tell me what's happened with Maisie.'

'She was in the garden with Ted,' he took a deep breath, 'she came in while I was on the phone to Sal, she went upstairs. I never heard her come back down or go out again, but when I went to find her she'd gone. Disappeared.'

'You've looked round the farm.'

'Of course I've looked—' He pulled himself up, softened his tone even though he wanted to hang on to the anger. 'She's not on the farm, Beth said they'd keep an eye out.'

'Why would she go? Has something happened?'

'You.' He stared at her, and the truth slowly dawned on him. Maisie wasn't just missing, she'd run away. 'This wouldn't have happened if you ...' The words hung, he shouldn't have said that.

'If I what?' She looked at him quizzically.

'We. Not you. We. If we hadn't been involved this wouldn't have happened.'

'What's that supposed to mean?'

'She's not just wandered off. She's run away because she was upset that nobody loved her, we weren't seeing you anymore and ...'

'Oh, Charlie.' She closed the gap then, and put a hand up to his face. Her palm cool, skin soft, and he wanted to lean into it, close his eyes. Cry. Instead he gritted his teeth. Rested his hand over hers.

'It doesn't matter about you and ...'

'Charlie, me and Jamie are planning something for Sally. A surprise, with Matt. Sorry I should have told you before, I know I should, but it was getting the right time when Sal wasn't about, and Maisie wasn't in hearing distance. I'll explain later, okay?'

He nodded, not really caring. All he wanted right now was to find Maisie. 'She's taken her coat and her bag, I don't know what's in it. Hell.' Frustration coursed through him, rippling through the worry.

'Bag?'

'The school bag, rucksack, it's gone. I was only on the phone for a few minutes, ten minutes tops. She'd come back in and marched upstairs and I never heard her come back down. But she was upset, about the costume.'

'Costume?'

'The flaming nativity, I said I didn't know how to make a costume, she said to come and ask you, but I said we couldn't.' He pulled his shoulders back, tried to ignore the tightening band around his forehead, the throbbing in his temple. 'She was upset, nearly crying, but I thought she was okay. Christ, Lucy I was only trying to do the best thing, calm Josie down, but I wasn't doing the right thing for Maisie. She misses you like hell.' He shut his eyes briefly. 'So do I.'

'I miss her.' Her voice was soft. 'I miss both of you.' She took a breath, then seemed to focus, switch into common-sense mode. 'Right, let's ring around and get the whole village checking. You call Matt and the landlord at the Taverner's and they can check at that end, I'll call Sally and Jamie, I'll ask them to get hold of Jim, and if I tell Jill she can let Timothy know.'

'You don't think it's a bit ...'

'It's fine, if the whole village knows then somebody will soon spot her.' She'd picked up her mobile and Charlie followed suit. 'We'll soon find her, she can't have gone far.' She looked at him reassuringly, her voice soft. 'She might be home in her bedroom by now.'

'I hope so.' There was something therapeutic about making the calls, the calm responses and the feeling of doing something, but after the two short conversations he suddenly felt helpless again. His daughter was out there somewhere, on a freezing November afternoon. At best she'd be cold, lost and frightened. At worst … Well he couldn't think like that. But they had to find her before the light began to fade, before it got even colder.

'You get back to the farm, Charlie and organise a search there. I'll stay here for a bit just in case she does make her way here.'

The words she didn't say hung between them. If she was heading there, why hadn't he passed her on his way over?

'Thanks, Lucy, look I know I've made some bad decisions, and I think trying to keep away from you is one of my bigge—' The jangle of his phone stopped him dead.

'Charlie? It's Beth Wright here, lovey.'

'Has she …?'

'No sign of her yet dear, but I'm sure she'll be back soon. Your little dog has turned up though. Yapping away he was, and he's a right state, a right mucky mess. Smells like he's been in a ditch.' Charlie felt his heart lurch. If the dog had been in a ditch, where was his daughter?

'From the state I'd say he's been across the fields so we're going to have a look down by the bottom field. We've brought the cows in, so don't you go worrying about them.'

'I'm on my way back.' He glanced at Lucy. 'Did you hear?'

She nodded. 'You go, I'll let everybody know and then I'll follow you over. We'll soon find her Charlie, she can't have gone far or Roo wouldn't have found his way back. Go on, go.'

A muddy Roo was ecstatic to see Charlie, and bounced around like his namesake but was absolutely no use at all when he was asked where Maisie was. He sat down and barked. Then lay down, his chin on his paws and fixed his puzzled gaze on Charlie.

Fishing out a spare lead, he clipped it on to the dog's collar. Even though the terrier was showing no inclination to lead the way, maybe if they got close to where Maisie was he'd take over and take Charlie to her.

Jim's Landrover pulled up as he made his way back outside.

'Lucy just rang me, lad. I've got an idea. We'll find her, Charlie boy. Timothy is checking round by the school and on the green just to be on the safe side, and Jill is going to stop by the church and village hall, she said Maisie was quite taken with the church when they took them down there the other day. Right lad.' He patted Roo on the head. 'I'll get out of your way. I think from the state of that dog this is a job for boots and a stick.' He gave Charlie a friendly thump on the arm, and grabbing his walking stick from the back of the vehicle he set off in the direction of the cow shed.

# Chapter 18

By the time Lucy had rung round everybody with an update it was 1 p.m. She bit her lip as she pulled her scarf and jacket on, painfully aware that soon the light would start to fade and the slightly chilly day would turn distinctly colder.

She'd half expected Charlie to call her the moment he got back to the farm, saying that Maisie had turned up. But he hadn't.

Piper looked up expectantly as she pulled her boots on, and after a moment's hesitation she clipped the puppy's lead on. The dog was only young, but she always had her nose to the ground, sniffing out exciting smells, and she did like Maisie, and Lucy was pretty sure that a dog's hearing was better than a human's. If Maisie did cry out, then maybe Piper would respond. It was a slim hope, but right now Lucy would do anything that might mean Maisie was back with them quicker.

She tried to push the horrible thoughts of Maisie being lost or stuck somewhere to the back of her mind. If she was hurt, stuck out in the dark all alone ... It didn't bear thinking about.

Slamming the door shut behind her Lucy headed back up the lane towards the veterinary surgery. She'd have one quick look there before walking on towards the farm – and she would scour the ditches and hedgerows on the way.

The fingers of her hand clutching Piper's lead were soon frozen, she'd lost all feeling in the tips, and as she shoved her hands in her pockets a sudden pang of fear clutched her. If she was this cold already, how did Maisie feel?

The surgery was in darkness. All shut up, the blinds down. She'd popped in earlier to see what Sally's puppy party was about, but the party was over now, the building empty and quiet.

With Piper beside her she walked round the edges of the car park before checking round the building. The outhouses around the back, where the surgery kept supplies, were firmly locked but she banged on the doors and shouted just in case. There was no answering bark or shout. She edged her way behind the bins, desperately hoping to find Maisie curled up somewhere. There was no sign of anybody. She knew Sally and Jamie had joined the search and had no doubt checked the surgery before they went, but there was always the chance that Maisie had got there after they left.

But she hadn't. There was no sign that anybody had been there.

Biting her lip, Lucy hurried up the lane, breaking into a trot, Piper loping along at her side. Just past the surgery she knew there was a stile and a public footpath that would take her across the fields and straight to Wright's farm. It would be a lot quicker than heading back into the village square.

She was glad now that she'd spent the summer in Langtry Meadows, and not headed back to her old home. It had been a good summer, and she'd spent many happy days exploring the place with Jim as her guide. He'd instantly bonded with little Maisie, his gentle manner soon making her forget her shyness, and he obviously loved the company. As they'd wandered along the footpaths he'd pointed out flowers to her, showed her where the mice had built their nests, told her tales about the old woodland and how he'd helped lay the hedges when he was young.

Oh she'd give anything now to know that they'd be able to do the same next year; that Maisie was okay. She glanced at her phone again to check she hadn't missed any messages. Jim had told her he'd head for the farm as he had his Landrover which would make easy work of the muddy fields.

There was the smallest chance that Maisie remembered their walks, this path, and that she'd been heading back to the surgery this way. At least that would explain why Roo was muddy.

She clambered onto the stile and paused astride it, scanning the fields from the higher vantage point. In the distance she thought she could just make out the figure of Ed Wright and his quad bike, and heading over one long, slightly sloped field was a lone figure that could have been Jim, or even Charlie.

Jumping down onto the damp grass she urged Piper, who wanted to stop and sniff everything, into going faster. Soon she was slipping and sliding along the muddy edge of the field, very relieved that there were no cows in sight, as she peered under the hedges, and stopped every now and then to shout first Maisie's name.

Out of breath, with mud spattered up her jeans, Lucy finally reached the back of the farmhouse and made her way round to the yard at the front. Charlie's car was parked at the front next to a Landrover she was sure belonged to Jim.

It seemed sensible to go straight to the building that Charlie and Maisie called home, and she was soon rapping on the door. Pausing only for a minute she pushed the door open.

'Anybody there?'

'In here love.' Beth Wright waved from the open plan kitchen. 'Just getting the kettle on and making a few bacon sandwiches.'

Disappointment hit her. She'd been willing them to be here. For everything to be alright. 'No sign?' It was obvious that Maisie wasn't there, that Charlie hadn't returned, but she asked the question anyway.

'No love, but I'm sure these will be welcome when they get back. Poor little nipper, she'll not have got far on those little legs though. I remember being told about my Ed doing exactly the same when he wasn't much older, ran up the fields he did because he thought he'd got foot and mouth and would be shot.' She shook her head. 'It was chicken pox, the silly fool, but you don't always know what goes on in a child's head do you?' She tapped the side of her head to demonstrate.

'Very true.' Lucy sighed, and sank down onto one of the kitchen chairs. 'Charlie blames himself.' She'd hoped against hope that she'd find Maisie wandering along the footpath, but there had been no sign – no little footprints, so she was sure she hadn't been that way. Now she felt surprisingly deflated.

'Ah, but we do, don't we love? All that parental guilt, can't do right for doing wrong can we? Right, get your coat off love and give me a hand, there's enough of them heading out in the fields at the moment and we can join them if she doesn't turn up in the next hour.

Though it might be worth you checking under the beds, you know what a man-look is like? Sometimes they can't see what's in plain view.'

Lucy was glad of the friendly chatter, which held a lot of common-sense. 'I'll go and check, just in case.' She headed upstairs, sure that Charlie had checked everywhere, but more than happy to double check. She was on her hands and knees peering under the bed for the second time when her mobile phone rang.

'Charlie? You've got her?'

'No.' The worry echoed in that single word. 'Not exactly, but I think Jim might have found her. I'm in the bottom field, but he went off on his own. I just got a very strange text from him, I'll forward it to you, see what you can make of it.'

*Stuk in a dich, in to aker feeld by pit nead help*

Lucy frowned at the message and felt the first glimmer of hope since the distraught Charlie had arrived to break the bad news.

'Beth?' She scrambled down the stairs into the kitchen. 'Does the two acre field near the pit mean anything to you?'

'Course it does, lovey.' A broad grin spread across Beth's round face. 'Ah, now that does make sense now you mention it. Hang on let me wipe my hands and I'll give Ed a ring and get him over there, I'm not sure where he is at the moment but I'm sure he can find

Charlie and take him.'

'It sounds like Jim or Maisie has had an accident, I reckon Jim got Maisie to send this text because he's, well I think it means stuck in a ditch?'

'He's not, is he? Silly old bugger. Hang on, love, let me ring my Ed.'

'I'll let Charlie know.' She tapped out his number, and he picked up immediately. 'Beth knows where they are, she's calling Ed, have you seen him?'

'Other side of this field I think, we split up, so we could check out the copse and the ditches.'

'Get over to him, but I think he'll call you once Beth has passed the message on. I'll wait here Charlie, oh God I hope they're okay. I'll ring off so he can get hold of you.' She sat down, her legs suddenly wobbly. Piper sat on her feet and looked up. 'She's okay, she's going to be okay.' She fondled the dog's ears.

'Here you are love, nice mug of sweet, warm tea. Our Ed is on the way over there, and he's already picked Charlie up on the quad bike.'

Lucy gazed out of the window. She wanted to be at Charlie's side, she wanted to be holding his hand so he knew he wasn't alone in this. She wanted him to know that Maisie was already a big part of her own life, that whatever Josie said or did, that would never be taken away.

She blinked away the threatening tears. She knew

Maisie didn't need a mother, she had Josie. But the emptiness in her stomach, the fear that was churning inside was telling her something that she'd been trying to ignore. It wasn't just Charlie that she loved; she cared for Maisie far, far more than she'd admitted to herself.

She'd told her mother that they weren't a family, that her and Charlie couldn't even be a proper couple at the moment, that it wasn't like that. And what was it her mum had said back? *'Tell the world whatever you want, but inside you know exactly what you are.'* She hadn't known, or hadn't been ready to acknowledge it. Until now.

Maisie had to come back, she *had* to be safe.

'They'll find her, love.' Beth patted her hand and sat down beside her as she wiped a tear from her cheek with the back of her hand. 'Never underestimate old Jim.'

Lucy sniffed. She had to pull herself together, for Charlie's sake. What good would she be – sitting here wailing? She nodded. 'That message had to have been sent by Maisie,' it had, there was no doubt in her mind about that, 'so she must be okay. They both must be, because Jim would have told her what to write, and it was his phone that the message came from.'

'She must be fine, love. She must. Oh now, would you look at that, Ed's ringing again.' Beth bustled away to answer the phone, and Lucy was itching to follow her. Desperate to find out what was going on. 'Ed says they're safe and sound. Your Charlie is making his way back with Maisie, but he says they've had to ring for an ambulance.' She shook her head. 'Sounds like old Jim's done some damage. They tried to get him on the quad bike, but the poor man was in too much pain so they've rung for help.' She was on the move again. 'You stay where you are love, I'll ask our Helen to keep an eye out for the medics and point them in the right direction when they get here.' She bustled out of the house in search of her daughter, and Lucy let out a sigh, her whole body trembling with it as shock and relief hit with equal measure.

Maisie was okay. They were all going to be okay. Apart from of course poor Jim.

Lucy was sure she could hear excited barks. At first she convinced herself she was hearing things, but then she was sure. Positive. And Piper confirmed it, she sat bolt upright, her ears pricked, her tail doing a very slow wag, whooshing over the floor.

It felt like she'd been sat here waiting in the kitchen for a lifetime. Her and Beth had both jumped up when they saw the blue flashing lights of the ambulance, and they'd rushed out to make sure that Helen had given clear instructions to the cheery crew. Then they'd despondently gone back into the warmth, not sure how much longer they had to wait.

Lucy dived for the door as the noise got louder, and was unmistakeable. It had to be Roo, which meant one thing.

Charlie was striding across the yard, and Lucy ran across to meet them.

'Where's Roo?' Lucy looked at Maisie, who was wrapped in a large blanket, her small hands clutching Charlie's shirt, and she couldn't help but smile.

Her auburn hair was wet, clinging in ringlets to her pale face, her features cold and pinched, tears streaming down her face. 'I want Roo, and he got lost.'

'Oh, Maisie.' Lucy was laughing through her own tears as she wrapped her arms round both of them, then pulled back, not wanting to frighten Maisie with a rush of too much emotion. 'Roo's fine. Look,' her voice was uneven, and she swallowed hard. She had to sound normal, for Maisie's sake. 'He's run inside, which is where we should all be. There's a big fire, and we can even make hot chocolate if you like?'

'With marshmallows?'

'With marshmallows.'

'Roo's not going to get lost again?'

'He wasn't lost. He came here, home, to tell us where you were.' Charlie rolled his eyes as Lucy said the words. Okay, she was stretching the truth a little bit. Roo had been no use at all in showing them the way, but he had at least headed home and put them, well Jim, on the right track.

'How's Jim?'

'They should be on their way back with him soon.'

'Ahh, there you are. Get inside, inside quick, you'll all catch your death of cold.' Beth herded them in, then deftly caught Roo as he made a dash towards the open door, and lifted him up. 'Now look at this little horror, he's all cold and dirty isn't he, a right mucky pup. How about Ted and his sister giving him a bath for you? How's that?' Maisie nodded. 'Then you can have him back when he's all sorted.' She tucked the wriggling dog firmly under her arm. 'I'll be off and get him sorted, and give you some time on your own. He'll be back in a jiff.' She glanced from Charlie to Lucy. 'If there's anything you need, just give us a shout. I've thrown some more wood in the stove, and there's more butties over there if you're hungry.'

'Thanks, Beth, you've been amazing.' Lucy gave her a hug.

'Oh stop that with your nonsense, just being neighbourly. Right, I'll be off and get the kids to clean up this pup for you.'

Tiredness hit Lucy as she closed the door quietly behind Beth. She sank down on the sofa next to the warm bulk of Charlie, and Maisie stirred.

'Roo was keeping me warm, we cuddled by the tree,

then he got scared when a big bird made a horrible noise,' Maisie made a squawk noise, 'and he wriggled away.' Tears brimmed up in her eyes again as she gazed up at Lucy. 'I couldn't find him.'

'Well he's home safe now, and so are you.'

Maisie nodded and put her thumb in her mouth, her eyes half closing as she relaxed against her dad's warm body. 'I showed Roo the tree, I went to see Jim's tree, got to show Lucy the big tree ...' Her voice drifted. 'Jim came, where's Jim? Jim's hurt his leg and I had to do his phone cos his fingers are too big.' She rubbed her eyes, then yawned and snuggled in closer. 'Jim's my friend.' She sighed. 'Jim said I belong here now my name's on the tree.'

Lucy looked at the exhausted little girl, and a shattered Charlie, who was hugging his daughter tightly in his arms as though he was never going to let go.

'Is Jim okay?'

Charlie wiped his palm over his face, and tried to shake off the fatigue. 'We managed to get him out of the ditch, but there was no way he was coming back on the quad bike. He was in agony every time he moved. I think he's got a dislocated knee and God knows what else he's damaged. I was going to try and pop it back in, but he was in such agony the last thing I wanted to do was cause him more pain. I passed the medics on my way back with Maisie, they'll strap it up, give him some painkillers and get him over to the hospital.'

'At least the ambulance got here quickly.'

Charlie nodded. 'And we managed to get him out of that ditch. The cold and damp wasn't doing him much good, he's not as young as he likes to think he is. Good job he knew where to look though.' He brushed Maisie's hair back from her face, and gazed down at the sleepy child. 'He said she was curled up next to the tree, still cuddling Roo's tug toy when he found her.'

'Jim's tree?'

'Well it isn't exactly Jim's tree.' He gave a tired smile. 'I think most people who grew up in this place think it's theirs. I've not been down there for years, but it used to be one of my favourite haunts when I was a kid. Why didn't I think of it?'

'You've taken Maisie down before?'

'No.' A frown creased his brow. 'No, I haven't actually. I didn't even know she'd been. Jim took her off for a walk more than once over the summer though.'

'He's a good man.' Lucy had always thought that was a bit of a glib, meaningless comment, but she realised now what it really meant. Jim was a good man. He was one of those people who always seemed to be there when you needed him, but gone before you really had a chance to say thank you. 'Do you think he's lonely without Annie?' Lucy knew that Jim and his sister were close, they had steady teasing banter that you only heard between people who loved each other.

'I'm sure he misses her, but he's always looked out for people.'

'I hope he's okay.' Lucy looked down at their hands, which had somehow found each other. 'I better get back and lock the hens up for the night, and feed the rest of the animals.'

'You'll come back?'

She stared into his deep brown eyes for a moment, then smiled. 'I'll come back.' She nodded. 'I won't be long, but I better pop in and let Elsie know as well, she'll be worried. I did text round and let everybody know as soon as we knew Maisie was safe, and I rang Elsie, but I'm sure she'll be happier hearing the full details. She sounded,' she paused, 'worried.' Her voice had wavered, and when Lucy had put the phone down she'd felt uneasy. Elsie had sounded old, almost panicked in the way she'd insisted on Lucy repeating the information, assuring her that everybody was safe.

'Leave Piper here if you like, and take Jim's Landrover.'

'Jim's?'

'Well he won't be in any state to drive it. You could drop it off at Elsie's where it's handy, and then you can drive back here in your own car. It'll save you a walk, Luce, you look knackered.'

'But ...'

'I'll walk round from the surgery in the morning and

shift it onto his drive.'

There was a flash of lights, and Lucy walked over to the window. 'They're just loading Jim in, on a stretcher.'

'Do you mind having Maisie for a mo? I'd like to see him.'

She nodded, and took Charlie's place on the sofa, gathering Maisie up into her arms as he headed outside.

'You'll never believe who has just turned up.' Charlie was back within a few minutes, and didn't give her time to reply. 'Timothy Parry!'

'Really?' Who was the last person Lucy would have guessed. 'What's Tim doing here?'

'He's going to follow the ambulance over in his car, I was a bit worried that nobody would go with Jim, but Beth is already in the ambulance with him holding his hand, and Timothy was not to be deterred.' He grinned. The first proper grin she'd seen on his face all day. 'No doubt he's been ordered to give Elsie a full report, you know what that pair are like. Thick as thieves. Here,' he reached down and scooped Maisie out of her arms. For a moment they were almost nose to nose and Lucy reached up impulsively and kissed him. 'I'll put her to bed.' His voice had a gruff edge to it. 'You get back home and do what you have to, it's getting dark.'

Lucy was surprised to see just how much the light had

faded when she got outside. She glanced at her watch, she'd completely lost track of time.

The yard was deserted. Strangely silent now that the ambulance had left, now everybody had gone home. An eerie glow from the dairy, where no doubt Ed was still milking, lifted the gloom, and the farmhouse looked bright and welcoming. It felt peaceful rather than intimidating as she walked across to where the cars were parked, a wave of tiredness creeping over her. She'd been running on adrenalin for the past few hours, and now that had gone she felt weirdly empty, worn-out.

It was only late afternoon but the air was still, and the sky clear. It was going to be a cold night, with a definite threat of an early morning frost. A little shiver ran down her arms, they'd been so lucky that Jim had been around, that he'd instinctively known where Maisie was. Without him things might have ended quite differently. It was such bad luck that he'd injured himself, why did bad things happen when people were doing their best to be good?

Climbing into Jim's Landrover she made her way carefully down the potholed driveway, then headed down the lane towards her home. The cobbled square was quiet, the cottages with their curtains drawn against the winter evening, with only slips of light breaking through, showering the square with uneven shards of light. From several of the chimneys there were wisps of smoke that teased at her nostrils as she opened the door.

The windows of Elsie's house were spilling light onto her large garden, and Lucy was sure the old lady had been keeping an eye out for her arrival. She'd decided to pop in here first, check Elsie was okay and set her mind at rest before sorting her animals out, grabbing an overnight bag, and making her way back to the farm.

The door opened the moment she reached it, and Elsie ushered her in.

'In you come child, you look freezing.'

'It is a bit cold, it looks like we could have a good overnight frost.' She wasn't looking forward to slip-sliding her way into school tomorrow, or for the walk to the church that they'd planned with all the children. Hopefully by the afternoon the weather would have warmed up.

Molly didn't stir from her spot on the rug in front of the blazing fire.

'A tot to warm you up?'

'Sorry?'

'Whisky dear, my father always swore by it. Settles the nerves and warms the stomach.'

Lucy laughed. 'I've got to drive back to Charlie's, I promised to make him some supper. I'm not sure I'll be capable of either if I start drinking whisky on an empty stomach.'

'Well I'm sure you've got time to pop the kettle on and make us a cup of tea, you know where to find everything, don't you?'

Lucy nodded, and tried to check the time without it being too obvious. It was unusual for Elsie to delegate the tea-making duties, and she realised why when she carried the tray through to the front room, there was a definite tremble in the old lady's hands.

'So, Maisie has been found safe and sound?' She launched straight into the matter, before Lucy had even poured.

'She has, she's cold and tired, but apart from that she seems fine.'

'Children are surprisingly resilient, we worry too much. She was down by the oak tree, Timothy tells me?'

'She was. I've never been there, but from what she's said I think Jim took her in the summer.'

'That tree is quite a magnet, a strange place for the child to go though.'

'I think,' Lucy paused, she'd not quite got it all straight in her head yet but she had her suspicions about why Maisie had headed there. 'She'd got upset and felt that nobody wanted her.' Elsie raised an eyebrow. 'Me and Charlie had thought it best to keep a bit of a distance, because it was winding Josie up, Maisie chattering about what we were all doing together. It would have been totally wrong to tell Maisie not to tag *Lucy said* on the end of her sentences,' the last thing she wanted was to ask the little girl to cover things up, 'so it seemed sensible for us just to spend less time together.'

'But that caused a new problem of its own?'

'It did.' Lucy sighed. 'It was well intentioned, but we never really thought about how Maisie would see it.' Which was so stupid of her. She knew what it was like to lose somebody, she knew she'd felt abandoned and not good enough when she'd thought her dad and her friends didn't want to talk to her any more. How could she have got this so wrong? A pain in her chest grew as the truth hit her. She should have known. 'She thinks her mum has abandoned her, and now I have too, on top of that Charlie's been so busy, so—'

'She felt that nobody wanted her?'

'Yes.' She nodded. 'I should have known how she'd feel, oh Elsie.' Her hand trembled and she put her cup of tea down.

'No.' Elsie shook her head decisively. 'Now look at me Lucy. Your situation was quite different. That little girl hardly knows you, you're her teacher and a friend of her father. I'm not going to insult your intelligence and say that your absence played no part, not seeing you could well have been the straw that broke this particular camel's back, but what you did was perfectly reasonable. It's her mother at fault here, and I'm not going to pretend any different.' She tapped her stick on the floor. 'Charles has done his absolute best, but that woman has thrown nothing but obstacles in the way.' Her eyes narrowed. 'Your mother had no choice but to leave your father and sever all contact, the only regret is that she left it so long to explain to you.' Her voice wavered. 'But leaving things is often what we do to protect ourselves.' There was silence for a moment, as though Elsie needed to gather her thoughts, then she seemed to pull herself back into the present and frowned at Lucy. 'But why did she go down there?'

'Jim had told her she was part of the village when she scratched her name on the tree.' The full significance of it finally dawned on Lucy, and her words slowed. 'That it meant she belonged here. It offered her security I suppose.'

'You and Charles make her feel secure, Lucy.' Elsie's voice was soft. 'But sometimes when we're upset or angry, even if we're only little, then we need a little bit more.'

'Jim understood, even if we didn't.'

'Jim is a smart man.' Elsie picked her cup up in hands that trembled slightly. 'He understands about belonging to a place. Is he injured badly? I could get no sense out of Timothy, sometimes all that man does is waffle.'

Lucy knew her eyes had opened wide in surprise. Elsie and Timothy were very close, and she'd never heard either of them criticise the other. Although Elsie, who was a master at disguising her feelings normally, did seem quite shaken, and maybe this showed just how upset she really was. 'To be honest I haven't seen him myself, but Charlie said he'd wrenched his knee quite badly. I think he dislocated it.' She gave a little shudder. 'Which sounds painful.'

'But he has gone to hospital now?'

'Yes, the ambulance left just before I came back. Charlie had a word as they loaded him in, and he said he's had painkillers and seemed comfortable.' Lucy reached out and laid her hand over the older woman's. 'I'm sure he'll be fine, Charlie would have said something otherwise. And Beth Wright insisted on going in the ambulance with him, and Timothy was following in his car.'

'Good. I'm sure he will update me.' Elsie's shoulders seemed to relax.

'I'm sure he will. Jim was so fantastic though, if it hadn't been for him we might never have found her. He's a hero.'

Elsie suddenly smiled, the beam reaching her eyes so that some of her old spirit returned. 'How nice, a hero. I suppose he is, he'll be very pleased to hear that.' She put her cup down, her hand steadier. 'Well, with all this excitement I feel quite weary. Thank you for popping in dear and updating me, one does worry these days when one can't get out. Now, I suppose you need to get off.'

Lucy smiled. She'd been dismissed. But as she walked to the door and let herself out she had the distinct impression that Elsie had been much more interested in Jim's welfare than Maisie's.

Roo and Piper were curled up together on the rug by the log-burner when Lucy got back to the farm. They looked cosy, happy together. Like maybe she and Charlie could be one day.

Piper flapped her tail in a welcome gesture.

'Is Maisie okay?' She kept her voice low as she pushed the door closed quietly.

'She's tucked up in my bed, she was worn out.' He patted the seat next to him. 'None the worse for wear though, unlike me.' The smile was strained, but he looked much more relaxed than he had when she'd left a short while ago. 'I feel like I've been steamrollered.'

'Me too.' They shared a smile, and there was no need to add any words of explanation. They were both shattered, the worry and emotional turmoil taking far more out of them than anything physical would have done. 'Sorry I was so long.'

'No problem, it gave me time to settle her. Animals okay?'

'They're good, all fed, watered and locked up. Although Mischief wasn't too keen about being locked up in his shelter, that pony can be so stubborn at times. Good job I've got the measure of him now, a handful of carrots and he soon forgot his principles!' Luckily after a few months of looking after Annie's animals she knew most of their quirks and could whizz through the tasks in half the time it used to take her. 'It wasn't them that took the time, Elsie wanted to chat. She seemed quite worked up and worried which isn't like her at all, but I think she was fine once I updated her.'

She sat down, glanced his way under her eyelashes and he was studying her. Then he moved in closer, draped an arm over her shoulders.

'Good. I missed you.'

'Missed you too.' And she knew that they weren't just talking about her brief trip back to the cottage.

'We've got to sort this Lucy, haven't we?'

'We have.'

'Josie is going to have to accept my life as it is, Maisie's here with me and I can't just live life on her terms.'

'She's agreed to talk to Timothy you know.'

'I didn't.'

'He emailed her the other day, threatened to call in the heavy squad as he was concerned about Maisie's welfare. She's calling next week, so that might help. He wants me to sit in, on the off chance she'll talk to me. She has to realise as Maisie's teacher I'm part of her life.'

'She has to realise you're more than just her teacher.' He kissed the top of her head and a little shiver ran down her spine.

'We'll get there.' She hesitated. 'Look, the thing with Jamie ...'

'You don't need to tell me, I trust you.'

'I want to tell you, but we've just not seemed to have a moment on our own when nobody's been listening. I took Piper to Sal's puppy party, then at the end she was busy tidying up, so Jamie and me sneaked off for a chat.' Charlie raised an eyebrow. 'Jamie and Matt are planning a surprise for Sally, seeing as she missed out on a proper wedding. I mean Jamie knows she didn't want the full works here, but he also knows she likes a bit of a party and he reckons she's a tiny bit sad she missed out on having a proper wedding.' She smiled. 'He's madly in love, he'd do anything for her. So ...' And she told him all about the plan, and about Matt roping Jill in to help, and about how she really thought it was time Matt and Jill actually went on a date.

'You're a right matchmaker aren't you?' Charlie chuckled and pulled her in closer to his warm body. 'Worse than Elsie.'

'I've got a feeling about Elsie.'

'A feeling in your waters as my mother used to say?' He was grinning when she looked up, lovely crinkles fanning out from his warm brown eyes.

'A feeling in my ditch waters. I think she's going to admit what her guilty secret is soon.'

'And what makes you say that?'

She tapped the side of her nose, thinking of Jim as she did. 'It was something I saw in her eyes earlier, I've never seen her look like that.'

'Like what?'

'Maternal.'

# Chapter 19

'My mam says that if you bend my halo there'll be hell to pay.'

Lucy stifled the smile, and stared at the font, wondering if it was really such a bright idea to do the school nativity play in the church. But it was, as Timothy had told her, tradition. And Langtry Meadows held a great store in tradition.

It had seemed appropriate to hold the dress rehearsal in here, and try and put the children in the right frame of mind for the real thing, which was approaching far too quickly. But the children weren't the biggest of her worries. What really bothered her was the idea of having real live animals next to the crib. They'd settled for a baby Jesus made out of rubber and plastic, why couldn't the cow be?

Next time they were here there would be chickens, a cow and a donkey. Or a fat pony pretending to be a donkey. And the risk of wind, or something much, much worse that the church floor might never recover from.

'Daisy, will you stop swinging baby Jesus by his foot please.' Jill's voice echoed around them.

'It's not a Jesus, it's a she.' Daisy, dangling the doll by a chubby ankle, held it up as high as she could. 'Look, it's got pink knickers.'

'My mam says if God was a woman there'd be a lot more common-sense.' Sophie shook her head, and her halo rocketed from side to side as if it was on a spring. 'What's common-sense?'

'Thank you, Sophie.'

'It's a she cos it's my baby sister's and she calls it Elsa,' Daisy continued as though she'd never been interrupted, and pulled at the pink knickers in indignation.

'Well Elsa is going to pretend to be Jesus, just as you're going to pretend to be a king, Daisy.'

Daisy, looking very unregal in a costume made out of what looked like an old shower curtain (the loops gave it away), adjusted her cardboard crown and rustled her way closer to Sophie. 'Why do we all have to pretend to be boys? Kings are boys, shepherds are boys, Jesus is a boy.' She drew a breath, running out of examples. 'I want to be a queen, or a princess.'

'I'm a sheep. Sheeps are girls.' Billy who'd been quiet up until that point folded his arms. 'And I want a wee.' He scratched his bottom, and Lucy started to wonder if a cow might be less trouble after all.

'You went before we set off Billy, so I know you can wait until we get back. Right,' Lucy clapped her hands, 'let's all stand in our places so that I can have a look at these beautiful costumes.'

Harry eyed Daisy up suspiciously as she lobbed the baby back into the crate that they'd brought with them as a makeshift crib.

'Ah, here are the other children.' Lucy let out a sigh of relief as the church doors opened and the older children filed in, led by Mrs Potts who was brandishing a clipboard.

'Hallelujah, Jesus is saved,' whispered Jill in her ear, as the older Mary and Joseph took their positions and Mary carefully turned the baby over, straightened it's skirt so that the pink knickers were no longer on view, and tucked a blanket round it.

Daisy glared, lunged forward and made a grab for the doll. 'Amy said I'm the only one that can touch her Elsa.'

The Hargreave twins swapped places, Timothy wandered in smoking a pipe, and Lucy wondered if a braying donkey might actually be a godsend.

With the younger children intimidated by the presence of the headmaster and the older pupils, the rehearsal went much more smoothly than Jill and Lucy had expected. If you could ignore the king's very noisy costume that crinkled alarmingly every time Daisy moved (which was quite often), Joe knocking over the biggest pile of hymn books Lucy had ever seen, and Sophie the very un-angelic angel seeing if her halo would make a noise if she bobbed her head hard enough. It didn't make the whistling noise she was hoping for when she set it bouncing backwards and forwards, but it was moving so fast she nearly took the vicar's eye out, and Lucy made a mental note to stick with cardboard and foam, and to ban metal coat hangers next year.

The best bit about the afternoon though had to be that by the time they got back to school, took the costumes off and sat down, it was nearly home time.

'What's an acre?' Some of the children had already spotted their parents and run off across the playground, and Maisie was next in line. She slipped her hand into Lucy's and smiled up at her. 'Jim said we were in the two acre field.'

'An acre is a way to describe the size of a field.' It was the first time Maisie had mentioned her little adventure. 'But I think that's the name of the field as well. Is it a nice field?'

'I suppose so.' Maisie frowned in concentration. 'It's big and it's got a pond, and it goes up and down a lot. But it's cold and muddy. I've been there before. Jim took me and Roo. It's got a very, very big tree, Daddy has put his name on the tree.'

'Has he?'

'And Jim has, and Sally. Everybody has. Even I have. I wanted to take you and show you but Daddy wouldn't let me see you except at school. Don't you want to see me?' Maisie's grip on her hand tightened slightly.

'Of course I want to see you, Maisie. It's just a little bit difficult sometimes, but I'd love to see your tree some time.'

'You have to put L for Lucy and J for Jacobs.'

'I will do.'

'There's a big hole as well, that's what Jim fell in and he said a rude word.'

'Ah. I think that's because he really hurt his leg.'

'You shouldn't really say rude words even if you're hurt, should you?'

'Not really.'

'He said bloody, and hells bells.' Lucy tried not to smile. 'He got stuck and very muddy. He had cake as well.'

'Cake?'

'The first time he took me. He didn't have cake this time because it's winter, and you don't have picnics in winter. But he had a big coat he gave me. He said Roo hadn't run *away*, he'd run to get help.'

'He did, he was very clever, and Jim knew exactly

where you'd gone.'

'I went to see the tree. Daddy's by the gate, can I go?'

'You can. See you tomorrow, oh and Maisie?' Maisie glanced up. 'Tell him I like your costume.'

She grinned. 'It's a stripy tea-towel!' Then giggling, she turned and ran, flinging herself at her father's legs with a force that sent him staggering back.

'Maisie seems a lot more settled now.' Jill was straightening up the chairs when Lucy went back into the classroom.

'She is, a lot of that was down to Jim though I think.' Lucy grinned. 'He's very fatherly isn't he?'

'He is.' Jill smiled back. 'Though talking about fatherly, he's always our Father Christmas; it looks like we'll have to find another one this year.'

'Oh hell, I hadn't thought about that! I've been too busy worrying about the cow.'

Jill chuckled. 'Matt picked out a lovely quiet one, slobbery but sweet.'

'Slobbery sounds fun.' Lucy pulled a face and tried not to think too much about drooling. 'Then there's the donkey.'

'He had a brainwave on that as well, fingers crossed his friend at the sanctuary has got a very old one that isn't at all grumpy.'

'I'm crossing everything, living in the country is one

thing, but taking it into a church seems a step too far.'

'Oh stop being a city-girl wimp.' Jill laughed. 'Where's your sense of adventure? What's the worst that could happen?'

'Oh God, don't get me thinking about the worst. I have nightmares about cow poo and what will happen if Sophie Smith skids her way through it. Gawd knows what her mam will have to say about that.'

Jill grinned. 'But you have to admit, a donkey making more of a racket than Sophie bellowing out her version of *Silent Night* might be quite a good thing.'

'True. I've never heard it sung quite like that before, I'm pretty sure the vicar hadn't either.'

'Anyway, you should be more worried about Timothy hitting the mulled wine, just before he introduces posh George.'

'Now that might be worth seeing, and I won't care. As soon as the kids finish their bit, I'll be joining him.'

'You do know that Matt's been known to add an ingredient or two of his own?' Jill's eyes were twinkling.

'Believe me, I won't care. Elsie did mention it, she also said she thinks we should prime the vicar so he can start ringing the church bells if George's speech gets out of hand.'

'Or him and Timothy start fisticuffs.'

'Don't!' Lucy frowned. 'You don't mean that?'

'Oh chill! Honestly, it will be fine and the chaos adds

to the fun. It gives everybody something to talk about for months afterwards.'

Lucy had to admit, Langtry Meadows always seemed to surprise her, so maybe this would be the best Christmas celebration she'd ever been part of. 'Oh heck, I didn't realise it was that late. I need to get a move on or I'll miss visiting hours at the hospital. I can find out if Jim'll be fit to play Santa, though from what Timothy said he'll be strapped up, then be on crutches for a bit.'

'Oh don't worry, we'll soon find somebody else. I could maybe even persuade Matt?'

'Matt eh?' Lucy raised an eyebrow at the second mention of Matt in so many minutes, and Jill turned bright pink. 'He's being very helpful.'

'He is.' Jill shuffled an already tidy pile of books about. 'He's surprised me actually.' Her voice was soft. 'Under all that jokey stuff he's kind.'

'So, when are you two going to ...?'

A smile suddenly lit up Jill's face, and she looked much younger, and slightly mischievous. 'Now don't go jumping the gun, we're keeping it casual.'

'But you do like him, don't you?'

'I do, and,' she paused, 'it's nice to have a man in my life again. When I lost Mark, it was like I'd lost everything, it never even crossed my mind for a second that there would ever be anybody else. For ages it just never even occurred to me. Does that make me sound mad?'

'It makes you sound like you were in love, Jill.'

'It was like it was meant to be.' She looked down, self-conscious. 'I met him at college, and we never looked back.'

Lucy waited, hoping that Jill would say more. She'd never, ever mentioned anything about Mark before – other than that he'd died, and Lucy had a feeling she'd not really been ready to openly chat about it.

'He was gorgeous, in his heart he was the nicest man you could meet. I always wondered why he even looked twice at me.'

'Because you're gorgeous too, Jill. Inside and out.' Kind wasn't a big enough word for Jill, the children loved her, the whole village did, and Lucy had been working at the school for some time before she'd even had the slightest hint that any kind of sadness lurked behind Jill's happy smile. She'd been shocked, and felt very guilty, the day that they'd been discussing past problems, and Jill had told her that her husband had died. And then she'd brushed over it and moved on, and Lucy had let her because she'd been a stranger then – why would Jill confide in her?

'I never thought it was going to end. I mean you don't, do you? Then we found out.' She took a gulp of air.

'You don't have to ...'

'I want to. I had that outpouring of grief straight

after, but it hit me the other day when I was chatting to Matt about him, that I've not actually talked to anybody about Mark for ages. I talk to him at home, chatter when I'm doing things, like some mad woman.'

'You're not mad.'

'It doesn't feel mad, it feels natural now. But to anybody else.' She shrugged. 'You lose the habit of telling people though, they're not interested any more once the initial grief has gone. You're supposed to move on.'

'I wouldn't imagine anybody would just move on.'

'To tell the truth, Lucy, I don't want to. I don't want to forget him, but it's getting harder. I used to be able to smell him on his clothes, sheets, towels, and it's all fading. When I look at his photo I can still imagine him laughing, but I can't hear him quite the same, he doesn't talk to me like he did.'

'Maybe he's helping you move on, maybe he knows you're ready.'

'Maybe.' She sighed. 'For ages after I really wasn't bothered at all about dating, then I felt a bit guilty for even thinking about it.' She shrugged. 'But you could be right, it feels okay now. Mark would think it was funny, he always said Matt had hidden depths.'

'Sally said much the same to me.'

'Mark was always trying to matchmake for me, after we found out he was ill. He made a game of it, joking about what kind of guy I needed. Who'd live up to his high standards.' She blinked. 'I think he told Matt to look after me, he said he was solid, he wouldn't let me down. Maybe he knew something I didn't.'

'Mark sounds a smart guy.'

'He was.'

'Sally reckoned Matt just needed to meet the right person.'

Jill laughed self-consciously. 'Well I don't know about that.' I think I do, Lucy thought, but didn't dare say it. 'Who'd have thought my first date would be with a flirt like Matt Harwood?'

'He's fun, and actually *I'd* have thought it. He has been after you for so long, lurking by the school gate. Anywhere else he'd have been arrested! And he got me in trouble with Charlie, who was convinced that he was hanging round me, not you.'

'You're kidding?'

'Oh you know what he's like, all huggy and easy going. Charlie just took it the wrong way. He even took it the wrong way when he caught Jamie at my place the other week, what does he think I am?' Lucy laughed. Charlie really had jumped to the wrong conclusion about her and Matt, but that was a long time ago. Before they really knew each other. Now she was sure he trusted her, they trusted each other.

'He has been rather stressed out, he's not normally

like that. In fact I've never seen him jealous. I reckon,'
Jill grinned, 'it's because you're so important to him.
He's scared.'

'Scared? I'm not scary!'

'Of losing you, you noddle. I mean put yourself in
his shoes, he thought he'd lost Maisie and she means
the world to him.'

'He still could.' Lucy suddenly felt gloomy.

'He could, but there's a good chance he won't. Isn't
there?'

'I hope so.' Frustration gnawed away inside Lucy. It
was a waiting game, and she kept feeling on the verge
of losing her nerve, of having to storm in and ask Josie
what she was playing at. But it wasn't her battle. She'd
only make things worse. Charlie was doing everything
his solicitor Malcolm advised, being fair, being open,
not allowing himself to be drawn into any arguments
or agreements that could influence a court. 'Josie has
gone very quiet since Maisie ran away, and I'm half
expecting everything to turn nasty at Christmas. She's
coming home, which is nice for Maisie.' But could be
horrible for her and Charlie.

'Lucy, I'm not going to say it'll work out fine because
we don't know. Everybody said it would be fine for
Mark at first, but we knew there were no guarantees.
You've just got to make the most of every day, and hope
that you get another one. One day at a time.'

'I know.' Lucy hugged her. 'Oh Jill, I'm so pleased for you and Matt.'

'I might just be another notch ...'

'Rubbish. He wouldn't do that to you. To Mark.'

'Go away Lucy Jacobs before I get all maudlin. Go on. Shoo. Give Jim my love, he's a star.'

'I will.' Lucy grinned, and picked up her bag.

'Here, don't forget the card Maisie did for him.' Jill picked up the still-damp painting, which showed a very big tree, a diminutive stick figure with one foot in what looked like a very big plaster cast stuck out at right angles (which Lucy decided had to be Jim), and a dog that was floating mid-air. 'I think you need to read it.' She tipped her head on one side and smiled, so Lucy took the sticky card and carefully peeled it open.

'*Deer jim. Thank yoo. I howp yur leg is beter soon and we can tayk Lucy to the tree so she can beelong heer to. From Maisie and Roo x*'

Tears sprung to her eyes, and as she blinked them away the lump in her throat was a physical pain. They had to find a way of all belonging here.

# Chapter 20

Jim looked quite out of place lying on the crisp white sheets in the sterile environment of the hospital. He was however surrounded by cards, and had the biggest bunch of grapes Lucy had ever seen.

'Well now, if it isn't my favourite teacher.' He patted the chair at the side of the bed. 'Come and sit down, love and fill me in on what I've missed.'

'You're the biggest story of the village, Jim.' Lucy leant forward impulsively and kissed him on the cheek, before sitting down. 'You deserve a medal.'

'Nonsense.' His voice was gruff and he coloured-up with pleasure. 'So how's the little 'un?'

'She sent this.' Lucy grinned, holding the card by a corner. 'It's still a bit damp I'm afraid.'

Jim took the paper, oblivious to the smears of paint he was daubing the pristine sheet with, and guffawed at the picture, then blinked when he read the words inside. 'Little treasure.' His voice was gruff as he pointed to the tray at the foot of his bed. 'Prop it up on there, love then I can see it. Okay then is she?'

'She's fine, and that's all down to you. She had a good night's sleep and was back at school today none the worse for her big adventure.'

'Nothing wrong with running away, I've done it more than once myself.'

Lucy didn't like to say that times had changed, and when a child disappeared for as little as an hour then it caused palpitations – even in a lovely village like Langtry Meadows.

'How on earth did you know where she was? We'd looked everywhere.'

'Well,' he stroked his beard and grinned knowingly so that she could see his chipped tooth. 'Soon as that pup came back all muddy, I had a feeling,' he tapped the side of his nose, 'that they could have been down by the fishing pit. Spent many a day down there as a lad I did, draws kids like a magnet.'

'I'm surprised she found it, she said you took her down over the summer?'

'Aye well, that was my fault. Took the little 'un down there one day I did.'

'Fishing?' Lucy tried to temper the incredulous tone in her voice. 'She wasn't at all keen when we had a pond-dipping session at school a few weeks ago.'

'No.' Jim shook his head. 'The pond is what a lot of

them like, but it's not that she was interested in, it was the tree.'

'She did mention something about a tree, on the way out of school.'

'Very taken with it she was.' Jim shuffled about, pulling himself up on the pillows, and made himself more comfortable. 'It's a big old oak tree there, like on that picture she's painted. Been there forever it has. If you want to find out who's lived in Langtry Meadows, that tree is even better than one of Elsie's photo albums.'

This was sounding a little bit crazy, and she wondered for a moment exactly what painkillers poor Jim was on.

'I went there as a nipper, my old man took me and he helped me scratch my initials into that tree. "E'd done the same as a lad, even posh George has done it,' he chuckled, 'though he's got so many flamin' initials it's like The Lord's Prayer. Worse than one of his speeches, if you can believe that.' There was another deep chuckle, which rumbled its way through his body. 'Anyhow, I took the nipper down there in the summer, when Charlie was busy. He'd come out to look at one of Ed's cows and brought the lass and dog with him. Turned out a bigger job than he'd thought, breech calf I think, anyhow I'd come to drop a bit of cake off that Elsie had made. Does it as thank you she does, like an exchange because Ed gives her bags of muck for the roses.'

Lucy was glad she'd sat down, this was turning into quite a story. But however long it was, she was happy to listen – without Jim they might never have found Maisie. And she wanted to hear about the tree that had made such an impact on the little girl.

'No hardship for me to entertain the kiddie for a bit, she's a clever one, chatters away for Britain once she gets going, and it cheers me up it does.' He paused for breath. Lucy had never heard him say more than a couple of sentences at one time, even though he was always kind and friendly. 'Well, I showed the lass where I'd scratched my initials in, and I found Charlie's too. Quite taken with it she was, asked me where yours was and I told her you were new like she is, so hadn't been there yet. She wanted to take you down there, desperate to she was. Giggled when I showed her where Timothy Parry had done his neat little mark and where my Annie had tried to draw a goose, but it looked more like a two-legged giraffe.' He sighed. 'Bloody mistake trying to cross that ditch though.' Grimacing he put a hand on the top of his leg. 'You'd think I'd have learned.'

'You certainly would, you should know better at your age.'

They both turned at the clipped tones, and Lucy was surprised to see Elsie Harrington, dressed as immaculately as ever, her grey hair drawn back into a neat chignon, high heels on her feet despite the weather and her age, standing at the foot of the bed. 'You never grow up, you boys, do you?'

Jim chuckled. 'And you never stop telling me off, Elsie Harrington.' He winked at Lucy. 'Been doing that since I was in short trousers. Even Elsie here knows about that old oak tree though, don't you?'

'It's one of the few living things in this village that's older than me.' Her tone was dry, but there was a hint of a smile at the corner of her mouth.

Lucy smiled and pulled a chair up next to his bed for the visitor. 'He did an amazing job of finding her, nobody else had a clue.'

'It sounds like you won't be fit to clear my garden or take Molly out for a while.' Elsie looked disapproving, then her voice softened as she sat down. 'She misses you.'

'I miss her too.' Lucy was surprised how gruff Jim's tone was, he did a lot for Elsie and was obviously fonder of her than he admitted to. And the feeling was mutual from the look on Elsie's face, despite her slightly tart words. 'And how would you know about how long I'll be out of action?'

'The consultant tells me you'll be on crutches then you might need ligament surgery, which to my mind isn't a five minute job. I only asked because he was getting a coffee when I was. I suppose,' she pursed her lips, 'plenty of light exercise is what you will need afterwards, once the splint is off, so your dog walking will be ideal.'

'Ideal.' His eyes twinkled as he glanced from Elsie back to Lucy. 'Wrenched the bugger I did, twisted it, meant to jump the flaming ditch but I landed right plonk in it with one foot, and got stuck fast. I was daft enough to try and turn, and ping.' He threw up his hands, and Elsie flinched. 'I think my whole knee popped out, hurt like buggery it did. Good job the young 'un was there, though I was bothered I'd frighten her.'

'A good job *you* were there.' Elsie sounded slightly more conciliatory, but Lucy was sure this was about a lot more than her losing her odd-job man and companion, she was genuinely upset and doing her best to hide it under bluster and sharp words. The very fact that she'd made her way over to the hospital was a surprise.

'Poor lass was lost, she'd had fun with the dog in the pit, then he'd scampered off and didn't come back, hadn't a clue which way home was. And she was cold, poor mite.'

'I doubt she's ever been that far down the fields on her own.'

'Bright little thing she is, I told Charlie. Lad was beside himself he was, and was all for shouting until he saw the look on her face. I couldn't get to grips with the phone, hard enough hitting them bloody silly little letters on a good day, but I could hardly see to do it. Once I got the number up though and told her what to write she was a little gem. Spelling them words out like a trooper.'

'She is bright.' Lucy nodded. 'She's a good girl.'

'She is that, and I told Charlie not to be hard on her, even though he'd had a scare. Had quite a chat we did, me and little Maisie while we were waiting.' He gave Lucy a piercing look. 'Not much escapes her.'

'I know.'

'Can't be easy for her, all the moving. I was born in Langtry Meadows and I've never been anywhere else. Got my roots down as firmly as that flaming oak tree.' He chuckled, and shook his head. 'Poor little thing.'

'Charlie is doing his best, it's difficult.'

'I know it is.' He nodded. 'But kiddies don't understand good intentions do they?' Lucy tried not to flinch. 'They understand the things you *do*, not what you're *thinking* about doing. That's no good to them, is it? Got a bit confused she has, if you ask me. I always says it's best to keep things simple, if you know what I mean.'

'I think you're right, Jim.'

'Nothing that a few hugs won't put right.' He frowned. 'And what are you giving me that look for, Elsie Harrington?'

'I don't know what you're talking about.' Elsie sniffed.

'I think your medication must be too strong.' She tapped her stick on the floor.

Jim's eyes were twinkling, he knew Elsie far too well to be upset by her words. He winked at Lucy.

'Well she's quite attached to you she is Lucy, reckon we all need our mothers at times, and if they're not there then we need somebody to stand in.'

Elsie made a harrumph sound. 'And what would you know about that, Jim Stafford?'

'Well I know that when our mam went, our Annie stepped up to the mark she did. Made sure I was okay.'

'You were a grown man!'

'Aye, doesn't matter how old you are, now does it Elsie? We all need a hug sometimes, even you, you daft bat.'

'I'm not sure ...'

'And you're the one little Maisie wants to turn to, aren't you, Lucy?'

Lucy nodded. 'We just thought it might confuse her, and it might aggravate the situation.'

'The only one it will confuse is that mother of hers, and she needs a shake if you ask me. Right now, enough of that, what's the verdict Doc Elsie? When are they going to let me out of here? I've Christmas plans to make.'

'I'm sure they'll be only too glad to see the back of you, but from what that man said to me you won't be planning anything. You'll be home soon but that leg will be in a splint and it will be crutches for a while.' She gave a tut. 'And who ever heard of Father Christmas with crutches? Then they'll be sorting out some physiotherapy sessions.' Lucy thought Elsie sounded very well informed for somebody who'd made a casual enquiry by the coffee machine. 'I've told Timothy they'll have to manage without you this year.'

'But I always ...'

'Jill had a chat to Matt,' Lucy thought it was time to chip in, as Elsie's chin had set at a stubborn angle, and Jim was about to point an angry finger. 'He's really excited about being Father Christmas just this once. He wants to talk to you, for advice, as soon as you're home.'

Jim shook his head. 'And what am I supposed to do with myself?'

'You will be looking after the mulled wine,' Elsie said with a note of finality. 'It's about time we all made it through the evening without the bootleggers' version. You are one of the few people I'd trust in this village.'

Jim looked slightly mollified.

'If you're heading back, I could do with a lift my dear.' Elsie picked her handbag up, as though to say her job here was done.

Lucy nodded. 'Of course, Elsie. As long as you're sure you're ready to go? I can go and grab a coffee and wait a while if you want to chat to Jim for longer?'

'No, no. I think Jim is ready for a rest now, and I know you need to get back and do your marking, or whatever you teachers have to do.'

Lucy tried not to let the smile show. 'I've not got much marking at this time of year, just a few things to sort for the nativity. I was going to pick your brains actually about the best place for the crib. Matt told me one thing, and then Timothy said something quite different.'

'Splendid. We can pop into the church before I go home, and then you can see the photographs I have.'

'And you can both leave a man in peace, there's a programme on the TV I need to watch, thought you'd never go.' Jim winked to soften the blow of the words, and Elsie tutted at him, but Lucy was pretty sure that she was missing him. He was a regular visitor to Elsie's home, taking her dog Molly out and generally keeping an eye on her. They made an unlikely couple, but the more Lucy saw them together the more she saw how compatible they were. 'And don't you be forgetting to go and see Maisie's tree with her, Lucy. It was important to her that, takin' you there.'

'I will go Jim, definitely. Maybe you can take us, when you're up to it?'

'Mebbe. Though I don't think I'll be skipping across fields for a while, best you get Charlie to take you.' He peered at her. 'Soon.'

'And I,' Elsie stood up, and patted Jim on the shoulder in a rare intimate gesture, 'will be back tomorrow to talk to that consultant of yours, we can't have you lolling around here on your backside when there is so much work to be done. I'm sure they'll be ready to see the back of you by tomorrow.'

Jim gave Lucy a thumbs up behind Elsie's back, and she stifled a giggle. She was pretty sure Elsie hadn't missed a thing, but was choosing to ignore both of them.

'I need to talk to you, my dear.' Elsie slipped her hand through Lucy's arm as they reached the door of the ward, and ushered her through it.

'About the nativity? Are we doing something wrong?'

'Oh no, not about that my dear. This is a personal matter. We will talk when we get home. Right, where is your car parked?'

Much as Lucy loved the changing seasons, and the crisp clean air of winter, she had to admit that she preferred the warm hues and mellow evenings of autumn, to the dark nights and December chill. Winter was about cold mornings that were gloomy when she got up to get ready for school and afternoons when it was already dark by the time she left the village primary school.

The cold air bit into her bones as they made their way across the car park and she wrapped her arms round her body. All she wanted was to get the fire lit, and curl up in her favourite armchair with a mug of hot chocolate and bowl of pasta.

But Elsie was obviously missing Jim, and more upset about his accident than she was letting on. The least she could do was take the old lady home and stop for a short chat.

\*\*\*

'I think we will leave the church visit until tomorrow, my bones are creaking.' Elsie struggled out of the car, then made her way slowly up the garden path. 'You will stay for a quick chat?'

'Of course I will.' Lucy watched her with concern, Elsie admitting she still felt under the weather was worrying to say the least. The old lady was smiling though when Molly greeted them at the door, her tail swishing from side to side with delight.

It was Lucy who put the kettle on, and laid the tea cups and cake out on the tray, and when she went into the living room Elsie was settled in her normal chair by the roaring fire.

'None of us are getting any younger, are we?'

The words took her by surprise.

'When you are young like Maisie, you take life for granted, but the older you get the more uncertain things are. The more you try and value each day.' She lifted the tea cup, and eyed Lucy over the rim with an unwavering gaze. 'The more you realise that there are no guarantees.'

'Well no, I mean yesterday did shake us all up. Charlie was so upset, I think it's made him more determined than ever to make sure he does the right thing.'

'And it had made me more determined as well, my dear. A shock helps clarify the situation, the important things are magnified, and the little worries fade into insignificance.'

'And the important thing?'

'Is to do the right thing for my,' she hesitated over the word, 'son. If he missed out on seeing tomorrow, and I never had the opportunity to explain. Or if anything happened to me before I had a chance to explain ...' Her hand trembled. 'You do understand?'

'I do Elsie.' Lucy felt the heat of tears in her eyes. She put out a hand to cover Elsie's frail one. 'I really do.' Elsie rarely let her guard down, and it was easy to forget just how old she was sometimes.

Elsie sniffed and straightened. 'Splendid.' Her normal brisk tone resumed. 'I will resolve the issue as soon as possible, in the meantime I want to talk to you about your mother.'

'My mother?'

'She is lonely where she is.'

'She is?' Lucy blinked in surprise. That was news to her, and she'd only seen her a short time ago. She'd insisted on staying a week to make sure Lucy was okay, and to deliver soup to Elsie and keep her company until she was sure there was no risk of pneumonia. Then she'd headed back home, promising to return to watch the nativity.

'She is. That place never suited her, and her job is far too demanding.' Elsie poured more tea, and picked up a biscuit. 'You know I spoke to her after she'd visited you to see Jasmine Cottage?' She tipped her head on one side. 'She's very much like you, sensible and caring. We had quite a chat and swapped phone numbers, then of course she popped in when she came to visit you again the other week.'

'Ahh.' Lucy had been quite surprised at just how much time her mother had spent with Elsie when she'd visited last time, but she didn't know whether to be cross or pleased to discover that she'd told the old lady more than she'd told her daughter. 'She never said she wasn't happy.'

'Well why would she?' Elsie's voice had a tart edge. 'You're her daughter! She did tell you how much she liked your cottage though?'

'She did.'

'And the village? She told me you seemed happy here.' She paused. 'And settled.'

'I am, to both. The solicitors and estate agents all seem to think that the sale will go through just before Christmas.' She smiled. 'I can't wait to start work on the cottage, it feels,' she paused, 'it feels like I belong there.'

'Your mother told me she thought you'd finally found the place you belong, your home. She never did like where you were before.'

Lucy drew a sharp breath, and Elsie raised an eyebrow. 'Not that she isn't very proud with what you have achieved, but she didn't feel that it was the right place for you. More of a stepping stone.'

'Well, I'd not thought of it like that, but yes.' She'd never seen her mother quite as emotional as she'd been when she'd shown her the cottage, and it was only now, with Elsie's words that she realised why. Mum was right; she finally felt like she was where she should be. Home.

'Which I think is why it has dawned on your mother that maybe now is the right time to start thinking about herself, to question where she belongs.'

'Oh.'

'And she tells me that Langtry Meadows is very much like the place she'd dreamed of when she was younger, that she'd hoped for when you moved to Stoneyvale.' Elsie put her cup down carefully. 'I am not getting any younger, my dear, and I'm turning into rather a selfish old lady. I need a companion, someone to live in and help me, and I rather think your mother could fit that bill.'

'But she's not ...' The word 'carer' was on the tip of Lucy's tongue.

'I only need a companion.' It was as though Elsie read her mind. 'Not a nurse, I am not *that* infirm yet.' She huffed. 'And of course I have to consider Molly. With Jim out of action for a few weeks, she'll miss her strolls.'

'She will.' And, Lucy thought, Elsie would miss the companionship. Seeing Jim each day meant she always felt part of what was going on, even if she didn't get any further than the village shop.

'Your mother thought the position would suit.'

'You've talked about all this? You've sorted it all out?' Lucy couldn't believe that her mum hadn't said a word.

'I only offered her the solution yesterday. I wanted to be sure.' Elsie shook her head. 'She, of course, wanted to put you first and be sure that you'd approve. She is well aware of what a small community this is.'

'Of course I'd approve, if she wants to of course, I mean, well ...' The thought of living close to her mother again had never occurred to Lucy. Trish had her own home, her own life and was as independent as her daughter. Lucy would never have asked her to uproot herself, but both of them it seemed had been under the same misapprehension that the other would mind. 'I'd love it if she moved to Langtry Meadows.'

'Good. Well that's settled then. You may pop in on your way home from school tomorrow and I will take you to the church, dear. I'm sure you want to get off now,' she tapped her stick decisively, 'and I'm rather tired.'

'Jim will be okay Elsie.'

'Of course he will. I know that.'

'The doctor said he's very well in himself, but the torn ligaments will take time to heal.' She stood up. 'You should be proud of him, he's a real hero.'

'Of course, of course. He's a good man. You can show yourself out?' The conversation was obviously closed, and Lucy didn't want to push it.

She nodded and made her way to the door, glancing back just the once to see Elsie's eyes were closed, but her fingers were fondling Molly's ear.

'I'll go home, give Mum a call.'

There was the faintest of nods from Elsie, and the slightest satisfied lift of the corner of her mouth.

# Chapter 21

'Here, let me hold that for you, love.'

Lucy handed over the halo that she'd just removed from Sophie's head, then paused. 'Shouldn't you be helping Elsie, Mum?'

'Oh she's fine, she's with Jim. It's making her feel very useful, being able to support him, even though he keeps saying he really doesn't need any help.'

'Make way.' Elsie's strident tone rang out and Lucy glanced round. She was startled to see that while she'd been concentrating on getting the children into their positions, the church had filled up. It was crammed full, but on Elsie's orders the crowd had parted to give Jim a clear path through to the chair that she had insisted was provided for him.

Jim winked, then settled himself down with Elsie beside him. 'Aye isn't this splendid? Now I know what it's like to be a VIP.' He chuckled. 'VIP Jim, that's me!' And waved a crutch which startled the cow, which up until that point had been quite happy trying to eat Ted's hair. It took a step backwards in alarm, its big eyes wide and Jamie, who was minding it, was taken by surprise. He yelled out as it stamped on his foot before nearly pinning Timothy against a pew.

Matt laughed. 'You daft bu—' He stopped himself just in time. 'Wake up you dozy idiot, Jamie.' He had the lead rope of a very sleepy donkey in his hand. Its head was so low it was almost on the ground, and it seemed totally oblivious to what was going on around it. Which had to be a good thing. 'Should have put you in charge of hell raiser Harriet here instead.' He patted the head of the donkey, which blew through its nostrils, showering the nearest children with something that had to be in violation of normal health and safety rules.

'I'm a ghost.' Joe had spun the tea towel that was on his head round so that it covered his face, and was blowing as hard as he could trying to make it move.

'No you're not.' There was a crinkle as shower curtain clad Daisy leant forward and tugged hard, nearly pulling a handful of his hair out.

'Ouch, geroff.'

'Well that's two people who Father Christmas won't have to worry about, isn't it?' Liz Potts gave them both the eagle eye and they slunk back into position.

'It's snowing.' Billy, getting bored and upset he wasn't the centre of attention, had started to pull small white fluffy bits off his sheep costume and was busy trying to throw them up in the air. Before Lucy had a chance to say anything, his mother had shot out of the pew and cuffed him over the head.

'That's my best angora sweater that is, you do that again and you'll be the first sheep that's ever performed shorn naked.' With a warning scowl she headed back to her seat and the startled children fell silent. Until the cow passed wind.

'Thank you, thank you for all coming out on this dark night.' The vicar positioned himself centre stage, oblivious to the chicken that was burrowing its beak under his robe at the back and looked like it was about to disappear into the darkness. 'The children will perform for us in a moment, then we will convene outside for a short carol service before George does us the honour of turning on the Christmas lights. I do hope,' he peered over his spectacles, 'that you will all sing along with our wonderful youngsters.'

Lucy shot Ted a warning glance as he took a step forward, his gaze fixed on something on the floor – which was no doubt a spider or some other creepy crawly. He froze, grinned and stuck his finger up his nose.

Harriet the donkey coughed and Timothy cued them in for the start of *Silent Night*.

Sophie Smith had been told by her mother to 'sing

up'. So she did. No night had ever been less silent. Lucy was sure her bellow could have been heard from one end of the village to the other, and beyond.

The chubby little girl fixed her gaze on her mother, took a deep breath at the start of each line and gave it her all. Unfortunately, this year the donkey was not interested in braying. It wasn't even bothered when baby Jesus was accidentally lobbed out of the crib and landed a few inches from its nose.

Instead, with a weary sigh it sank to its knees, then dropped down before flaking out on its side.

'Does that animal need a vet?' Jim's voice boomed out, and he pointed with one of his crutches.

King Daisy rustled over for a closer look and a cry went up of 'Vet, vet' and 'Where the frig is Charlie when you need him?' before Charlie, who had all his attention fixed on little shepherd Maisie realised they were calling his name.

'It's not dead, it's resting its eyes.' Bellowed Matt. 'Aren't you Harriet?' He gave her a nudge with the toe of his boot and she opened one eye. So Charlie sat back down again, just as a chicken jumped onto the donkey's back and started tugging at its mane.

'It finks it's a worm.' Announced Ted. 'Why don't you get slugs in the winter? You get worms except they get stuck under the ground.'

'My cat had kittens and they looked like slugs,' Poppy

chipped in, 'they were yuk.'

Timothy tapped his conducting stick on a pew to try and restore order, and they all burst into a rendition of *Away in a Manger* with Harry bellowing out 'no crisps for a bed' at the appropriate moments.

By the time the nativity play had finished, the donkey had been coaxed back onto its feet, the chickens had been gathered up and the cow had been put in the pen outside the church, the Right Honourable George Cambourne was impatiently tapping the microphone with a pen.

There was a distinctly chilly edge to the air, and several people were glancing heavenwards as though they expected it to start snowing any moment.

Timothy elbowed George out of the way none too gently.

'No love lost there then.' There was a gentle humour in Jim's voice and Lucy smiled at him. He seemed different today, buoyed up and as happy as she'd ever seen him. Which given the fact that he was on crutches, and being relentlessly bossed around by Elsie was a bit of a surprise.

'As the weather seems to be taking a turn for the worse I think we should complete the Christmas carols, and our little prepared twelve days of Christmas dance, in the village hall.' Timothy glanced at his watch then looked pointedly at George. 'Shortly. Once the lights have been turned on. I suggest you all grab a tot of our wonderful mulled wine to warm yourselves up. Over to you George.'

George took his place back at the microphone, just as most of the crowd headed towards Jim for a top up of wine.

Like the natural politician George was, he paused until order had been restored. 'Ahem.' The crowd waited expectantly, with a few rolled eyes.

'You need to wait, George.' Elsie was not to be trifled with, and for the first time Lucy had seen, George fell silent like a schoolboy. 'Jim needs to be comfortable.'

Jim caught Lucy's eye, and she tried not to laugh. She was sure Elsie was causing disruption on purpose.

'Right,' Elsie waved a hand, 'you can start, but keep it short we all need a drink after that performance.'

George had barely started speaking when the donkey, revived by the fresh air, shook itself violently then started to bray.

'Can somebody shut—'

Nobody it seemed, least of all Matt, who had disappeared from sight, was capable of silencing the animal. Every time George started to speak, so did the donkey.

'I think I quite like that donkey.' Lucy, who had been dreading the chaos, was starting to feel quite attached to little Harriet, who after a sleepy start seemed to want to take a starring role. In fact she was feeling so fond of it she was beginning to wonder if it would like a new home, away from the rescue centre. Which wasn't a good thought at all, considering her ever expanding menagerie.

'Always said Georgie Porgie could talk the hind leg off a donkey.' Jim chuckled. 'The poor animal thinks he's one of them, ee-aww, ee-aww.' Lucy tried not to laugh at Jim's very good impression. 'Hope it doesn't keel over again.'

'Well at least we won't need the vicar to ring the bells,' muttered Elsie under her breath.

Soon it wasn't just Jim who was chuckling, and with a resigned sigh George leaned forward. 'I should have known better in this place I suppose.' He was grinning, a genuine happy grin. 'Happy Christmas Langtry Meadows, there's no place like it.' And with a flourish he pressed the switch and the Christmas tree lit up.

'Can we see Father Christmas now?' Maisie tugged at Lucy's hand, and she looked over the little girl's head to smile at Charlie. 'I'm sure you can.'

'Are you coming with us?'

The warmth in his smile sent her stomach tumbling. 'Well I think my job here is done.' She squeezed Maisie's hand. 'So why not?'

'Right, Father Christmas, then over to the village hall to hear the finale.'

'Don't you think he's rushing through them a bit?' Charlie hissed as Matt practically tossed Poppy Brownlow off his knee, promising her everything she wanted for Christmas, providing she was good, then beckoned Maisie over.

'He's frightened of being late.'

'Late?' He looked at her blankly, and she elbowed him in the ribs as Sally (dressed as a rather naughty elf) waved in their direction. 'Oh, late. Oh yes,' it finally dawned on him, '*late*.'

Several people turned to look at them. Lucy blushed and Charlie went into a bluster. 'Late, going to be late to surgery tomorrow, if, if ...'

'Shut up Charlie.' Lucy giggled. 'Whose idea was it to make her Santa's little helper?'

'Mine.' Lucy hadn't heard her mother sneak up behind them, and she whirled round. 'Do you? You, you know as well?'

Trish Jacobs nodded and grinned. 'We thought she needed to be kept busy. This mulled wine is excellent.'

'That's because it's got a bottle of brandy in it, Mum. Does everybody know?'

'More or less. Well Elsie and Jim do, and I think Elsie told Jamie to tell the vicar, then ...'

'Shh, shh she'll hear.'

Sally it seemed was too busy to overhear anything though. Matt had her running backwards and forwards, collecting gifts, swapping unwanted gifts, tidying up wrapping paper and writing lists at such a pace it made Lucy tired just watching. And in between it all, Matt managed to wink in her direction and give her a discreet thumbs up behind Maisie's back.

'Shall we, er, go to the village hall then?'

'You can't leave yet, Sal.' Matt, who must have been told to use delaying tactics to keep Sally out of the way until everybody was at the village hall was proving himself more than up to the job. 'You've got to put my costume away. Here.'

Lucy saw him peel the beard off as she ushered Maisie away.

'Matt, you're being a pain in the bum. I was asked to be a *helper*, not tidy the whole bloody square up.' It sounded like Sally had decided being Santa's little helper was not quite the fun role she'd expected.

'It's not the whole square,' he said reasonably, but even at this distance Lucy thought she detected the slightest tremble of laughter, 'we're doing that in the morning. Now stop whingeing and put the lid on the mulled wine, we're taking it with us.'

\*\*\*

'Matthew Harwood, if you tell me one more time to lift my end up I'll stran—'

Sally's words died in her throat as a big roar went up, and if Matt hadn't been prepared the mulled wine would have gone flying.

'What the ...?' She looked up in bewilderment at the massive banner stretched from one side of the village hall to the other, saying *Congratulations,* she did a double take, *on Your Wedding.* 'But ...' The whole village were there, glasses of bubbly in hand. All looking at her.

'I thought you deserved a party darling.' Jamie had made his way out of the crowd, and took both her hands in his. Looking straight into her eyes in that way she loved. 'I hope you're not cross, I mean I know you didn't want a big wedding, but,' he paused, the hint of a smile twitching at his beautiful mouth, 'maybe a good party?'

'Oh Jamie.' The tears were rushing to her eyes in a very embarrassing way, so she buried her head in his neck.

'You don't like it?'

'I love it.' She pulled away, wiped the back of her hand over her eyes then stared again. 'Everybody ...'

'Everybody is here love.' It was her dad, appearing as if by magic from the side of the room, two glasses of champagne in his hands. He handed one to Sally, and one to Jamie, before clapping Jamie on the back and nearly sending him flying.

'But ...'

'As I never got to give my darling daughter away on her wedding day, then I'm going to do it now. You don't think I'd miss out on that, do you?'

'Oh Dad.'

Sally didn't really hear much of her dad's speech. She just stared at him for a while, tears filling her eyes, then looked at her mother, who was wiping her own tears away even more frantically than Sally (but smiling the whole time), then she looked at Jamie.

'You did this for me.' It came out as a tiny whisper, but he heard.

He nodded.

'You knew ...'

'I knew you wanted to get married your way, and so that's what you did. But the whole village love you, Sal.'

'And they all love a bloody party.' Matt bashed his brother on his back. 'Right get that bubbly down your neck. We've got to listen to the school's twelve peacocks flying or whatever it is, then we can get this show on the road properly. Right,' he rubbed his hands together, 'get the kids sorted Timmy boy, and I'll start serving the beer.'

Timmy boy shot one of his terrifying headmaster stares in Matt's direction, but the effect was spoiled slightly when he blinked and took a slight stagger back. Matt's grin broadened, and before he could say anything, or anybody else could notice, Jill leapt in and gently steered the headmaster to the side of the hall.

'You sit down and enjoy it, Mr Parry, me and Lucy will sort it out. You deserve a rest after all the hard work you've put in.'

Lucy tried not to grin, and with the help of Jill did her best to gather the children together.

The Hargreave twins formed a mini chocolate-fuelled whirlwind, Poppy and Ted were cross-legged on the floor in the centre having a heated argument about slugs and newly born kittens, and Daisy decided it was the right moment to release the chicken that she'd smuggled in under her shower-curtain king costume.

Maisie started to giggle as Charlie made a dive for the hen, which decided it wasn't ready to give up its freedom. It headed off towards the buffet table as fast as its little legs would take it, neatly dodged Jamie, who collided with Charlie, and then with a squawk of indignation leapt in the air and landed plonk in the middle of Jane Smith's trifle – sending a shower of cream and jelly over Billy. He whooped with delight, and set off doing what looked a bit like a rain dance as the chicken flapped frantically splattering everybody in sight with hundreds and thousands, before it strutted off across the white table cloth in indignation leaving a trail of blancmange and jelly footprints behind it. For a second it hesitated, and everybody held their breath, then it shook one of its tiny feet and the piece of fruit that had got skewered on one of its nails flew off, span slowly through the air and landed on Timothy Parry's head.

Jim, who should have known better, lunged forward and deftly caught the chicken, then pushed it down firmly on his lap. 'It can watch from here. Daft bugger.'

The children by now were far too excited to remember any of the dance steps they'd been taught. The combination of a chat to Father Christmas, followed by all the adult cheering and an escaped hen had sent them all a bit giddy, and even Liz Potts hadn't got the heart to insist they did it properly.

The song, Lucy decided, had probably never been sung quite so quickly – which was probably a good thing given the hyper state of the lords-a-leaping and ladies dancing, and she really didn't trust the twelve drummers drumming, even if they were normally sensible Year 6's. Thank goodness that they'd ditched authenticity and gone with a cardboard cut-out partridge, which was flapping rather violently as Sophie shouted out the final line with vigour each time they came to it.

'Aren't they sweet?' Jill nudged Lucy, who jumped. Sweet wouldn't have been the word she'd have used right now. Why Jill was whispering was also a bit of a mystery, even the donkey couldn't have made itself heard above the might of the Langtry Meadows Primary School children when they were in full flow.

'Sweet?' Okay, she couldn't keep the incredulous tone out of her voice, but Jill chuckled as Maisie skipped on the spot, her earlier reservations about being a 'silly dancing lady' now gone.

'Them, you idiot.' She nodded in the direction of Sally and Jamie who were looking very loved-up indeed, and Lucy gave a sigh of relief.

'Oh, them! For a moment I thought you'd lost your marbles.' She sighed, they did look happy. Sally had been bowled over by the surprise party. It was just a shame she couldn't solve her own and Charlie's problems so easily. 'He gets her, doesn't he?'

'It looks that way.' Jill smiled. 'It took them a long time to get together, but we always knew that one day ...'

The children clattered to the end of the song, and the Hargreave twins let go of the pear tree which hit the ground with a loud thunk, followed by a flutter as Sophie cast the partridge on the top. The audience decided that signalled the end, so after a good round of applause they gathered up their children and directed them towards the hot dogs and pizza that were being served at the far end of the room.

'Phew, I think I need a drink.' Lucy let out a dramatic

sigh as laughter echoed round the room. She linked her hand through Charlie's arm. 'What do you think?'

'Sounds like a good idea to me.'

'I think it's past my bedtime.' Timothy, who'd been watching the proceedings like a genial uncle who didn't have a care in the world (which could have been down to three glasses of mulled wine) cleared his throat. He patted Lucy's arm. 'Excellent job today my dear, you've all done an excellent job. Splendid team, splendid. Oh,' he paused, 'nearly forgot.' He held up a finger. 'Elsie wants a word, something that's been playing on her mind. See you on Monday morning, bright eyed and bushy tailed. Now, what did I do with my scarf?' He pottered off, in the general direction of the door, his scarf already firmly knotted around his neck.

'I'll get refills shall I? While you see what Elsie wants?'

'You still find it strange calling her Elsie don't you?'

'I do, she's been Miss Harrington to me since I was,' Charlie grinned, 'knee-high to a grasshopper. In fact, I still don't think I dare call her Elsie to her face. Go on, she's summoning you.' He dropped a light kiss on her lips. 'I'll check Maisie's okay. Mulled wine or bubbly?'

'You are kidding me? If I have one more glass of Matt's rocket fuel I'll fall over, bubbly please.'

Elsie, Lucy realised, had her gaze fixed firmly on them, but as she got closer she realised the old lady was looking uncharacteristically nervous. There were pink splodges of anxiety on her cheeks, and the slightest of trembles in the hand that rested on her knee.

'We,' she shot a glance in Jim's direction, 'have an announcement.'

Lucy's mother, Trish, smiled encouragingly and Jim, one hand on his crutch, patted her arm with his other.

'I didn't want to make a fuss, but,' Elsie took a deep breath, straightened her backbone and seemed to find conviction from somewhere deep inside. When she spoke again the words rang out in her normal forthright tone. 'I would like you to meet my darling son.' She paused, then waved a hand with a dramatic flourish, just to make certain there could be no confusion. 'Jim.' And there could be no doubt at all of the note of pride in her voice.

Lucy looked from Elsie to Jim, then at her mother, who had the softest of smiles on her face.

'Here we go.' Charlie held a glass in front of her face, but Lucy didn't really see it. 'Sorry, is there something wrong, am I?' His tone dropped to one of uncertainty.

'No, Charles, there is absolutely nothing wrong at all.' Elsie, who had obviously gained confidence now that she'd spoken the words once, smiled. It was the happiest smile Lucy had ever seen. It lit her eyes, which were damp with emotion, brightened her whole face. 'I have news, a baby.'

When Lucy glanced up, Charlie had a startled look

in his eye, and she grinned.

'Meet my son, Charles.'

'Your?'

'Jim is my son.' Elsie looked delighted with her power to shock, and was positively chuckling. The same familiar chuckle that Lucy had heard from Jim a thousand times, just not quite as deep or rumbling. They had the same nose, the same direct stare, the same urge to nurture the village, the same kindness.

She'd had the slightest of suspicions when Jim had his accident, when Elsie had been so distraught and had vowed to tell her son the truth. But she'd not seen it clearly until now. When they were sat side by side. So different and yet so alike.

Jim had obviously been drawn to his mother, even though he didn't know that was who she was. He'd called on her, helped her out when he could, was company. And Elsie had watched him silently, from the side-lines, as he grew up. Watched him as a baby, a boy, a man.

Now she looked relieved. At peace.

Lucy smiled. It had taken a lot of bravery for Elsie to talk to Jim. She was frightened of being hated, of being shunned, but how could lovely Jim have done that to her?

'But now, if you'll excuse us, we have a lot to catch up on.'

Jim nodded as Elsie stood up, then helped him to his feet. The roles had been reversed. For so long he'd been there for Elsie, now she was grabbing the opportunity to do what she'd always wanted to. Look after him. Her child. 'Not had much of a chance to chat, have we? Been a lot to sort with the party and everything.' He tapped his crutch on the floor. 'Right then, we'll be off will we?' Wavering on his feet, he grinned at Lucy and Charlie. 'Summat good came out of the nipper running off then. If I hadn't buggered this leg up then who knows when the old fool would have told me.' He shook his head, but the look he swapped with Elsie said it all, the gentle affection that had always existed between them had moved to a deeper level.

'Things usually happen for a reason.' Her voice was soft.

'I'll stay on here for a while, if that's okay?' Trish's tone was gentle, she wanted to give them space. Time together.

'Splendid. We will see you later.' Then Elsie took a step forward and did something totally unexpected. She put her hands on Lucy's arms and kissed her. 'Thank you, dear. Thank you so much.' The words were so soft, Lucy was sure nobody else could hear them. Tears sprang to her eyes as Elsie drew back.

'And thank you.' Lucy whispered back as she glanced over at Trish, and Elsie followed her gaze. This was what life in Langtry Meadows was all about. People. Helping each other.

# Chapter 22

The grass was crisp, crunchy beneath their feet as Lucy and Charlie made their way across the field, Roo and Piper running ahead with Maisie in hot pursuit.

The last time Charlie had been in this field had probably been when Maisie was missing, and Lucy glanced up to see if it bothered him.

He looked down at her at exactly the same time, and the corners of his generous mouth lifted into the small, private smile she loved to share with him.

'Okay?' She kept her voice low.

'More than okay.'

'I do love you, Charlie.'

'Love you too.' He squeezed her hand in his. 'We're lucky to be living in a place like this, aren't we?'

'Daddy, Lucy, hurry up, stop talking.' Maisie skidded to a halt in front of them, then whirled around and headed back across the field. 'Follow me, I know the way.'

Lucy laughed. 'Very lucky.'

'How's your mum settling in with Elsie?'

'Oh she loves it.' Lucy had been surprised just how quickly her mother had settled into her new home in Langtry Meadows, and as she'd done so she seemed to have cast off a heavy cloak that had dragged her down for so long. 'She's happy; happier than I've ever seen her.' She'd been blind to how her mother felt as she'd been growing up. Too busy with her own problems to appreciate her mother's sacrifices, how she'd left Stoneyvale, Dad, her abusive husband, so that she could bring up her daughter in safety. To be independent.

That life had haunted Lucy until she'd moved to Langtry Meadows – the place she'd least expected to save her. And now, it seemed, it was saving her mother too.

'This way, Daddy, Daddy.'

Charlie suddenly laughed, and started to run, taking Lucy with him. Her feet slid on the damp grass, Roo ran circles round them barking with excitement and Maisie giggled as they reached her and Charlie swept her up into the air.

'You are a bossy madam.'

She squealed and pummelled on his back until he placed her back on the grass, then slipped her small hand into Lucy's. 'Close your eyes.'

'Is that safe? What about the dangerous ditches round

here?'

'I won't take you to the ditch.' Maisie waited patiently.
'You're peeping.'

Charlie's deep, warming laugh rang out and he took
Lucy's other hand. 'Come on, trust us.'

The tree was old and gnarled. Bigger than Lucy had
expected, spreading its ancient boughs over the ground
below as though it wanted to protect the land from the
elements.

There was something magical about the way the thick
branches twisted and turned, earthwards and skywards,
like a magic tree, the type you drew as a child, the type
you read about in fairy stories.

'It's amazing.' She spread her arms wide and turned
slowly, the weak winter sunlight shimmering through
the mass of barely clad winter twigs.

'You should see it in summer.' Charlie's soft voice
was at her ear, his breath bathing her neck.

'Look, look.' Maisie was dancing around with excitement like a demented imp, and took Lucy's hand to try
and drag her closer. 'MY name, look, and that's Daddy's,
isn't it?' She glanced up, and Charlie nodded. 'And Uncle
Jim's.' She'd taken to calling him uncle after he'd found
her, and Lucy wasn't sure if they'd reached some kind
of agreement that day, or if it was just Maisie making
sense of things in her own way. 'That's Jim's ditch.'

Maisie waved a hand in a vague direction. 'And that's the pond, but Jim called it a pit. That's the headmaster's scratchy bit.' She turned back to look at Lucy, her face solemn, her big, trusting, brown eyes wide. 'You've got to scratch your name, then you'll belong too.'

Lucy was surprised to realise her hand was shaking as she reached out to scratch her initials in the bark of the tree. She'd never felt like she belonged anywhere, well not since she'd been the same age as Maisie. But now, at last she knew she'd found her peace, found her place, in a tiny village called Langtry Meadows. Now she was ready to say a final goodbye to the one demon in her past – her father.

Charlie put his warm hand over hers. 'Okay?'

She nodded, blinking away the tears and smiling – the last thing she wanted was for Maisie to think she was sad. Now was not the right time to talk about this. 'I'm good.' She'd got a job here, she'd bought a house – well very nearly bought one – and she'd be spending Christmas here with her mother and the man she loved. A man who was so much more of a father to Maisie than her dad had ever been to her. Seeing Charlie and Maisie together had made her realise just how fractured her own childhood had been. Made her see how little he'd done for her, how lucky she was to have a mother like Trish.

Charlie covered her hand in his, helped as she formed

the letters, squeezed her against his warm body.

'We all belong now, me, Daddy and you.' Maisie pointed at each of them in turn. 'Now I've just got to tell Mummy to do it. Can we go and get hot chocolate now?'

Ah, out of the mouth of babes, thought Lucy as she caught Charlie's eye.

'We certainly can, first one back gets extra marshmallows.' He grinned, and pulled Lucy into his arms, not giving her time to object, as with a yell Maisie set off as fast as her little legs would carry her.

'I don't know why, but I've got a feeling next year is going to be better than this one.' He rested his forehead against hers for a moment, staring into her eyes with a look that was so much like Maisie's, then he brushed his stubbled cheek against hers and kissed her neck. 'Whatever happens, Maisie's happy and she'll always come back here even if she has to leave.'

'She will.' She caught his face in her hands, ran her thumb over his lips. She hoped like mad, for all their sakes, that Maisie wouldn't have to leave, but she didn't want to say the words out loud. Tempt fate.

'Come on, or she'll be trying to make that hot chocolate on her own and you know what happened last time she had the run of the kitchen.'

They ran across the field hand in hand, until they were slightly breathless, catching up with Maisie before she reached the gate.

***

'You're quiet.' Charlie had tucked a tired Maisie in bed and joined Lucy where she was curled up in front of the fire. Piper half on her knee, Roo sprawled across her feet.

'Sorry, it's just ...' She didn't want to spoil a perfect day, but ever since she'd found the article on the internet it had been gnawing away at her insides.

'Go on.' His voice was soft as he pulled her against his solid body. She glanced up. 'You can tell me anything you know.'

'I know. It's just ...' she took a deep breath. She could tell him anything, everything, and she had to. She wanted to get this off her chest, see what he thought she should do. Even if, in her heart, she knew she couldn't let it lie. 'I know I shouldn't, it was silly, but last night after the party, everybody was so happy, you and Maisie, and Elsie had told Jim and ...'

'Go on.' He nudged her gently, willing her to continue.

'Mum's always been brilliant, she's done everything for me.'

'I know, but ...'

'But even though I know everything she's said is true, and that we had to run away from dad, and that he was horrible, mean, and he was never a proper dad to me ...'

'You want to know what happened to him?' Charlie's voice was little more than a whisper.

'I didn't want to see him, just to know, is that crazy?'

'No.' He shook his head, then rested it on hers. 'He is your dad.'

'Was.'

'*Is*, Lucy.' His voice was soft. 'He still fathered you.'

'No,' she shook her head. 'Was. I couldn't sleep so I googled him, I know I shouldn't I just wanted, well I don't know, but ...' Maybe she'd hoped to see some picture of a monster, a man easy to dismiss, she didn't know. She shook her head. 'It doesn't matter, but I found this.' She picked up her mobile phone from the sofa, opened the tab she'd saved.

Lucy really hadn't known what she was looking for, but this was the last thing she'd expected to see. A local newspaper report, a hazy picture of what could have been her childhood home, a woman, a child, a man who had familiar features. There was something of her dad hidden deep in the face that stared out at her – the line of his nose, the piercing gaze directed at the camera, the thin lips that he'd so often pursed in disapproval when she hadn't been good enough. But his hair was thinner, shorter, his face broader. It looked like him, it looked like the house that was once her home. But she couldn't be sure, not absolutely sure.

Charlie scanned through the report, then put the phone down without a word. Shock was spattered across his face, and he cleared his throat, swallowed before speaking.

'That's him? Your dad?'

'I think so.'

'He did ...'

'I think so.' She didn't need to read the report again; the words were imprinted on her mind, words that would be hard to shift. The man who'd fathered her, but never really been a dad had hung himself. But first he'd killed his family.

The news had been splashed over the local papers, but been of no interest to anybody else. It was cut and dried, a note had been left explaining everything. Her father's wife had wanted to leave, but she'd not been as clever as Trish. She'd told him. And he'd wreaked the ultimate revenge – nobody was going to show him up.

'I can't tell Mum until I'm sure it's him.' She felt strangely detached; he'd been a stranger for so long. She was sure that the shock would hit, but right now all she could think was that could have been them.

She'd cried into her pillow not because she'd lost her dad, that had happened far too long ago, way before the last time she'd seen him as an eight year old girl. She'd lost him when she was younger, when the mental abuse had first started. No, she'd cried for his family, she'd cried for her mother, she'd cried for Charlie who was a real dad but could lose his daughter, and for the injustice of it all. Then she'd fallen into a deep uninterrupted sleep.

'I need to go back to Stoneyvale, Charlie.' She met his gaze. 'I need to check the graves, see our house and know it's the one in this photo.' She needed to know for sure that it wasn't some weird coincidence, then she'd tell her mum.

'You don't have to, we can hire somebody, check out it's him without going.'

'No. I need to go. I can't move on completely until I've gone back, but don't tell Mum, will you?' Today, at the oak tree, her resolve had strengthened. She belonged here, but going back would mean she'd banished the bad part of her past forever. She'd know he could never come back and hurt her. If it was him.

'Of course I won't tell her, not if you don't want me to.'

'I don't want to upset her, not until I know for sure.'

'I'm going with you.' He kissed the top of her head. 'No arguments.'

'Thanks.'

*\*\*\**

'You'll be okay, Mum?'

'Of course we will, won't we Maisie?'

'We're going to make mince pies.' Maisie folded her arms and gave a heavy sigh. 'If you ever go.'

'You'll be okay too, won't you love?' Trish's eyes sought out Lucy's, and there was a question in them. 'You'll be careful, you won't ...?'

'We'll be careful, I'll look after her, I promise you.' Charlie's reassuring voice swept over them in a comforting wave and Trish relaxed slightly.

'He won't be there, Mum.'

Trish twisted the tea towel in her hands, and Lucy felt a pang of guilt. Her mum had been happy since she'd accepted Elsie's job offer. She'd only been here for a few days, but they'd been perfect. Now she was risking it. Upsetting her mother. But she had to go. She had to close this last door before she flung open the new one. In a very real sense as well as in her head.

She'd moved on so much since arriving in Langtry Meadows in the spring, but she wanted to tie up this one last loose end before December was out. She had to see for herself.

In a few days' time, the school term would end, and then before she knew it Christmas day would arrive and a new year would be looming. A bright, shiny year full of hope. She wanted closure on the part of her life that had given her, and her mother, so much sadness and hurt. That had fed childhood insecurities until they bloomed like mushrooms in the dark.

She'd mentioned it to her mum, knowing that she wouldn't like the idea, but the force of Trish's vehemence, the fear in her eyes, had surprised Lucy. 'I can't ever go back to that place, Lucy. I said my goodbyes a long time ago.'

'I understand, I really do, but can you understand that I have to?'

'But what if he talks you into staying, Lucy he's clever, he's ...'

'I'm not going to see him, Mum. He won't be there.' She wanted so much to show her mother the report, to set her mind at rest. But what if it wasn't him? What if she'd made a mistake? Then it would be far worse. 'I'm going to see our home, my school, the village. I'm going so that I can remember the good bits, not the bad. I won't see him. Promise.' It was hard to put into words, but the need to go back had been growing in Lucy over the past few months. She couldn't close the door on the past hurt, the feeling of failure, until she'd proved to herself it no longer had any power over her, it didn't scare her.

Knowing her father could be dead hadn't lessened the need to go, if anything it had strengthened her desire. Because if she didn't there would always be that question mark.

'Promise.'

She'd hugged her mum close. 'I promise, Mum. Trust me, okay?'

So here they were, mum looking after Maisie, and her and Charlie setting off to cover the relatively small distance that felt as wide as an ocean. And, probably just as deep and dangerous.

'See you soon.' Lucy waved at Maisie, who tugged at Trish's hand. But all of Trish's attention was on her daughter. Her eyes were pained as she looked straight at Lucy, the worry etched into her face.

'I'm sorry.' She said the words softly, but she knew they wouldn't help. 'I've just got to do it.'

'I know, darling.'

'We can make mince pies now, can't we?' Maisie was tugging at Trish's sleeve.

'We can.' As Lucy climbed into the car, she watched Trish push the door shut. At least Maisie would be a good distraction.

Lucy's palms started to sweat before they'd even left Langtry Meadows, and by the time they joined the motorway she was having to take deep, calming breaths or she knew she'd start to panic. Dad had tried to trap them in that house, he'd bullied her mother, he'd scared off her friends. But she'd not understood, not known.

She'd loved him, he was just Dad back then.

What if this article wasn't about him, what if he was still there, what if she saw him?

The warmth of Charlie's hand drew her back to the present. 'You don't have to do this you know? You've nothing to prove, just say the word and we'll turn round.'

'I do have to do this.' Her voice was raspy even to her own ears. She swallowed hard, trying to take the dryness away. Be brave. 'You know how sometimes you have to do something, you have to prove you're brave enough?'

'I do.' He squeezed her knee, his lovely mouth set in a twisted smile. 'I keep getting this voice in my head saying that when everything is settled with Maisie, then I have to do a DNA test.' He shrugged. 'I know it's stupid, she's my daughter whatever, but some tiny part of me ...' His voice drifted off and he put both hands on the steering wheel as though he needed to concentrate on the road. 'One day,' he swallowed hard, 'I need to be able to tell her if she's not mine.' He rolled his shoulders back. 'Not far now, this is the turn off isn't it?'

Lucy glanced down at the map on her phone. The little red marker taking her ever closer. 'It is.' The dot on her phone hopped forward and she looked up, gazed out of the window, waited for a familiar landmark.

There was none. The sigh escaped. Part frustration,

and part relief. She'd not had any idea how she'd feel when she returned to the village she'd been brought up in.

Fear that she'd see the bullying father they'd run away from? Anxiety that she'd feel unwanted still? A worry that those old feelings of not being good enough would bubble up and set her heart pounding?

But the rush of emotion didn't hit. This wasn't the Stoneyvale she'd known. It was different, it had moved on – like she had.

She was fairly sure that they'd always followed a country lane, with open fields as they drove into the village. But now there was tarmac and bricks. Modern houses had sprung up on both sides of the road – which was wider than she remembered.

If she hadn't seen the sign as they entered the village, she'd have thought they'd taken a wrong turning.

Charlie slowed the car. There was very little about Stoneyvale that was familiar as they drove towards the centre of the village. It was bigger than Langtry Meadows, but it lacked the pretty features. There was no village pond or green, just a large play area for the kids.

The place had sprawled out in an ungainly fashion since Lucy and her mum had left. Langtry Meadows had managed to fight a lot of the developments, but Stoneyvale it appeared had surrendered.

'Can we stop?' Lucy had spotted the sign for the

primary school, the place that had held part of her heart victim for far too long. It had seemed a vast lonely place back then, but now as she looked, a smile tugged at her lips. It was tiny. Not much bigger than the school she was teaching at now.

A new extension had been tacked on one side, to accommodate the new influx of villagers. Part of the playground, the corner she'd often stood alone in, was now rubber tiled.

She climbed out of the car, and walked over to the fence.

'This was your school?' Charlie draped an arm over her shoulders, reminding her he was there for her.

'It was.' She pointed over to the small playing field. 'That tree over there was our tree,' she smiled and glanced up at him, 'nothing like your oak tree. We'd sit under there and make daisy chains.'

'Sweet! I can imagine you in your short skirt.'

He winked and Lucy laughed, and gave his arm a playful thump. 'This was primary school you idiot!'

'Shall we walk, or would you rather?' He inclined his head towards the car.

'We can walk.' She said it lightly, but felt the tremor in the words as they crept between her lips. They wouldn't bump into her dad, he didn't do Sunday strolls, and anyway he probably wouldn't even recognise her. She slipped her hand into Charlie's. 'I'll show you where we got the tomatoes from.'

As they strolled down the main street there was a vague familiarity, a gentle stirring of recognition, but so much was different. She did a double take as she realised that the small glossy supermarket had replaced the corner shop which had been a favourite for sweets and ice-creams. Where once there had been a greengrocer's there was now a café.

They turned a corner, and Lucy took a step forward, then ground to a halt. What had been a small entry lane leading to the nursery and allotments had been tarmacked over. The black surface was already pitted with the odd pothole, showing that it wasn't a recent development. She stared, out of all the things she'd thought she'd feel she didn't expect this to shock her most. Now the sweet smell of the vines, one of the really good memories of her childhood had gone forever and she felt hot tears prick at the back of her eyes as she stared at the group of modern houses, with their tidy front lawns that reminded her more of her home on the edge of Birmingham when she'd been teaching in the city. 'I suppose that's what they call progress?'

He laughed softly, the familiar sound curling round her. 'It makes you realise how lucky we are in Langtry Meadows.'

'It does.' She felt her fingers tighten round his, and the hollow feeling in her stomach grow. There was one last ghost she had to face, the most important place of all to visit. 'Do you mind if we drive up to the house?' Her legs felt weak, she'd feel safer in the car.

'Of course.' He pulled her tight against him, hugged her close. 'I love so many things about you, you know. You're gorgeous, clever, funny, but most of all you're brave.'

She tried to laugh, but it came out uneven. She didn't feel brave. 'Flatterer.'

'But you're rubbish at baking.' He gave a dramatic sigh, the same one she'd heard from Maisie. 'I suppose I can't expect perfection. Though I might give you some lessons.'

'Cheeky bugger! Don't forget I've seen your baking attempts. You and Maisie looked like you'd had a flour fight last time you cooked together.'

'You've got me.' He grinned. 'Oh well, I guess we have a future of takeaways ahead of us.' He kissed the tip of her nose, and the little shiver brought out goosebumps on her arms, but warmed something deep inside her chest. A future ahead. 'Ready?'

'Ready.' Or at least as ready as she'd ever be.

Lucy stared out of the car window. Her childhood home was smaller than she'd remembered. The vast garden she'd seen in her mind reduced to an overgrown square of lawn, weed filled borders in place of the mass of colour she'd remembered. There was a neglected air about the place that her father would have never allowed. He liked everything tidy, organised. In order.

It was unmistakeably the same house that had been in the newspaper report, but it looked different, more familiar in real life.

And then she saw it, the For Sale sign that had fallen onto the ground, a bright red slash of 'Sold' across it. The house was empty. Her father was gone forever.

'Do you want to get out?'

She shook her head. 'There's no need.' She stared at the upstairs window, her bedroom window, the one she'd spent hours looking out of. Watching the other children play, being prevented from joining them. Her gaze dropped to the downstairs, to the large bay window where once her piano had stood. Until he'd got rid of it, stopped her doing what she loved most. 'I'm going to get a piano, when I've moved into Jasmine Cottage.' The place was small, but she'd squeeze a piano in somehow.

'Good.'

'I don't want to go to the churchyard, I don't need to now.' It would feel voyeuristic, wrong to see the graves of his wife and child, meaningless to look at his name on a headstone. 'I know it was him.'

Charlie squeezed her hand, but didn't say anything.

'He was never a proper dad – like you are to Maisie.'

She'd told him about her dad before, but she suddenly needed to explain, while they were here. Now. 'He was just a man, a man who made a baby.' Her eyes were damp and she knew there was a wobble in her voice.

Her dad had never protected her, looked after her. He'd not been the man who'd celebrated her achievements – he'd been the one who always told her she had to try harder, she wasn't good enough. He'd not been there to rub her bruises better, he'd been too busy complaining, telling Mum that she wasn't even capable of bringing their daughter up properly.

'I don't think he ever even tried to find us when we left, even though Mum didn't want him to. I mean it would have been awful if he had, but I think he just wrote us off, moved on. He was never going to admit that he'd failed was he? I never got that before, but I do now. I understand.' She leaned in against Charlie's comforting, warm body. A man who cared, who was solid. 'If I'd have run away like Maisie did he wouldn't have worried.'

'You can't know that.' Charlie's voice was soft. 'Any parent would worry, would care.'

'He wasn't a normal parent, Charlie. He never cared. Me and mum were just belongings, not people he loved. He needed to control and manipulate us, and if he couldn't.' She paused. He hadn't been able to with his new family, but she couldn't go there, couldn't dwell on something that might have been. She swallowed away the tightness in her throat. 'We never shared a tree, anything. Whatever I loved he got rid of.' Charlie hugged her even tighter.

'You okay?'

'I am now.' Something inside her had lifted. She was, she would be, and when she got home (and it really was home) she'd be able to set her mother's mind at rest as well. 'Thanks for bringing me, Charlie.'

There were no real memories here for her now; good or bad. The last ghost of her past had been laid to rest. There was nothing left in Stoneyvale that could cheer or hurt her. She smiled up at Charlie. 'Shall we go home?'

# Chapter 23

The beep was insistent. Going on and on. It was no longer the reversing tractor in Charlie's dream, it was something real. He opened his eyes and reached out groping for the alarm clock and instead found a warm body.

Lucy muttered in her sleep, then flung an arm across him and he knew he was smiling. They'd spent far too few nights together since the summer, when Maisie had come back into his life, but last night had been perfect. Waking up next to her on Christmas Day was special, even if, he glanced at the time, hell it was the middle of the night.

The beep started again. It wasn't an alarm clock, it was his phone.

With a groan Charlie picked it up.

'Morning.' The cheery bellow made him cringe. 'Got a bit of a problem with one of the cows.' Except it sounded like coos. 'Wouldn't bother you if I didn't need to, with it being Christmas Day and everything.'

'No problem, no problem at all Mr Brownlow.' He rolled out of bed and reached for his trousers as the farmer carried on a monologue about 'the trouble with cows'. 'I'll be right there.'

'What's the matter?' Lucy, who had now spread-eagled herself across the bed opened one eye and peered at him through her hair, her voice muffled and sleep-laden.

'Nothing. Go back to sleep, I've got to go up to Brownlow's.'

'I'll look after Maisie.' She closed her eyes again and cuddled into the pillow that still had the indent of his head.

'She's not here.' He chuckled softly and thought she'd never looked so beautiful. There was something about Lucy in bed, when she opened up, dropped the barriers. The chats they had, curled up in bed together, were the best they had.

She started, and rolled onto her back, then stared at him as she woke up, and remembered. 'Oh yeah, Josie. So,' she sat up, fully awake now, 'I can come with you.'

'Do you know what time it is?' He pulled a second sweater on. 'It's four o'clock in the morning, and you've told me anything before 7 a.m. doesn't exist.'

'It's different. It's Christmas.'

'And it's freezing.'

'Snot a problem.' She padded off naked towards the bathroom.

\*\*\*

'You're clever aren't you?' Lucy slipped her arm through his, and moved in closer. 'My hero.'

Mr Brownlow chuckled. 'Aye, he's a clever one. That's a good strong calf, that is.'

Charlie had been relieved that the situation hadn't been as bad as he'd feared. The calf had been stuck like a cork in a bottle, one of its forelegs bent back, but with a little bit of manoeuvring and a gentle pull it had slithered out onto the straw and soon been up on shaky legs.

'Cuppa tea before you goes home?'

The warmth of the kitchen hit them as soon as they walked in, and Mrs Brownlow grinned. 'Bacon's already on, you will stay for a quick bite won't you?' She cracked an egg into the pan without waiting for a reply. 'And a Happy Christmas to both of you, cow alright is it?'

'It's grand.' Mr Brownlow kicked his wellingtons off and sat down by the Aga, sticking his cold feet out in front of it.

Charlie made an apologetic face at Lucy, this wasn't exactly what he'd planned for their first Christmas morning together. Lovely as the Brownlow family were he'd had a lazy morning on their own in mind.

Lucy grinned, and blew him a kiss. 'Happy Christmas, Mrs Brownlow. That smells lovely, just what we need.'

Right now, Charlie thought, it really wasn't possible to love Lucy more. Josie had always hated the inconvenience of clients, even though she was a vet herself, but Lucy understood.

'Oh call me Sarah, love. Black pudding?'

'Happy Christmas, Miss.' Lucy turned round to see Poppy, already dressed, clutching a black and white kitten. 'Do you want to see my kitten, Miss Jacobs? It don't look like a slug anymore, it went fluffy.'

Mr Brownlow shook his head. 'Now don't go pestering love, Miss Jacobs is on holiday. Come here.' She went over and climbed on his knee, as Sarah piled the breakfast on to large plates. If they ate all of that they wouldn't need Christmas lunch.

'You just eat what you want, love.' She smiled at Charlie. 'It's a long time to lunch though and you need something to keep you warm.'

An hour later, as they slipped and slid their way across the yard which had frozen over like an ice-rink, Charlie slipped his hand into Lucy's and spun her round to face him just as they reached the front door. 'Happy Christmas.' She shrieked in surprise, nearly losing her balance and grabbed out for his arm, before sobering up at the look on his face.

They studied each other for a moment. Making the most of the quiet stillness.

The lights were on in the farmhouse, and soon Ed Wright would be out to milk his cows, but right now it seemed like it was just them. The world was theirs for the taking.

'I do love you Lucy Jacobs.' He tucked her hair behind her ear, ran his thumb over her cheekbone, loving the softness of her skin, the way her blue gaze locked with his.

'I love you too, Charlie Davenport.'

'You're cold.'

'I'm fine.'

He pulled her close, wrapping his arms round her and breathing in the smell of her hair, enjoying the warmth of her body that fitted against his so perfectly. 'Oh you're more than fine.'

She giggled then, a soft murmur of sound that he never wanted to be without. Then she pulled back slightly. 'Maisie will be here soon.'

'You don't have to go.' He wrapped his arms tighter around her waist, willing her to stay, but knowing he shouldn't ask.

'I do, I've got to sort the animals out and get ready. Pick me up at two o'clock?'

'I didn't mean that.' He didn't want her to feel that

because Josie was on the scene, things had changed. He didn't want the early morning magic to disappear.

'I know. She might want to chat though, Charlie.' Her voice was soft. 'You don't need me here, it will complicate things. Spend some time on your own with Maisie, it will be the only quiet time you get together today, just the two of you.'

'Thanks for coming to the farm with me, it was nice.'

'It was lovely.' She rested her head against his chest again, and the sweet smell of her perfume played with his nostrils. 'I've not seen a calf born before, and it was so cute.' Then she pulled away reluctantly and this time he let her. 'I really do need to go.' Piper barked, and she laughed. 'See, even Piper agrees.' She stood on tiptoes and kissed him. 'Happy Christmas, Charlie.' Then she put a finger on his lips, in the same place she'd pressed her lips. 'See you in a bit.'

Lucy had only been gone ten minutes when Roo's barks, followed by a rap on the door announced Maisie and Josie's arrival. Maisie dived into the house, her cheeks flushed. Her arms full of toys. 'Daddy look! I get two Christmases.' She put the presents down, and gave him a hug before moving on to Roo. 'Mummy, mummy come and see my room.'

Josie followed reluctantly, not sure of her welcome, and they looked at each other for a moment before

Charlie nodded. 'Come in for a bit, there's a jug of coffee on if you want a cup?'

She shook her head, her auburn waves, the exact same shade as Maisie's curls, swishing around her face. 'I won't stay, Mum and Dad will be expecting me back for sherry. They've got guests coming for pre-dinner drinks.' The smile was apologetic, but they both knew that having a reason made this easier. 'I'll come in a minute poppet. You play while I talk to Daddy.'

'I'm going to see Treacle, he's in the utility room and he's going to get sprouts today.'

'I'm sorry I've been such a cow, Charlie.' Josie sat down at the kitchen table, and took the mug of coffee he'd poured out anyway. 'You don't deserve it. You've never deserved all this ...' she waved a hand, 'shit.'

He sat down opposite her, not trusting himself to speak. Once upon a time he'd trusted Josie, now he didn't know which way she was going to turn, what she had planned next. Lately when she'd been reasonable one day, like she had over the Christmas arrangements, she was nasty the next.

'Thanks for letting me take Maisie to Mum and Dad's last night.'

'She's your daughter too.' He shrugged, trying not to let a bitter note creep in.

'Maybe, but I've been a bit of a crap parent lately haven't I?' She held a staying hand up and gave a short, nervous laugh. 'Don't answer that.' She took a gulp of the too-hot coffee, fixed her gaze on the table. 'He doesn't know.'

A chill ran through Charlie at the unexpected words, and his fingers tightened round the handle of the mug, until the blood leached out leaving them white.

'The one, the man I had a, well.'

She didn't have to explain what she meant. He knew all too well. The man who could be Maisie's biological father. The man she'd had an affair with.

'I'm making a hash of this, like I have of everything lately. He was married, it was stupid, a drunken ... it didn't mean anything, it was never meant to mean anything Charlie, it was just me trying to run away, burying my head in the sand. Look, I know you don't want to hear all this, I know, I'm just being selfish again, trying to explain for my own sake.' She pushed the coffee away and took a deep breath. 'I'm just trying to say that I never told him I was pregnant, the only man who's ever been her dad is you.' She stood up. 'I'm going abroad again in the New Year, it would be nice to see Maisie again before I go.' There was a question in her eyes, hanging in the air. And now she did look up, look him in the eye.

'Of course, she wants to see you.' He had to say this. 'But is it fair on her, you coming and going like this?' You wanting to take her with you, he could have added, but daren't. 'Putting the job first?' Which was a joke, seeing as she'd left him because she'd said he was married to his work.

'It's not just the job. Charlie, I've realised that I can't just settle here, I'm crap at it, I'm just not the right person to be a wife or mother.' Her gaze didn't waver from his, but her hand was trembling. 'You're much better than me at this parenting stuff Charlie. I like what I'm doing out there, I want to travel. I know it's selfish, but I do care about Maisie and I think she's far better off here with you than with a hopeless mother like me.'

He held his breath, not sure that this meant what he hoped it did.

'One day, maybe all this will be out of my system and I'll want to settle. Who knows?' She shrugged her slim shoulders. 'Then I'll come here Charlie, and we can work it out between us. We can do what's best for Maisie. I want her to grow up knowing who I am, I want to share her life, but ...' Josie took a step back. 'I've written to my solicitor saying I want Maisie to be here with you, but us to have a shared arrangement so that I can see her when I can, and we can have equal time with her when I move back. She'll talk to your solicitor and they can do whatever paperwork they have to. Is that okay?'

Her voice was gentle, for a moment the old Josie was

back, but all he could do was nod. He didn't trust himself to say a word, the emotion would spill out, he'd be crying with relief.

'We don't need all this court case drama, do we?'

'No, Josie.' He swallowed, tried to keep his voice steady. 'We don't.'

'I'll pop up and see her room,' her voice was soft, 'and then I'll go. Mum will wonder where I've got to.' She took a step, then stopped, only a couple of feet from Charlie.

He looked at the woman he'd loved, hated and now hoped one day he could just like. There was the hint of a smile on her face, a hopeful, forgive me look that made him think instantly of Maisie. She'd inherited her mother's hair, smile, the wistful look when something was just out of reach.

'I am sorry about everything Charlie, truly.'

He nodded, and for the first time in a mixed-up year he knew he could believe her.

'I did love you Charlie, but we were never really right together were we?' Her gaze flickered upwards. 'But we did do one good thing.'

'We did, she's the best thing that ever happened to me Josie.' His weakness, the person she could use to hurt him. But for some reason he felt he could say it now, know that the battle was over. At least he hoped it was, that he could trust his instincts.

364

'I know. Happy Christmas, Charlie.' She ran lightly up the spiral staircase and Charlie felt a strange sensation. A lightness. It took him a moment to work out what it was.

Hope. Relief.

# Chapter 24

'Want a hand, Mum?' It seemed a bit strange to be in Elsie's house for Christmas dinner, and it should have felt even odder seeing her mum bustling around the large kitchen, a tea-towel slung over her shoulder.

But somehow, despite being here for such a short time, Trish looked completely at home. And she was singing.

A lump formed in Lucy's throat. It was a long distant memory now, but being here had stirred it up. Her mum had always hummed and sung as she cooked, in fact she'd often swept Lucy up into her arms and danced round the kitchen with her, stirring pots in passing. But that had been years ago. Before Dad had started to mete out his punishments if everything wasn't just as he liked it. Before they'd fled the village and ended up in a horrible house, and cooking became a chore not a pleasure.

'You can give that cranberry sauce a stir if you want love.' Trish gave her a hug, then pointed at the pan. 'Now isn't this lovely, us cooking Christmas lunch together?'

'Well I've not made much contribution yet.' Lucy grinned.

'Well you know what I mean. You used to stand on a chair next to me and help stir things when you were little.' A brief cloud seemed to pass over her face, then she blinked it away. 'Having Maisie with me making mince pies the other day took me right back, pass the salt will you, Lucy?' She tasted the gravy, then shot Lucy a sideways look. 'I'm going to do everything with my grandchildren that I wanted to do with you.'

'Don't give me that look.' Lucy shook her head in exasperation, but still couldn't quite keep the hint of a smile off her face even though she was trying her hardest. 'I'm not even married.'

'And since when did that stop anybody? Cranberry, love,' she pointed, whilst still managing to stir the gravy and check the pigs in blankets, 'it's bubbling.'

Lucy turned the heat down and stirred, wishing she could cool her cheeks down as easily.

'Elsie loves entertaining children so I can be granny for you and still do my job here.' She was sure a *pfft* noise escaped from her lips, but her mother was undeterred. 'It's not like she needs a carer or anything really, just a hand with the shopping and cleaning, and a bit of company. And once Jim is back on his feet properly he'll be around a lot as well. Be a love and get the plates out of the warming drawer before they get too hot.'

Lucy was fast realising that there was absolutely no point in objecting, or trying to reason with her mother that she was loving her job, and hadn't even had the slightest urge to have a baby. Diversion tactics were probably the best way to play this. 'You do like it here with Elsie, don't you?'

'It's wonderful. It's a lovely place to bring up kids.' Lucy squished a cranberry with unnecessary force against the side of the pan. 'This is just the type of place I imagined when me and your dad moved to the country. It's a shame it didn't work out, but things happen for a reason.'

'Mum, how can you say that? You would have had a much better life if—'

'Well, if I hadn't met Dad I wouldn't have you, and,' she stirred the gravy a bit too vigorously, 'if things hadn't gone wrong we wouldn't be here now, would we?'

She couldn't fault the logic, but Lucy was sure her mum hadn't deserved the hard life she'd had.

'You didn't mind uprooting, moving here to work for Elsie?' The one thing that had bothered her about her mum's move was the fact that she'd always been so totally selfless, had done everything for Lucy. And Lucy really didn't want to think that she'd dragged herself away from her job and friends because she still felt her little girl needed her.

'Tosh and nonsense. I wouldn't have accepted her offer if I had, would I?' Trish put the spoon down, the first time she'd taken her concentration away from the cooking, and turned so she could look at Lucy. 'I didn't have any roots, darling.' The words were soft. 'Elsie hasn't offered me a job, she's offered me a whole new life.' She patted Lucy's hand, then went back to stirring. 'She's a very clever lady. I could never have afforded to rent a house here, or give up that job, even though it's been getting a bit much for me. Now I know if anything happened I'd be out of house and home, but you can't think that way can you? Sometimes you just have to bite the bullet and go with your heart.'

'You do.' Lucy knew that all too well. As she watched her mum drain the sprouts, and take the perfect crunchy roast potatoes out of the oven it hit her. This was how her mum had wanted things to be, how she'd thought their lives should be. They'd taken several wrong turnings but they were here now. They'd both come home.

'Now, I think that's everything.' The normal 'get on with it' tone was back. 'If you'd like to take the turkey through, Jim's been sharpening the knife on and off for the past hour. I was tempted to take it off him earlier because that click-click was a bit unnerving. I don't know whether it's because he's excited, or he knows we've been sold a tough old bird.'

Lucy laughed. 'Nobody would dare sell Elsie anything but the best.' She kissed her mother on her cheek, then lifted the tray, hoped she didn't trip over a dog on the way, and headed for the dining room.

'Now then little 'un, what are you doing with those sprouts?' Jim chuckled, and gave Maisie a nudge. She giggled.

'They're for Treacle.' It was a stage whisper that every-body heard. 'My guinea pig.'

'I think he'd prefer them raw.' Charlie was fighting a losing battle to keep the smile off his face. 'We will give him some when we get home.'

'O-kay.' Maisie wasn't convinced.

'And in the meantime maybe you could put them back on your plate and eat those?'

Maisie grinned, and opened her hands wide. 'They were on my knee but they've disappeared!'

Lucy laughed as Roo and Piper, who'd been keeping a vigil under the table by Maisie's feet, both slunk out. Piper dropped a sprout, then nudged it with her nose, looking at it with suspicion. Roo, who was less fussy, had his head tilted to one side and was munching and screwing his face up at the same time.

'That was fabulous.' Charlie patted his stomach. 'I'm

totally stuffed.'

'It's so lovely to be cooking for a family again.' Trish blushed as she took his empty plate. 'There's Christmas pud next though, so you better have left some room.'

'Of course he has.' Elsie smiled, looking much more relaxed than she had for a long time, her eyes twinkling mischievously. 'Or he'll be first up for charades and that will clear some space in his stomach.'

Charlie groaned. 'Not charades, please tell me she's kidding.'

'Charades, charades.' Maisie jumped up, clapping her hands, and the last sprout catapulted off her skirt, flying across the room like a missile and landed on Piper's back. Before she could react, Roo had leapt over her grabbing it on the way. Maisie paused. 'What's charades, Uncle Jim?'

Jim, basking in his new roles of uncle, son and turkey carver pushed his chair back, and gestured for Maisie to sit on his knee.

Lucy stood up to help clear the table, and followed her mother through to the kitchen. 'I'm glad you're happy, Mum.'

She'd always been a wonderful mother, and it had never occurred to Lucy that she must have missed it. Looking after others. Elsie seemed to know though, and offering her a job had brought the old 'mum' back. The one from when she was a toddler, before their home life went wrong, and before it had been just the two of them – and all of Trish's energy had to go into making both ends meet.

Elsie had seen what Lucy had missed, had, with the simplest of gestures, offered her the role she'd always wanted, made her happy.

'I am, love, very happy, and I'm glad you are.' She brushed a lock of hair back from Lucy's face. 'We've done okay, haven't we?'

'Always. Happy Christmas, Mum.'

'Happy Christmas, love. And you know I'm here if you want a hand smartening up that house of yours, don't you? Not that I'll stick my nose in if it's not wanted.'

'Of course I want you to help, as long as you promise not to talk about babies!'

Trish smiled. 'Good. Now, can we trust Jim to light this brandy for the pudding, or would it be safer to give it to Charlie?'

The Christmas lights were twinkling in the square when Charlie, Lucy and Maisie waved goodbye to Trish, Elsie and Jim and headed home.

When Lucy had accepted the permanent job at Langtry Meadows she'd started the new school year with a stirring of hope in her heart that she'd found a place she loved, a man she loved, a new beginning. But now, she couldn't believe quite how much had changed in the last few months.

It was so lovely to have a proper family Christmas, in Elsie's gorgeous period home that was just made for events like this. Even Maisie had stared open mouthed at the enormous Christmas tree which Jill and Matt had decorated, under Jim's supervision.

Elsie and Jim seemed to have easily adjusted to their new relationship, without it being awkward and Lucy was pleased for both of them. They deserved to be happy.

She tightened her grip on Charlie's hand, then glanced up, met that deep dark gaze full on and smiled.

Things had to go right for him and Maisie, didn't they?

# Chapter 25

Lucy leant on the work surface, her coffee cup warming her hands, and studied the snow covered garden. In two days' time she'd be back at school and, she smiled to herself, she'd be starting a new adventure.

Piper nudged her leg, then jumped up, both paws on the edge of the work surface to see what she was missing. 'You're a nosy one, aren't you?' The dog wagged her tail, and smiled her happy-dog smile, tongue lolling out of her mouth, before jumping down and barking. 'Yes, yes, we're going out in a minute.'

The puppy ran over to the door, poised. She could swear that dog understood nearly everything she said to her.

Seconds later there was a rap on the door, followed be a cheery shout as Charlie opened the door and Piper abandoned her post by the back door and went hurtling through the cottage to greet him. He strode into the kitchen, bringing a waft of cold air with him and shaking snow from his jacket.

Lucy laughed. 'You look like you've been rolling in it!'

'Not far off.' He gave a wry grin. 'Snowball fight with Maisie, but she cheated and called in reinforcements.'

'Isn't she with you?' She glanced round, half expecting the little girl to come bounding in.

'No, she's building snowmen with your mum.' He stepped closer, ignoring the fact that Piper was doing her best to trip him up. 'So we could do something to warm us up?' He wrapped her in a hug, and when she met his gaze he gave her that look of his that could have melted an avalanche of snow.

Lucy giggled. 'Thinking of hot chocolate were you?'

'Hotter!'

'Later,' inviting as a heat-warming afternoon with Charlie was, she just had to share her surprise with him. Before she burst. 'I want to show you something first.' Since the phone call an hour before she'd not been able to sit still, and waiting for Charlie to arrive had felt like a lifetime.

'Spoilsport.' He grinned good-naturedly, but relaxed his hold slightly. 'Come on then, what's this surprise you text me about?'

'It involves putting your boots back on.' She wriggled her way out of his grasp, before she was tempted to give in.

'No clues?'

'Nope.' She pulled her jacket on and grabbed his hand.

Luckily most of the snow and ice had melted, and the footpaths were slushy but not too slippery as they made their way across the village square. Much as Lucy loved to see the countryside blanketed in white snow, she wasn't that keen on the slush, and hated ice. If anybody was going to go flying and land on their bottom it was her. She was the one who always looked like an old lady as she edged her way along, putting one foot carefully in front of the other. Going slowly today was not an option, so she was relieved that in her boots she actually felt quite stable.

Charlie laughed as she did her best to chivvy him along. 'Are we going far?'

'Nearly there.'

'Thank goodness for that, you'd give Piper a run for her money!' He was totally perplexed though when they got to the village green and she led him across it.

Lucy stopped, she was actually quite out of breath, but she'd been far too excited to even think about slowing the pace. If she had done she'd have ended up telling him. 'Close your eyes.' She was rubbish at keeping people in suspense, at hiding things.

Charlie pulled a funny face but did as he was told.

Lucy fished about in her pockets, having a moment of panic when she couldn't find what she was looking for, then her fingers closed round it and she let out a sigh of relief. Her heart was pounding as she held it up. 'Open.'

Charlie opened his eyes and stared at her. Not registering what it was she was holding up in front of him. Then all of a sudden his face cracked into a smile. 'You've got it?'

She nodded. Not trusting herself to speak.

'You've got the key! Jasmine Cottage is yours?'

When she'd got the key to her first house, Lucy had wanted to savour the moment on her own. Open the front door knowing it was hers. Take that first step in and act as madly excited as she wanted in private. It had been *her* moment, *her* triumph. But this time was different. This time she wanted to share the moment with the most important person in her life. She felt like she'd come home, that she belonged. But it wasn't just the place, this cottage – it was Charlie who made this place special.

'It's mine. It's really mine!'

Her words were lost as he swept her off the ground, and spun them both round, before putting her gently down, cradling her face in his large warm hands and kissing her.

She grinned, made to move away so that they could

go in, so that she could open *her* front door for the first time. But he held her back.

'I've got a bit of an announcement of my own actually.' He pulled her back to him, and all of a sudden he looked unsure of himself.

'Really?' She searched his face, wondering what on earth could be so important that he had to say it right now.

'Eric has asked if I'll be a partner in the firm.'

She twisted round so that she could study his face properly. This was good wasn't it? He should be pleased.

'He loves being back at work, but he says he's finding it a bit too much. He'll never be able to run the place on his own again. He says he was just looking after the place for my family, until I came to my senses,' he smiled, the lines fanning out from his gorgeous brown eyes, 'and was ready to take over.'

'And are you?' He had to be. Surely he was?

'I am.'

He was smiling still, just about, but Lucy could sense that there was something wrong, he didn't look as happy as he should. Her heart fluttered, couldn't he commit? Wasn't Langtry Meadows the place he wanted to make his home again? 'But?' It came out as a croak, but she had to ask. Was he telling her he was going, telling her before they opened her new front door together?

'It's just.' He paused. Brushed his thumb over her

lips, the words hesitant. 'It's just I wanted to check something before I said yes.'

'Oh.' She tried not to pull back, but it was hard. Something was wrong, he wanted something more than she did, than this place could give him.

His arms tightened round her, stopping her from getting away.

'Lucy, I know you've bought this place and ...'

He couldn't ask her to move away, start somewhere else. She loved this place, she loved this cottage. 'This is where I want—'

He put a finger on her lips to stop her saying more. 'I know you've bought this place, and it's yours and ... Christ I'm rubbish at this.' He let go with one hand, threaded his fingers through his hair, then took a deep breath, blinked hard and fixed her with a steady look. 'What I'm trying to ask is if you'd consider sharing it, if, well ... I know it's not perfect, and it's complicated and ... oh, hell. Lucy, will you marry me?'

It came out in a rush and she blinked, not sure she'd heard him right. Then realised, when he blushed scarlet, that she was just staring at him. Her mouth slightly open.

'Can you say that again?'

'I know it's complicated, with Maisie and ...'

'Not that bit.' It was her turn to blush, her heart pounding, and her voice with a definite wobble. 'The last bit.'

'Will you marry me?'

'Yes please.' She only got half the word out, his grip had tightened and his lips were over hers, and the dishiest vet she'd ever seen was kissing her like he was never going to stop.

# Chapter 26

*Three months later*

Charlie stared at the envelope. The letter inside would change his life. It shouldn't do. It shouldn't make the slightest difference, but he knew it would. And it scared him.

He propped it up against the sugar pot in the middle of the table and felt the same twinge of anticipation that he always had when a road traffic accident was brought in. When he knew he had to get the nerves under control, switch onto auto-pilot and try to stop a life ebbing away. That first cut of the scalpel was always the worst, once he was in it was different. However bad the situation, he knew what he was dealing with.

It was the same with this envelope. Except he had a horrible feeling he wouldn't just be able to stitch up the gaping wound in his heart if the contents were what he was dreading.

'So, that's it.'

He hadn't heard Lucy come into the small kitchen behind him, and he jumped as she rested a hand lightly on his shoulder.

'It is.' He glanced up, meeting her gaze only briefly, because God knows he didn't want her to see the fear he was sure was leeching out of his own eyes.

She sat down opposite, so that he couldn't avoid her. 'What if ...'

'Charlie, you've been waiting for this since Malcolm gave you the go ahead.' Her voice was gentle, not pushy.

'But if it's ...'

'It won't make any difference at all, will it? Not really.'

Charlie wasn't so sure. He normally liked everything black and white, which was why once everything he and Josie had discussed, once the child arrangements order was in place, once he knew that Maisie couldn't be whisked away, he'd asked his solicitor if it was safe to go ahead.

But once you'd asked the question, there was no going back, was there? The answer was here, in front of him.

He'd deliberated long and hard about whether he was ready to take this step. To find out if Maisie was his biological daughter.

In the heat of the moment, when his ex, Josie had thrown a spanner in the works, shouted out that she didn't even know if the baby he'd seen into the world, the toddler he'd watched take her first step, the little girl that he'd photographed in her first school uniform, was actually his. Then, at that moment, when she'd stormed off, it would have been easy to do.

To let her go if she wasn't, to fight for his rights if she was. But now it was different.

Maisie would always be his. He'd always look after her, always love her. But if he got a negative result now, even though he knew that she was here to stay with him, would it make a difference? Could he really, honestly, be sure nothing would change once he knew for sure?

What if he wasn't as strong as he thought he was?

'Charlie.' Lucy tapped the back of his hand. 'You don't have to open it now. We can put it somewhere safe, give it to Malcolm.'

'She's the most important thing in my life.'

'So it doesn't make any difference, does it? You don't need to know. I'll tear it up for you.' She reached out.

He sighed, put his own hand over hers. 'I do. I'm only human.' And so was Maisie, one day she'd want to know. She deserved to know.

Josie had stuck to her word after their chat on Christmas Day. She'd spent as much time as she could with Maisie over the holiday, reassured her, promised her that she'd be back again soon and in the meantime she should be good for Daddy. Then she'd instructed her solicitor that they would look after Maisie between them, that she wouldn't take her out of the country without Charlie's consent, and that when she moved back she'd find somewhere close enough so that Maisie could see both her parents. She'd never broached the possibility that Charlie wasn't Maisie's father. She'd never questioned that Lucy was part of their lives.

They'd avoided a messy divorce, they'd decided – like adults – what was best for Maisie.

There was no biological father going to come forward and whisk Maisie away, but one day, if he wasn't that man himself he wanted to be able to explain – to give his daughter the opportunity to make up her own mind. He owed her the truth. And he wanted the time to prepare himself for that day. 'This is for her – not me.'

'She's not old enough to understand yet though, Charlie.'

'I know.' He reached out and laid the envelope flat. Picked up the knife off the table. Very deliberately slid it under the flap. Then with his throat dry, and a well of emotion clogging up his throat, stopping him breathing, he pulled out the contents.

Unfolded the sheets of paper. Prepared to take a step he could never un-take.

He blinked. Crumpled the sheet in his hand, the tears pricking hot in his eyes and Lucy reached out. Wrapped her slim hands round his.

'Oh, Charlie.'

'She's mine.' The words trickled out as though they didn't belong. All he could hear was the tick of the clock. For a moment it was as though he was in a vacuum, nothing was real. 'She's mine.' This time he believed what he was saying. This time he couldn't help the smile, the laugh that broke out of him, the wave of pure elation that seemed to be threading its way through his whole body.

He grasped Lucy's hands in his own and laughed as he looked at her, and then she was laughing back, leaning across the table to kiss him.

'She's mine.' And this time the words came out in a sane, sensible way. With the conviction they deserved. He stroked the back of his hand down Lucy's face, cupped her chin and let himself drink in every bit of her face. 'I feel like I've won the lottery, a daughter and you. I must be the luckiest man alive.'

'You know what? It's me and Maisie that are the lucky ones.'

Then he took the sheet of paper, held it high in the air and ripped it into tiny pieces that showered down on them like confetti as he pulled Lucy to him, and kissed her.

# A Note from the Author

Dear reader,

Thank you so much for picking up this copy of 'Blackberry Picking at Jasmine Cottage', if you've already read 'Summer with The Country Village Vet' then I'm sure you'll love this second book in the series. If you're new to Langtry Meadows I hope you enjoy your visit to the village!

As I write this, the school year is coming to an end and there are lots of excited children looking forward to a long hot summer of fun, so it's perfect timing. In Langtry Meadows the summer is nearly over, a new school year will soon begin and with it comes a new start for Lucy, and more than one of the other villagers.

New starts can be scary, but they can also be invigorating and bring a sense of freedom – as you let go of the past and make a new future. All that hope, and as yet unfulfilled promise of a new place, new year, new job or new life!

I do hope you enjoy the story – if you do, please leave a review on Amazon. Finding out, as I drink my morning coffee, that somebody loved one of my books really does make my day!  And if you click on the 'follow' button on my author page you'll be the first to hear about new releases.

I love to chat, so please do search me out on twitter (@ZaraStoneley), join me on my Facebook page (ZaraStoneley) or drop me an email (ZaraStoneley@ gmail.com)! It's also easy to sign up for my newsletter so you can be sure to hear my latest news – just visit my website www.ZaraStoneley.com.

Happy reading!
Zara x

# Acknowledgements

Big thanks as always to the fabulous HarperImpulse team, especially to the lovely Charlotte Ledger and Emily Ruston, you make team HI a very special place to be.

Thanks to my agent, Amanda Preston, for your advice and support, and your enthusiasm for my country vet and the village of Langtry Meadows.

As always I'm extremely grateful to everybody who has helped ensure that I've got all my facts straight – your support is invaluable and I really appreciate the time you spend answering my many questions. Special thanks to solicitor Philippa Sanderson for advice on all things legal.

Also, thanks to Carol Siwek who let me steal the wonderful name Piper for my cockapoo puppy, and to cockapoo owners Abigail Wrigley and Kelly Disley for advice and help. (Look out for more puppy adventures in Book 3.) I hold you all partly responsible for the new addition to our household – Harry the cockapoo. He's currently disrupting my writing schedule and eating my shoes!

I also need to thank the lovely Sian-Elin Flint-Freel for suggesting the perfect pet for Maisie - a guinea pig!

These acknowledgments wouldn't be complete without a mention of all my wonderful writing buddies (you know who you are), and the fabulous bloggers and reviewers. Special mention and hugs to fabulous authors Cressida McLaughlin, Mandy Baggot, Jane Linfoot and Christie Barlow for all your support and positive words and thoughts – they make a huge difference!

Massive thanks to Joanne Robertson (My Chestnut Reading Tree), Kaisha Holloway (The Writing Garnet), Alison Drew (Ali the Dragon Slayer), Shona Lawrence (Booky Ramblings of a Neurotic Mom), Lucie Poole (Not Left on the Shelf), Laura Bambrey, Kelly (Love Books Group), Agi (On my Bookshelf) and Rachel Gilbey (Rachel's Random Reads) who helped me introduce Langtry Meadows to the world, and are always incredibly supportive. Please do check out their blogs, these ladies are amazing!

I also want to thank Tracy Fenton, Helen Boyce and everybody else at TBC for all your incredible support. You're fantastic!

And lastly, a big thank you to you, the reader – this

story would be just words on a page if you weren't there to enjoy it and bring the characters and places to life in a head other than my own!

Printed by RR Donnelley at Glasgow,  UK